Heaven's Gate

Deborah Leitch

Heaven's Gate

All characters and events in this novel are a figment of the author's imagination. Any similarity to persons, individuals or events is purely coincidental. The Miramichi area in New Brunswick, Canada is real, as is Mullen Stream Falls, a truly beautiful place on earth and an area deserving to be "Heaven's Gate".

Special thanks to:

Mabel Luscombe, my friend and first reader!

Brenda Dockman, for her support and belief in me and in this book.

My sister - Anne Dunnett, for her never ending support and encouragement.

My brother - Ron Robichaud, for introducing me to Mullen Stream Falls and sharing his passion for nature.

Dedicated to my husband and son: John and David Leitch

"There is no dream too big."

(2013)

Chapter 1

"Is ET ready for its next mission?"

Simon Gallagher looked up from his workstation in the electronics lab to see his boss, Henrietta Storm smiling at him.

ET was the acronym they chose for the "Energy Tracker" application he invented. They laughed together when they selected the tiny alien face with the big eyes and the pointing finger for the on-screen icon. In some ways it all seemed linked. The work they were doing felt like it was indeed from another world, inscribed by an extraterrestrial race.

He finished inserting a miniscule GPS tracking module into the small hand held electronic device he was working on before replying.

"Maybe."

Simon might be a genius, but self assurance was not one of his strengths. It was also one of the things that made it hard for him to establish relationships. Henrietta was an exception to the rule. She had been his thesis advisor in quantum physics and although she was 30 years his senior they formed an immediate bond. She hired him as her research assistant as soon as he graduated. Was that really five years ago?

Henrietta was seldom without a smile and Simon found himself smiling at her in return. Her long grey hair was pinned in a knot at the top of her head. She wore her usual attire; a long gypsy skirt and t-shirt. Unlike him she was comfortable with herself. She had a lust for life and an intrinsic belief that under man's crusty outer shell, all people were basically good. Because she believed in you, you found yourself not wanting to let her down. It was hard to explain, but being around her made you feel good about yourself. She made you want to be the person she thought you were. Before meeting her, he had let many people down. She instilled in him not just the belief that he could do better but also the confidence to try.

In addition to their mutual passion for physics they shared an interest in the paranormal sciences. Their bond was fueled by their shared determination to answer a question that for different reasons haunted them both.

"Where does life's energy go when you die? If energy is neither created nor destroyed then what happens to it after it leaves the body?"

He loved testing theories, finding proof that explained the unexplainable. His mother said he was a born inventor, like his father. He hated the comparison. He did not want to be like his father. They came at life differently. Simon was driven by the need to understand why something occurred. His father didn't care about the why; he just wanted to figure out the how. His mother had been the go between, smoothing the waters between them, keeping the arguments to a minimum.

Which of the animals is ready?"

"Number 38 is very close."

"Ok, let's give it a go then."

Simon picked up the handheld electronic device he was working on and followed Henrietta to the animal lab.

The lab was a large rectangular room that was about forty feet long and twenty feet wide. It was located in the basement of the Medical Science Building on the Boston University campus. Thanks to the extravagant air handling system that the university insisted on, cool fresh air greeted them as they entered the room. Henrietta flicked the light switch to reveal stark white walls, sterile chrome work surfaces and a multitude of animal cages lining the length of the lab. Although the cages housed mice, frogs, rats and rabbits, the room was odorless. The room was aglow with the eerie green fluorescent electrocardiogram tracings that monitored each animal's cardiac rhythm and rate on a flat screen above the cages.

The rabbit cages were located at the far end of the room. Each cage had a large number attached to its front. They continued down the row until they came to the cage with the number 38 on it. Inside the cage was a large grey rabbit. The rabbit lay on its side, motionless. The only evidence of life was the green dot tracing an extremely slow ECG pattern and the barely perceptible, shallow and irregular breaths that moved the rabbit's chest wall.

"How long has he been this way?" Simon choked.

The last moments of life were precious; sacred somehow. He felt like an intruder; a trespasser who had no right to share in the most sacred of all moments.

"About an hour. He is very close now."

Henrietta's soft voice grounded him.

In her early career days Henrietta worked as a nurse on an oncology unit. She witnessed many people die. She described to him the feeling of awe, the stillness that came over the room, the tangible touch of life's energy leaving the body at the moment of death. He could feel that now. He knew this was just a rabbit, not a person yet he felt what she described; the stillness, the aura, the feeling of reverence that befell the room.

Simon carefully lifted the rabbit out of his cage and laid him on the table. He placed a gentle hand on the big grey rabbit's head and softly stroked his fur and long ears.

"It's okay, little guy." he whispered. "It's your time. Show us where you go."

He touched the little alien face with the pointing finger on the screen of the electronic device in his hand.

Henrietta flipped 3 switches to turn off all power in the room.

The overhead fluorescent lights, the sidewall emergency lighting, the cardiac monitors, the computer screens, printers, fridges and the air exchange system were shut down. The room became still and black.

The silence was loud in the absence of sound.

The everyday white noise, the constant hum that filled every human dwelling and workspace was not even noticed, until it was gone. The wonderful bliss of silence was something rarely encountered in a world filled with electronics and machinery. Simon revelled in the absolute quiet for a moment before placing the computer tablet on the table next to the dying rabbit.

He placed his thumb over the alien figure with the pointing finger on the electronic device that lay next to the rabbit. The screen display immediately opened to a graph of the room he was in and the surrounding buildings and streets outside the walls of the lab. Simon pressed the small "3D" symbol at the bottom of the screen. The graph on the screen immediately projected itself into a hologram directly in front of him and Henrietta.

"Ok, ET. Do your job"

The GPS application he installed just moments before made a faint beep as it linked onto the rabbit's energy emission.

Simon's hand on the rabbit's side felt the animal draw its last breath. He sensed more than felt the slight shiver that ran through 38's body as life's energy exited. The faint beep emitted from ET changed to a low buzz as the GPS began to track the energy rising above 38's lifeless body.

Simon and Henrietta watched in awe as the dot on the holographic screen rose above the now dead rabbit, floated in a circular pattern for several seconds and serpentined gently along the virtual display of the lab's ceiling. The buzzing sound emitted from the speakers grew less distinct as the energy stream moved away. At the end of the lab, the sound stopped all together. The green dot dimmed and went out. The energy was gone.

Neither Simon nor Henrietta spoke. Witnessing the departure of life's energy from a living thing left them with a feeling of reverence and humility. It was an overwhelming emotion. The moment of silence was fitting.

Finally Henrietta placed her hand over Simon's. "Run it back."

Simon touched the start screen on ET but this time he selected the spaceship icon from the drop down menu directing the application to rerun the recorded sequence of events they had just witnessed. Instantly, a 3D holographic image of 38's energy waves and its line of travel were captured on screen and projected into the space in front of them. The wave of recorded energy ended at the virtual walls of the lab.

"I think this confirms our theory." Henrietta said. "The more evolved the animal, the greater the cohesiveness of the energy. The cohesiveness keeps the energy waves together and it travels in streams instead of dissipating into space as it did when we tracked the energy from the frog and the hamster that died last week. We are getting there, but we still have a long way to go to determine life energy's final destination."

Simon nodded in agreement. Eliminating electrical interference from manmade energy sources such as lights, computers, and air conditioners helped them track the energy further but obviously not far enough. He hoped his latest enhancement to the GPS tracking unit might have allowed them to track the energy outside of the walls of the lab, however.

"Well at least we know it travels somewhere," Simon shrugged off his disappointment. "I think we need to take our work outside of the lab and outside of the city. If we are really going to be able to find out where the energy goes we need to get somewhere with less electrical interference. If we could come up with a hypothesis;

some idea of where it might travel and went there, we might have a better chance."

Henrietta broke into his thoughts. "Simon, come to my office. I want to show you a project that I have been working on that may have some relevance to what we are trying to do. It might just help us with that hypothesis."

Henrietta's office walls were lined with flip chart paper covered with coloured lines, formulas and arrows. She was a visual thinker and thought better when her ideas were plotted out on paper. She took Simon to a large geographical map representing the world in a topographical view of greens and blues that was taped to one wall in her office. The map showed overlapping lines indicating waves of energy with arrows pointing in different directions.

"This is an energy flow map that I have been working on," she explained. "I have been trying to determine if there are higher natural energy waves in certain areas of the world than others and if so, why. Look here."

She pointed to an area on the map with numerous converging red circles.

"I am seeing an interesting trend. There are a few areas around the world where there are higher energy flow patterns than in other areas of the world. You can see on this map, how it looks like energy actually converges in these spots and from the topographical photos you can also see how very lush these areas are. It might just be related to the soil and moisture in those areas but I believe something is pulling energy there. I don't know if it is related to the work we are doing on tracking energy but I keep getting these niggling thoughts that we should explore this more."

Simon studied the map closely. Indeed, there were great wavy circles of energy over numerous areas on the map including Egypt, the United Kingdom, Russia, Mexico, Peru, Africa and North America.

As Henrietta indicated, most of these sites were known for abundant vegetation and many had natural or manmade wonders that he could easily recall. He pointed to the spot on the map that was where he knew the Great Pyramid of Giza was located.

"I am not sure that is true of all the sites though, Henrietta. This spot on the map is definitely not lush with growth and life. In fact it is the exact opposite. The pyramids undoubtedly at the time of their erection were surrounded by lush land and must have had an ecosystem and environment that was able to support and sustain the significant population of people that lived there. Today, though Egypt is mostly desert."

"It may be an anomaly," Henrietta suggested but Simon's observation had triggered a series of questions in her mind.

She pointed to a spot on the map.

"If you look here you will also see that there is one of these points only a few hours from here in a small community in eastern New Brunswick."

She lifted the map to reveal another map underneath dated a year earlier.

"This map from a year ago shows that this area in New Brunswick actually had a significantly higher level of energy a year ago." She pointed to the greater number of circles around the area mapping energy flow. "I wonder if something is happening there."

Simon's heart instantly sped up. He stared blankly at the point on the map toward which Henrietta was gesturing. He knew the area well. The Miramichi. The river valley where he grew up. The town where his father still resided. His mind was filled with an image of his mother, smiling, arms outstretched in welcome and the look of blame in his father's eyes.

Intense loneliness clouded his senses. Loneliness wrapped in guilt. He had not been home since his mother's death.

Henrietta's voice broke into his memories instilling a sense of dread.

"I think we need to go on a road trip."

Chapter 2

"Dr. Thomas to ER. Dr. Thomas to ER."

The request resounded through the overhead speakers in every corridor of the small city hospital. Simultaneously the pager connected to Dr. Galen Thomas's belt began to beep.

He silenced his pager with one hand while laying his other hand on the lifeless forehead of the four year old girl who had just died. He gently stroked her hair.

Sara Dickson.

The bright eyed, blond haired, ball of energy he had come to know and love had succumbed to leukemia. He closed her eyes, returned his examining penlight to his pocket and raised his face to address her sobbing parents. Their emotion was tangible. Could there be any pain worse than that experienced by a parent as they watched their child die?

"Mr and Mrs Dickson I am very sorry." He kept his voice steady to keep his own emotion in check. "Sara was a brave little girl right to the end. There was nothing more we could do. There was nothing more *you* could do."

He paused for a moment.

"I am being paged to the emergency department now, so I need to leave. If there is anything you need to talk to me about please don't hesitate to call."

Knowing his comments were unheard in the ensuing grief that overwhelmed them as they held and gently stroked their child's lifeless body, Galen turned and left the room. He took a deep breath, let out a large sigh, and stepped into the elevator that would take him to the main floor of the Miramichi Hospital. There was no time for despair. There never was.

The elevator doors opened directly into the heart of the busy emergency department. Tirisa Case, the energetic blond haired charge nurse in the ER met him in the hallway. She immediately fell into step with his rapid stride, accompanying him down the hall to the trauma bay.

"Glad you are here, Dr. Thomas."

He sensed relief in her comment. Relief that there was someone here to help deal with this latest crisis. It was a nice feeling; being needed. It was what kept him coming to work every day. He liked Tirisa. She was always professional, knew her job. She was confident, quick. He was glad she was here too.

"It's not pretty," she started right in with the report. "65 year old man. Gunshot wound to the head. Case of domestic violence. His wife shot him. Not much left to his face. Not looking good overall. Pulse 140. Respirations 40. BP in the basement. Still conscious, but barely. Lots of pain. We started oxygen and an IV of Ringers full open."

Loud raspy breaths and agonizing moans of pain greeted them as they reached the trauma bay. Tirisa pulled back the privacy curtain surrounding the bed and held it apart so that the doctor could duck into the patient's bedside. A crash cart and ventilator were sitting outside the curtain ready to be used if needed.

The man lying on the stretcher was remarkably still alive. It didn't take an expert to know that he wouldn't be alive for long. The damage to his airway was too great. There would be nothing that could be done to save this man's life. The left side of his face was obliterated. A mangled mess of flesh, muscle and bone was all that remained. He made pretence of examining him and ordered Morphine 10 mg IV to help ease the man's suffering.

Tirisa quickly drew up the narcotic, inserted the needle into the IV port and pushed the drug into the man's vein. Within seconds the man's breathing slowed, became less raspy, and shallow. His painful withering ceased.

Thomas held his head, reached into his pocket for his examining pen light and aimed it inside the man's mouth just as he exhaled his last breath.

The room became silent and still.

He placed his stethoscope on the man's chest and listened intently for a moment. He did not call for the crash cart.

"That's it. He's gone. Time of death 0230 hours."

No one questioned Dr. Thomas's decision to not resuscitate.

"Where is his wife? " Galen asked.

"She is up on 2 South."

"The obstetrical ward?"

"She was eight months pregnant."

Tirisa was usually pretty stoic, but he saw the beginning of tears welling up in her eyes.

"He beat her up and she went into premature labor."

He noticed that she placed her hand on her own protruding abdomen. It was a subconscious gesture. Galen knew it was a way of reassuring herself that her own waiting baby was okay. That the life she carried was safe and for the moment not affected by this warped outside world, where a husband beats his pregnant wife and she in turn shoots him.

"I guess I better go up and see her. She will need to know that her husband is dead."

"Go easy on her," Tirisa said. She tilted her head and shifted her gaze toward the two police officers standing in the waiting area.

Mrs Creaghan's problems would not end with the death of her husband.

The obstetrical unit was hopping. Every labor room was full. The unit clerk told him that Mrs. Creaghan was in labor. Room 210.

The long hallway to her room had gleaming polished floors and walls that were covered with pictures of babies. Captured moments at the beginning of life. Photos full of promise of the life that lay ahead. He wondered when it changed. At what moment in the transition between child and adult does it change? When does corruption overcome the innocence so prevalent in all of these pictures?

At the door to Mrs. Creaghan's room he stopped. Listened.

He heard a nurse's voice comforting a patient. "Take some nice slow breaths now. That's right. You are doing great."

Familiar sounds on an obstetrical unit. It was what he didn't hear that told him what he needed to know however. The absence of the reassuring; thump, whoosh, thump, whoosh of a baby's heart beat being broadcasted from the speakers of the electronic fetal monitor. He stood outside the door, waiting, not wanting to intrude on these next terrible moments.

"Ok, now with this next contraction, you need to really push."

Screams of pain.

"That's right you are doing really good. Almost there. Now push. Push hard."

A loud cry of relief as the uterus succeeded in its job.

Silence. Then:

"Is my baby okay? I can't hear him. Is he okay?" The woman's voice was filled with anxiety. Fear.

The nurse might need help. Galen entered the room. The look on the nurse's face confirmed his expectations. Baby Creaghan was dead.

The nurse bundled the baby, a boy, gently in a receiving blanket and cradled him in her arms.

"Oh baby" she softly whispered and stroked the tiny cheek before bringing him to his mother.

"I am so very sorry, Mrs Creaghan." Tears streamed down the nurse's face. "Your baby didn't make it."

Tiny. Lost. Forlorn. Mrs. Creaghan looked defeated.

The woman in the crumpled blood stained and soaked bed held out her arms for her baby. The baby she had fought to protect. She gently unwrapped the blanket. Lovingly she touched her tiny son's face, his arms and legs. She held his tiny feet in her hands. She gently caressed him, kissed his head, and held him close. Silently wept.

Such senseless loss.

"I am so sorry, Mrs. Creaghan." Galen spoke through his own choked emotion.

"Who are you?" she looked at him in confusion, lost behind a blanket of grief and despair.

"My name is Dr. Galen Thomas; I was the emergency physician on call tonight when you and your husband were brought in by ambulance"

"Is he dead?" She asked flatly.

"Yes."

Mrs. Creaghan turned her face away and once more gazed at her baby.

"It's okay now. We are safe now," she whispered as she stroked his tiny head.

Galen turned and quietly left the room, leaving the woman to grieve in peace.

Chapter 3

"It's time to take this to the next level Galen. Innis only has another month to live at best. If he dies before you finish the energy conversion device we will not get one cent of the $500 million dollars in our contract with him. You know what that means. He is a tough bastard in life and will be even tougher in death. It is time to stop messing around and start coming up with some results."

The irritating voice of Devlin Matthews, CEO of Living Energy Corporation, the greedy self serving partner he had taken on in a moment of weakness greeted him without so much as a "hello" when he picked up the phone. Galen felt the bristles on his neck rising. Rudeness was never acceptable in his world. Anger rose from the balls of his feet and slowly seeped into the tightening muscles of his arms, his brow and his jaw. He detested Devlin Matthews. The man was an over bearing, obnoxious society climber and if it wasn't for the funding and resources that he lorded over him he would have found a way to break their contract long ago. Consumed by money and power Devlin had no appreciation for medical science, for human life or for the miracle that he, Galen Thomas was in the process of creating.

He took a deep breath and kept his voice from showing his rising rage.

"I am sorry to hear about Alfred." He answered in the soothing and controlled tone he had perfected from years of working with anxious patients. "Everything is moving along. It will be ready. You need to relax and trust me."

He was not ready to tell his pushy friend just how far he had actually come. There was no point in giving away all of his secrets yet, but he did allow himself to reassure Devlin.

"I have a few more experiments to try, but I am close."

He knew that the calm sense of control he was using would have its usual result and would serve to calm Devlin and defuse his anger. It never failed him in the past.

Devlin's voice was an octave lower and noticeably slower when he replied.

"Ok. Call me when it is ready, but don't take too long. We don't have enough time to wait for perfect opportunities. I have a contract with a rich billionaire who is about to die, and if we don't pull this off before he croaks, I will be bankrupt and you will be out of the research business."

Devlin disconnected the call before Galen had a chance to reply.

"The arrogant ass." Galen muttered to himself. He picked up the gleaming silver penlight that was sitting on his desk in his well manicured hands and immediately dismissed Devlin from his mind.

He polished the inscription that read "COLTEN" in small script on the base of the pen. "COLTEN" was derived from the words collection, transfer and energy. He marvelled at his own ingenuity in selecting the name for his invention.

His passion had always been healing and helping people. That was why he became a doctor. When he discovered that he could actually capture the energy that was within a body before it dissipated into the atmosphere at the time of death and was lost forever, he became enthralled with finding a way to re-direct this vital energy in a way that could sustain or extend life for others.

It had been so simple to create in the end. He slowly rotated the pen admiring the shining surface, revelling in the smooth cold, and hard feel of it in his hands. He gently depressed the button at the end of the pen. Fifty small metal arms shot out from around the circumference of the pen. Each arm held a small collection cell that resembled a minuscule solar panel. The cells were not designed to collect solar energy however. They were designed to capture a different type of energy. Life energy. At this very moment this amazing object in his hands contained the living energy of not just Sara Dickson and Mr. Creaghan but also another twenty people who had passed away in the ER over the past few months.

Since he discovered how to capture life energy upon death, it was amazing to him how easy it was. He visited palliative patients during their last breaths and collected their energy as it left their body. His shifts in the trauma bay in the Emergency Department and the many heart attacks and MVAs that poured in through the hospital doors provided him with donors to add to his energy collection. On a number of occasions, when it seemed appropriate and no one was watching, he helped the death process along somewhat - giving an extra dose of Morphine or taking a little too long to aerate lungs. To his colleagues there was no reason to suspect him of any untoward behaviour. Everyone lost patients from time to time. He never took the life of someone who was not destined to die anyway.

He looked at the digital display on the side of the pen. The two most recent strings of energy were largely different. One cell held 2 million units of quanta and one held merely 350 units. While one would think that it was the child who donated the lower number of units he knew that in fact, Mr. Creaghan, previous wife abuser, now consisted of a mere 350 units of energy while Sara, an innocent four year old had contributed 2 million units. While Creaghan's meagre contribution was not much in the vast scheme of things it was still more than he collected from the euthanized lab animals he experimented on.

By spending time with the "donor's families" he formulated a theory about the energy levels he was collecting that was based on the lifestyle of the donor. Donors who led vicious, aggressive lives and who contributed little to the betterment of society released small amounts of loosely linked energy quanta. Those whose families described them as caring, compassionate, supportive and loved, donated great amounts of energy with the quanta particles knit closely together. Children consistently had higher levels of energy than adults. He theorized that it was related to their level of

19

innocence. The energy collected from his latest donor combined with the comments from his wife supported his theory once again. If he was going to get enough energy by the time Devlin's client died, he was going to need to find donors who were worthy. Surely another opportunity such as the natural death of a child like Sara would present itself to him within the next month. In the meantime he needed to perfect the process of energy transfer.

He absent mindedly rubbed his forehead. At the moment he was facing two problems. How to consistently convert and transfer the energy from the holding cell in COLTEN to an assigned target and how to collect the volume and quality of energy that he required within the short time frame that Devlin was demanding. The time frame in which he had to work was dependent upon the progression of one man's fatal illness and could not be reliably predicted.

Always pragmatic, his mind began working out the steps he would need to take. If he could actually not only collect but convert and direct this energy he truly would be the ultimate healer. An unconscious smile played on his lips. He could already feel the swell of pride and accomplishment that would be his, the difference it would make to the world. He really was a genius.

***

Devlin Matthews paced back and forth in front of the floor to ceiling window of his executive office on the 27th floor of the Life Energy Corporation building in New York. Forty five years old and CEO of one of four major energy companies in the United States, he was not accustomed to depending on anyone. Right now he was depending upon a small town doctor with a God complex and he did not like it at all.

He had worked his way into the CEO position by being a man of action. He saw what needed doing and did it. He took risks. He didn't always play by the rules and he was not above bending rules either. In its hay day, Life Energy Corporation had been an unstoppable money making machine. He landed in the CEO position by a combination of good timing and some self made luck.

He was hired into the finance department at the tender age of 22 and fresh out of Business College. He was filled with ideas on how to take the fledgling company to new heights. Opportunities quickly presented. No one knew the role he played in making the company go belly-up. The diverted funds, the over the top contract "wages" he indicated were required to hire good people. He found ways to extrapolate dollars and resources to bring the company to the point of bankruptcy. When the company was ready to sell out, he used the money he diverted to buy it back and take over. He had many contacts who didn't mind throwing their weight around and they helped him make the company the richest in the oil industry.

That was then.

The recent down turn in the economy coupled with the drying up of 10 of the 15 oil wells owned and operated by his company was causing a cascading downward spiral toward bankruptcy. Desperation drove him to explore alternate energy options. In his search of the latest research related to energy, he stumbled across an article that Dr. Galen Thomas had written for the New England Journal of Medicine. He never would have searched the medical journals for a solution to his problems, but the search engine he used latched onto his company's name of "Life Energy" and matched it to the article that the physician had written.

It turned out that Galen Thomas was a small town doctor in a remote community in eastern Canada who was enthralled with living energy. He also happened to be brilliant. Galen believed he could capture life's energy as it left the body at the moment of death and later use that same energy to keep another person alive. It seemed a little hokey pokey at first, but the more he thought about it, the more enthralled and intrigued he became. He began to formulate a vision of becoming not just the richest man in the world; he would be the most powerful as well. He could offer eternal life to those who were willing to pay for it.

The dream did not come cheap. Much of the good doctor's work was still in the theory stage. In order to make it a reality he needed significant dollars not just for computers and software, but for product engineering, and the newest technology in replicators. Devlin had to create partnerships that would provide the kind of cash flow that would make the doctor's research come to reality before his company went bankrupt.

Luck was in his corner. The same town that the doctor lived in was the home town of an eccentric billionaire that Devlin had worked with in the energy business over the years. Alfred Innis was in his late 80s and somewhere Devlin had heard that he was dying of lung cancer. Seeing this as the perfect partnership, he gave his old acquaintance a call.

Alfred Innis was a man who was neither liked nor respected in his home town. In fact, the town people blamed Innis for his hand in the demise of their town. Innis had effectively sold off the many natural resources that the province had originally had: iron ore, lumber, and fish. He managed over a period of 20 years to rape the province, sell off all of its natural resources and leave the land in a devastated state. Devlin convinced Alfred that he could give back to the community, alter his reputation and at the same time fund a cure for his incurable condition. Posed with the offer for prolonged life, perhaps even eternal life, Innis was quick to sign a contract. He agreed to provide endless dollars, to not only support the doctor's work but to pay Life Energy Corporation five hundred million dollars. He had two caveats however. The first caveat was that all research had to happen in his home town and the technology and equipment was to be given to the town library so that the town would see him as a benefactor and perhaps lessen their bad opinion of him. The second caveat was that if he died, no money would be transferred to Devlin's company.

It was all working pretty good. The good doctor was set up with an elaborate laboratory in the basement of the town library. The library was a technological masterpiece with every known modern wonder available. The community held a lovely thank you ceremony to honor their benefactor. The fatal flaw was Innis' health. The original life expectancy of 2 years that he was given was drawing to a close. Dr. Thomas was still busy testing his miracle device. Devlin's business was drowning. The stack of bills on his desk and payroll that he was not going to be able to make this month were taking a toll on him. There was no more time to test the product. They needed to get the device ready and be ready when Innis croaked. The doctor seemed to be in no hurry and was hung up on doing more and more experiments. There was no more time for testing. He had to find a way light a fire under Galen.

Chapter 4

Mullen Stream Falls. According to the energy maps that Henrietta had created, a hidden away and little known about natural water fall in eastern New Brunswick was the location of the highest energy readings on the east North American continent. The irony of it was uncanny. Simon had successfully avoided returning to the Miramichi Bay area since he graduated from high school 10 years ago.

It was an eight and a half hour drive from Boston to Miramichi and he was not relishing the idea of going there. Henrietta was determined that they should drive so they could get the "feel" of the land.

They travelled from areas of dense population to areas of dense forest and from areas of wealth to areas of poverty. The contrast was also evident in the style and sizes of homes, the number of cars in driveways, the types of stores in the towns, villages and Indian reserves they passed through and the condition of the roads which were winding and littered with pot holes. North eastern New Brunswick was an improvised area. Henrietta was astounded at the differences between this world and the one they had just left. She began to doubt the energy readings recorded for the area.

Simon felt some inner compulsion to defend his home province and rationalize the stark conditions.

"This area used to be rich in resources with lumber, iron ore, coal, cod, salmon, lobster and endless wild life for hunting if that was your pleasure. That was before the large industrial companies from the United States, Norway, Germany and Sweden flooded in to capitalize on its natural resources."

Henrietta pointed out the window at a dilapidated building. Shattered window panes, faded and rusty metal siding, abandoned rusted out tractors; all contained within an eight foot chain link fence.

"Perfect example. An abandoned pulp and paper mill. A bottom line of profit was the only goal. Companies came in droves buying rights from our government. Rights to pillage and rape the land. They depleted and stripped the entire region of its natural resources investing nothing in the surrounding towns and leaving behind rivers, streams and air polluted with chemical residue. The forests once dense with fir, spruce and birch were pillaged and destroyed and are now wastelands of debris. As the resources dried up, the paper and lumber mills, mines and fish plants closed. The country side, once lush with life and promise was left like this; a waste land. The people were left without jobs or a way to make a living."

"Now entering Eel Ground First Nations Reserve," Henrietta read the sign on the side of the highway. "It seems like we have passed through a number of First Nations Reserves. Do you know what tribe lives here?"

"Mi'kmaq. The name Miramichi means "Country of the Mi'kmaq". If I can remember my history correctly, long before settlers from France, England, Ireland and Scotland arrived on its shores, the Miramichi was home to this native group and so the river was named for them. They were known for living in harmony with the land. Their spiritual belief dictates that you never take more from the land than what you need to survive. They respect the relationship between all living things-animal and plant. The mindless destruction of the land, when big companies moved in was devastating to them. They harbor a great deal of anger directed at the remaining white people who live here. They blame us for all of this. I have to admit, that even driving through their reserve makes me uneasy. We wouldn't want to break down here."

"So if all of these companies have left, what do people do here? How do they survive?"

"Well the river is still good to the people. There are lots of people who still fish, and of course eastern New Brunswick is famous for lobster. The Miramichi River itself is the most famous Atlantic salmon fishing river in the world. People from around the world come to cast their flies and experience the thrill of baiting the big fish. The tourist dollars help but there isn't enough to really boost the economy. Mostly the men leave home for seasonal work on oil rigs and manufacturing plants in other provinces. The wives work in grocery stores and offices for minimal wage. Somehow they manage to get by. Most people, who are born here, stay here. I seem to be an exception to the rule."

"Why do you think that is? I mean why do people stay here when life is so hard and they have to just scrape by when they could live a very different and comfortable life somewhere else?"

"I don't know. People say the river calls them back. In spite of the hardship there is a lot of camaraderie here. Everyone is accepted for who they are. There are no great expectations. People don't have much but they share what they have. There really is no crime because no one has anything worth stealing. Once you have experienced that kind of support it is hard to live without it. I mean face it Henrietta, how well do you know your neighbors in Boston? Would any of them know if you were in trouble or needed help? Would any of them even care? Here everybody knows everybody and everybody helps everybody. It is how they survive."

Henrietta let this information settle in her mind. Simon had a point for sure. Yet the poverty that surrounded them saddened her.

"Miramichi, 2 miles." Simon read the sign out loud. He couldn't explain the sense of excitement that he was feeling. Anticipation? He had dreaded returning here, now he found himself looking for familiar sights. Parks Ice Cream parlor was still here! And it was open! It was such a special treat when his mom and dad took him here for a chocolate dipped soft ice cream cone. The memory was so vivid he could almost taste it.

"Just drop me off at the Sheraton." Henrietta broke into his thoughts. "I want to get settled in and get my bearings. Maybe meet some of the local people on my own. I will catch up with you in a couple of days after you have had a chance to re-connect with your father."

His father, Marcus Gallagher. Yes, that was the plan. Never in his life had he believed in coincidences. The fact that he was back here in his home town surely meant that he was supposed to visit his father, to make amends for the past.

He dropped Henrietta off at the hotel and made his way down the familiar roads of his home town. Not much had changed in 10 years. Childhood memories greeted him at every turn. He slowed as he passed the elementary school playground and watched the handful of children on the swings and slide. It was June. Lunch hour. In his school days he remembered the playground was always full.

He passed the Catholic Church. With its high bell tower, great dormers and stained glass windows, it looked more like a cathedral than a church. He spent every Sunday of his childhood there. His mother had been a stout Catholic, and there was no excuse that would free him from Sunday mass or his obligation as an altar boy. He tried to squelch the painful memories of sitting in the front pew with his father at his mother's funeral. A funeral was supposed to provide the opportunity to say goodbye; to allow healing to begin. It had done neither for him. It was the priest talking of the afterlife and the glory that awaited in God's kingdom that affected him most. Where exactly was God's kingdom?

He crossed the railway tracks and pulled into the long driveway to the two story turn of the century house that he once called home.

The majestic elm trees that once lined the driveway were gone. The house and yard looked naked without them. The lawn had been freshly mowed but the long winding gravel driveway leading up to the house was in bad need of a load of gravel. The large white two story home with wrap around veranda looked otherwise the same. He always loved this house. Perched at the top of a ridge it overlooked the entire Miramichi River Valley. He parked, stepped out of the car and revelled in the view. It really was spectacular.

He didn't see the man sitting in one of the four white armadack chairs on the veranda until the wet nose of a golden retriever nudged his hand. He turned to look toward the house. He had not seen his father since his mother's funeral ten years ago. In many ways it seemed like yesterday. Other than the greying hair, he looked the same. Same green work shirt, same green work pants, same bottle of beer in his hand.

"Simon."

"Dad." Simon extended his hand to greet his father.

Neither knew how to start the conversation. The golden retriever nudged Simon's hand again and wagged her tail in welcome. Simon reached down to scratch the dog's ears, thankful for the opportunity presented to break the awkwardness of the moment.

"Who is this?" He asked.

"This is Randi. I have had her for about 5 years now. It got lonely here without your mother and with you away. Randi is good company," his father answered.

Simon wasn't sure if the criticism about his absence was intentional or not.

Hearing his name, the golden dog looked up at her master with unabated love.

Simon was not surprised that there was no open armed welcome as in the story of the returned prodigal son but he hoped for a slightly warmer reception. His excuse for not visiting or staying on the Miramichi after he graduated was related to both the lack of opportunity in the town, his guilt over his mother's death and his feelings about his father. He was not innocent of blame for the lack of relationship that existed between them. After his mother died, he didn't know what to do. He was only 17. His father began drinking heavily and didn't want to acknowledge that he was even around. When he was accepted into Dalhousie University in Nova Scotia he jumped at the opportunity. After completing his physics degree he went on to do graduate studies in Quantum Physics at Boston University and immediately been working with Henrietta. He had not been home since he graduated from high school.

"I need to be on the Miramichi because of a project I am working on. My boss is staying at a hotel in town, but I wondered if my old room might still be available?" Simon asked, determined to try to resolve the issues between them as Henrietta suggested, but quickly added: "If it is too much trouble, I can stay at the hotel too."

Marcus shook his head. "This is your home, Simon. Your room will always be your room."

Simon wondered if this was his mother's voice projecting through this father. How different it would be if she were here. His mother had the longest arms. They would reach out and welcome you, envelope you and comfort you. She was the steady force in the household. He looked at his father wondering not for the first time, why she had ever married him.

It was an awkward moment filled with silence as neither man knew what else to say.

Marcus took a drink out of the can in his hand.

"Ok then, I will bring my suitcases in," Simon mumbled.

He grabbed the two bags out of the trunk of the car and headed into the house glad to be out of his father's scrutiny. His old room was on the 2nd floor. His mind was filled with mixed emotions and he forgot about the narrow and uneven steps. He stumbled on the last stair, falling flat faced on to the landing in front of his childhood bedroom. He immediately sprung upright. Shook his head in disgust at his ever present clumsiness and snuck a look over his shoulder relieved to see that his father had not been watching.

As a son he had never been able to please his father. Extremely critical, intolerant and borderline alcoholic, Simon couldn't wait to leave home, to get away from him; away from his control and his ever critical eye. Nothing he did was ever good enough or was ever valued by his father. Even if Simon put hours and hours of work into a project, praise or commendation came rarely if at all. The lawn was never mowed precisely enough. His marks were never good enough. His hair was too long. His friends were geeks. He spent too much time on the computer. He was a klutz. He could never be the son that Marcus wanted. No matter what he did, he could never be worthy in Marcus's eyes. The death of his mother was the final nail that told Simon he would never be worthy. He had to leave to avoid the look of blame and disappointment he saw in his father's eyes every time he looked at him. Buried emotions began seeping to the top of his consciousness. The momentary enjoyment of being home was rapidly dissolving.

His room looked the same. The same bedspread was on his bed. His ball and glove were still on the dresser along with his hockey and swimming trophies. The room was clean. Even his books and journals were still in the bookshelf. There was no dust on the dresser or under the bed. His room was immaculate. He found himself frowning. His father would never pay for a housekeeper so he must have been cleaning it himself.

As he unpacked and put away his things his reflection stared back at him in the mirror over his bed. At 27 he didn't look that different from his father. He shared his father's tanned complexion, dark brown hair and deep brown eyes. They were both tall and slender with broad shoulders. He let out a deep sigh. So similar on the outside and so different on the inside. He had stopped trying to be the man his father wanted him to be many years ago.

He flopped down on the bed, stared at the ceiling and thought about the enigma of this man who was his father.

If anyone asked him to describe his father he would first say that he was an alcoholic, a functional alcoholic because he never lost work because of alcohol, but he was an alcoholic none the less. He would also describe him as an inventor. An inventor born of necessity. He had grown up at a time when money was hard to come by and if you needed something you made it or you made do. As long as he knew what was needed, he could figure out how to accomplish it with whatever he had on hand. When the water taps in the kitchen began to leak, he re-fitted them with valve handles, when he needed to water the garden he invented a barrel and siphon system that did not require any power, only gravity. He made a penny stretch a mile. He remembered a time when the gas tank rusted out of his old 67 Datsun truck. His father refused to pay the outlandish price to replace the tank and instead had rigged up a gasoline tank in the box of the truck with an intravenous tube to feed the motor gas! His "make do" attitude drove Simon crazy but it was his talent to fix things that had earned him a place of respect in the community. People came from everywhere to seek out his help and he was never too busy to help them.

He shook his head at no one in particular. Everybody likes Marcus Gallagher except Simon Gallagher.

The sound of the radio in the kitchen below his bedroom waffled up through the open floor grate, the only route for heat to rise from the first floor. He let out a sigh and headed down the worn stairs being careful of the uneven step this time. The stairs creaked with his weight and the banister was wobbly under his hand. The house had seen better days.

In the large country kitchen, Marcus was boiling water on the stove. There were two mugs and a can of condensed milk sitting in the center of the table. Simon couldn't help but smile. Tea had always been the family tradition for as long as he could remember, other than alcohol of course. Coffee was served only on rare occasions when company arrived that seemed to prefer the need to be stimulated as opposed to the desire to relax and slow down. He could always separate coffee drinkers from tea drinkers. Coffee drinkers were wound pretty tight and constantly on the move. Tea drinkers had a tendency to take life a little slower, to relish in the moments that present themselves. Alcohol drinkers, well they were trying to be happy with life but found a way to block it all out instead. He was glad his father was offering tea and not whiskey. Maybe some things had changed since he left.

"Your mother would be pleased to see you home." He knew his father was trying to find common ground that would not lead to an argument. He appreciated the gesture even though he suspected they would be unable to remain argument free for very long.

Simon took a slow sip of tea and felt it relax him. "The house looks good. I miss the trees though. What made you take them down?" He followed his father's lead and tried to stick to safe topics.

"The county told us they were diseased and had to be removed. Dutch elm disease. Every elm in the town had to be removed. It sure changed the look and feel of things around here."

Simon nodded. "I noticed that the town seems different. Do you think it is just the trees?"

Marcus looked at Simon curiously before asking. "What do you mean?"

Simon told about his observations as he drove into town, the lack of children playing, the dullness in the colors of the town, it was like the town was lacking vigor.

"Well maybe it looks different to you because you haven't been home for so long."

The reply was laced with a sarcasm that Simon tried to ignore.

"So what kind of research are you doing?"

He told his father about the work that he and Henrietta were doing, and the success they were having in tracking life energy as it departed the body at the moment of death.

His father sat in silence nodding occasionally as he told him about the number of sites in the world that had higher than average energy fields and how Miramichi was one of those sites. He also told him when they compared energy fields to previous years, the energy in the Miramichi area was actually diminishing.

"Is that what you mean by lacking vigor? You think that the energy around the Miramichi is actually declining and that our town is on the brink of dying?"

"I guess so, but I didn't make that connection until you said it." Simon shrugged indifferently.

"So what is all this about- tracking energy after it leaves the body? Where do you think it goes?"

"I don't know Dad. That is the whole point. If we could figure out where it goes, we could answer lots of questions about life after death."

"You know where it goes. It goes to heaven or hell. It is not up to you to get in the way of God or God's plans."

His father's voice changed from one of interest to one of domineering antagonism.

"That is what we always believed, but wouldn't it be nice to have proof? Wouldn't it be nice to know if the same energy that keeps man alive is the energy that keeps all living things alive? Maybe it is even related to all energy on the planet. The field of quantum physics says that energy is energy. Whether it is for heating homes, running motors, growing tress or growing humans, energy is energy. If we can figure out where that energy comes from, where it goes and what maintains it, we could influence many things in the world, maybe correct problems or prevent problems. The elm trees, for instance. If we knew why the tree's energy was susceptible to disease we could prevent their death. The same could be true with all living things. But that is way down the road.

Right now all we want to do is track where energy goes when it leaves the body."

"Some things are better not knowing. You are not supposed to know. You have to have faith. That is what religion is all about. Life is a miracle and so is death. God decides. Man has no business trying to alter God's work." Marcus's voice was loud and angry.

Simon felt his face grow hot and he struggled to keep his voice calm. "I am not trying to alter God's work. I am just trying to track it."

Simon knew there was no point in arguing with his father; it would only end in a bigger fight, one that he did not want to have on his first day home.

"I know you don't understand Dad. You asked me what I was working on and I told you."

He got up from the table and left the room, closing the kitchen door softly behind him even though he would have preferred to slam it.

The look of hurt that flickered across his father's face escaped Simon's notice. The sound of the fridge opening and the familiar popping sound of a can opening did not.

Chapter 5

The sound of chirping birds outside his window woke him. A glance at the alarm clock on his bedside table told him it was five thirty. He lay in bed listening, letting the sights and sounds flood his senses. An early sunrise softly lit his room. Subdued music drifted up through the floor grate from the radio in the kitchen. The squeak of the fridge door. Foot steps. Water filling a pot. A step back in time. His father first up, enjoying the early morning solitude, before the first sip of alcohol, preparing breakfast. Familiar sounds.

The shower was cold, just like he remembered. The ancient pipes and water heater were unable to meet the demand for instant heat to the second floor bathroom. Simon shaved, dressed in blue jeans and light t-shirt and descended the squeaky steps to the kitchen. The table was set for two. The smell of freshly buttered hot toasted bread made his mouth water.

Standing next to the stove and without a word of greeting, Marcus removed two steaming eggs from the boiling water and placed them on Simon's plate next to the toast. The events of the evening before were not mentioned. A comfortable feeling settled over him as he savored the hot buttered toast and planned his day.

Revelation was just around the corner. He could feel it. He could almost hear ET in his backpack urging him toward the source. The source. Could it really exist? Could there really be a place that was a source for all energy? Excitement of what lay in reach overcame him.

"What is the best way to get to Mullen Stream Falls?" he asked his father.

* * *

There was not a cloud in the sky. It was a great day to venture off into the wilderness. The dirt road into the falls was an old logging road that had long since been abandoned. It was overgrown with trees and brush and in some areas knee high grass. The SUV Simon rented bumped and tossed over the tough terrain. He wished he had rented a truck with a higher chassis or at least brought along a jack. Some ruts seemed to swallow the vehicle whole leaving the SUV precariously balanced and close to getting high centered or rolling over. He was deep into the provincial forest and there was not a sign of human habitat anywhere. He hummed a tune and focused his attention on navigating the winding road.

The sun flickering between the trees created a disquieting light show of dark and bright, shadow and blinding white as he travelled down the deserted wagon trail. His excitement at getting started was overcome by a feeling of apprehension that seeped its way into his consciousness. The hairs on the back of his neck bristled. He tried to shake it off. For a fleeting instant he saw a glimmering shadow moving within the brush. He looked over his shoulder and stole quick glances in the side view mirrors. Was someone following him? He stopped the car and peered into the brush both left and right of him as far as he could see. There was nothing there.

He tried to convince himself that he was being stupid; a victim of heightened imagination. A sudden loud creak and groan brought a rush of adrenaline through his veins. He feverishly pressed the brake pedal to the floor. Five feet in front of him, a huge jack pine thundered toward him, its branches scraping the front of his windshield and hood. Adrenalin pumping, arms tingling, he threw the gear shift into reverse. The tires grabbed dirt and spun the vehicle backwards away from the falling tree.

"What the Hell?" He jumped out of the SUV. Heart pounding. Two more feet and he would have been crushed! He listened intently. Looked in every direction. The air was still. There was no wind. It was a sunny day. What made the tree fall? He examined the tree. It was not dead. There were no cracks or cuts or axe marks. The bark was green and the inner pulp white and moist. The many branches were filled with plump green needles vibrant with color. What would make a healthy tree fall at this instant?

The road ahead was completely blocked. The tree was too heavy to move. There was no way around it. He checked his location on the GPS in the SUV. If he was going to see the falls today, he was going to have to go the rest of the way on foot. Shaken and a little unnerved, he gathered a few supplies from the car threw them into his backpack and set out on foot. Based on the GPS directions he should be no more than a mile or two from the falls. He whistled as he walked, partly to tell wild life he was in the area and partly to help shake off the jitters that had taken hold of him.

The trail he was on was an old logging road that had long ago been abandoned. The trees formed a dense canopy overhead and the road gradually disappeared, obliterated by the overgrowth of grasses, shrubs and small trees. He would not have been able to take the SUV much further anyway. He examined the route before him. There were several trails. Some made by hunters and teenagers who journeyed here to jump off the cliffs into the bottomless pool created by the falls and others that were most likely made by wildlife. Wanting to avoid the man made influences of the place; Simon chose the wild life path. The path was shaded by overarching fir, pine and poplar trees and the deep moss felt spongy under his feet. There were millions of ferns and delicate lady slippers on either side of the trail. The air was thick with the scent of green freshness. He took a deep breath and felt the exhilaration and sense of well being by inhaling the oxygen rich air that surrounded him. As he walked he marvelled in nature. Living in a large metropolitan city for the last ten years, he had forgotten how restful, how replenishing nature could be.

From time to time he had the feeling of being watched. He couldn't seem to shake it.

A soft humming noise filled the air around him. With heightened senses he made his way through the dense bush, gently moving aside heavy branches that blocked his pass. The trail was difficult. The brush was dense and the trail was steep. He climbed over fallen trees and sloshed through hidden bogs that had his Reeboks and socks soaked, water squishing between his toes with every step.

He had not travelled more than a half mile when he was swarmed by mosquitoes. Millions of them. They were everywhere. They encompassed his head and arms. He breathed them in and coughed and sputtered uncontrollably. Covering his mouth and nose with one hand and madly swatting insects with his other hand, he fought the urge to run through the brush. Running blindly wouldn't help. It would only serve to stir up more of them. How could he be so stupid as to come to the forest wearing short sleeves and no insect repellent? He cursed himself that he had not thought to at least bring along some Deet. He could already feel his skin welting under the greedy blood sucking bites of the multitude. He focused on slowing his breathing. They were an inconvenience but would not kill him. He looked around for something he could use to deflect them away from him. The underbrush was thick with ferns. He reached down and broke off two sturdy stems at the base. Perfect. He waved the broad reaching fronds up and down in front of him as he moved forward. The mosquitoes dispersed. He drew a large sigh of relief.

The sound of water drew him forward. He must be close. The trail headed south and he followed it.

Rounding the next bend in the path he heard a crashing noise coming from his left. He stopped and listened intently. There was a small clearing twenty feet in front of him. He edged forward slowly, moving away the branches of deep shrubbery to peek into the clearing.

Charging toward him was the largest moose he had ever seen. Its antlers stretched at least four feet on either side of its massive head.

Simon froze. He could do nothing but stare at the animal coming toward him; threatening to trample him in an instant. The familiar paralyzing fear held him in place.

Abruptly, seeing Simon standing in front of him, the animal stopped.

The air was still. Simon was afraid to breath.

Not a sound erupted from the forest around them. They stood, facing one another. Their eyes locked.

For some unexplainable reason all sense of fear dissipated. A sense of peace radiated from the animal. Simon's mind filled with visions of his childhood, his mother, father, Henrietta and his work. It was as though the animal reached into his very soul, the essence of his being. Then the moose slowly diverted his eyes, turned his massive head and ambled as quietly as such an enormous beast could, off the trail and into the forest.

Simon took in a deep breath. The oxygen rich air filled with the aroma of pine and spruce filled his lungs. A wave of peace came over him. He felt great. There were no more mosquitoes buzzing around his head. He looked around him and took in the wonders of the place. The sun was shining through the trees warming him and lighting the trail ahead. The sounds of wild life abounded. The welcoming call of the whip-or will, the singing of sparrows, the buzzing of insects, the land was alive. The apprehension that filled him moments ago dissipated. The tree falling in front of him was not an omen it was an invitation to get him out of his car and to experience the best that nature could offer. Had he remained in the car he would not have experienced this wave of exhilaration and well being that was now overcoming him.

The sound of splashing water beckoned him on. Pushing through a dense clump of willow shrubs he was confronted with the most awe inspiring scene he had ever encountered. It was worth facing the natural hazard of the trip, the falling tree, the walk, the mosquitoes and the moose.

The falls were the result of two converging streams. The waterfall itself was not large, but the ambiance created by the rock formation and plant life created an area that was simply beautiful. Over thousands of years the streams carved a notch through the bedrock, producing sheer cliff walls on either side of the falls. Steep cliffs over 30 feet high encircled the entire area creating a circular pool at the bottom. The entire area was surrounded by fir, spruce, poplar and birch trees to create what Simon thought must truly be one of Mother Nature's most beautiful spots.

The air was fresh and rich with oxygen. He inhaled deeply, feeling new energy surge through his body as he did. There was a reverence about the place that took Simon's breath away. Without thinking he made the sign of the cross, touching his temple, chest, left and right shoulders. This was a ritual he had not done since his altar boy days many years ago. He wasn't conscious of doing it now.

He took out his Geiger counter and scanned the area in front of the falls. The counter went off the scale. Energy abounded here! If there was an Eden, maybe he had found it.

He stepped to the edge of the cliff anticipating the usual dizziness he felt at great heights. Instead he only felt the warmth of the sun and the cool spray of mist on his face. He revelled in the sensation. Far below he could see the circular pond fed by the cascading falls. Churning water that foamed and climbed the walls of the canyon then fed into a circular pool directly below where he was standing. The clear water in the pool reflected the dark green and brown of its surroundings making it impossible to determine the depth. Simon knew from his reading that the pool was considered bottomless.

No one had ever been able to dive to the bottom.

He stepped back from the edge and peered up at the sky. A slight northerly breeze cooled his cheek.

The sound of twigs snapping and a rustling of leaves drew his attention away from the waterfalls. Still holding the Geiger counter in his hands he turned to the sound.

A man was standing there. He was holding a .25 gauge shotgun. It was pointed directly at him.

Jolted back into the moment, a bolt of raw adrenaline shot through Simon's veins. Adrenaline that would have made anyone else run for their life. It froze Simon to the spot.

"You have 3 seconds to get out of here before I shoot." The man with the gun spoke. The solid unfaltering look in this man's eye told Simon this was no joke. He was serious.

"One...two..."

Fear clutched his heart in a tight grip. He broke free of its paralyzing hold. He leapt sideways to get out of the line of fire. The move allowed instinct to take over. He darted forward, crashing through the bush along the trail he had come. Two steps. A bullet ricocheted off a tree right next to him! He charged ahead. Stumbled over a fallen tree and fell flat on his face.

In spite of the pounding of his heart and the rushing in his ears he was sure he heard heavy footsteps coming after him. Cracking branches, moving trees. He pushed himself upright and ran.

Another bullet whizzed by him.

This man was trying to kill him! Adrenaline overcame his clumsiness and cleared his thinking. Get off the path. The trees will provide cover. Bending low to the ground he dashed into the dense forest, serpentining between the trees in a weaving pattern back toward his car.

The white SUV was in the same place he left it. He said a silent thank you to God, jumped in, started the engine and thanked God again as the engine instantly came to life. He jammed the gear shift into reverse and sped backwards. He spun the car around in a small clearing and raced as fast as he could along the rough trail back toward the highway.

As he got farther away from the falls, his pulse began to slow down. Fear was replaced with anger.

What was that all about? My God that man shot at me! You can't just point a gun at someone in this day and age. Who does this guy think he is? Miramichi might be an Acadian village but shooting at someone?

The trek out was a lot easier than the trip in. Gradually his anger was replaced with resolve. He needed to talk to the local sheriff and get a permit to come on the land and he would report this idiot at the same time.

He was back in town within an hour and pounding on the Sheriff's office door.

"What did he look like?" Sherriff Donavan, a short fat man with balding hair asked, looking over his thick framed glasses

"I don't know. Not that old, maybe my age. I think he was native. Dark complexion. Pretty dirty. Long hair in a pony tail."

"Sounds like Peter Lifesong, Michael Lifesong's boy. Always thought he had a few screws loose," Donavan commented. "His father is an elder with the Mi'kmaq tribe. His whole family takes their role in protecting the environment and that particular piece of land you were visiting real seriously."

"Seriously? I would say shooting at someone is a little over the top, Sherriff."

"You know this land was first owned by the Mi'kmaq before the white man arrived. That particular piece of land has been an area that Michael's family has considered their job to protect. It has to do with some strong native custom that has been handed down through the generations. No one really knows what it is all about, but because they look after the place, no one has ever really argued it with them either. You have to admit, it is a little piece of heaven out there," Donavan explained.

"What?" Simon couldn't believe his ears. "The man just shot at me and you are making it sound like it is okay! You need to arrest him."

"Well now he didn't actually hit you, did he?" the Sherriff asked. "Before you go running off all steamed up, you will have to talk to Michael about the falls and his boy. There is lots of superstition and ancient custom involved and I am not about to go rising up any stirring with the Mi'kmaq. We all get along pretty well here. There is something about the pool and the falls that makes it a natural medicine wheel and it having some link to their spirit world. You know how those old Indian legends go; everything in the world is a circle, even life, there is no beginning and no end and everything is connected. Well it seems somehow the falls and the basin it forms is some symbol of that and the Mi'kmaq here take it very seriously. They aim to protect it from all outsiders."

"I am not an outsider. I was born right here. I don't intend to cause any damage to the area, I am just doing some energy readings for some research I am doing for the University. The falls is on crown land. Can't you just issue me a permit granting approval to be on that land?"

The sheriff shook his head. "I don't want to get in the middle of any dispute. Giving you a permit would be an insult to the Indians. You know how it is. The Indians don't care about crown land. They think it is rightfully their land. Giving you a piece of paper is not going to do anything except make it harder for you to be there. If you really want to be there, you will need to track down Michael, Peter's Dad. He is the Chief. You will need to work it out with him. Like I said, we get along well with the natives in this community and I don't need you coming in here and raising lots of trouble."

Simon was exasperated. "Where can I find him?"

"He is usually at the Lucky Lucy for breakfast every morning. That is your best option. But take my advice, know about their traditions and offer him a cigarette before you ask for any favors."

Assured that he would not be getting any help from the police, Simon stormed out of the station. He was going to need to find a way to deal with this on his own. He needed information and he needed a plan. Like he always did when he didn't know what else to do, he headed to the local library.

Chapter 6

It was just like he remembered. Entering the front door of the heritage house that once belonged to Lord Beaverbrook, for once he was comforted to see that nothing had changed since his boyhood. The shining hardwood floors, the polished oak staircase, the row upon row of oak book shelving filled with ancient volumes of information. Even the librarian's desk was in the same place as he remembered, although the same librarian was not.

Sitting behind the desk was a woman in her mid twenties. Glasses and hair pulled back in a bun, on first glance she looked like a stereotypical librarian. She was typing on a keyboard and looking at a large flat screen monitor in front of her. Simon casually approached the desk.

"How can I help you?" She peered over the rim of her glasses, a wide welcoming smile lit up her face.

She was not stereotypical at all. She was stunning.

"My name is Simon Gallagher. I grew up in these parts." He found himself stumbling over his words. "I haven't been home for a really long time. I am looking for information. Anything you might have on Mi'kmaq traditions, Medicine Wheels and Mullen Stream Falls".

"Francis Simpson," she reached out her hand to greet him, still smiling. "I know you, Simon Gallagher."

Simon looked at her quizzically, searching his memory banks for any shred of history about this beautiful woman in front of him. Nothing.

"We went to the same high school but I was two years behind you, so you probably never noticed me. But I knew who you were. I watched most of your hockey games. You played defence."

She had the most perfect white teeth. Her deep dark brown eyes twinkled with good humor.

Simon felt himself blushing. God, he had been a terrible hockey player. He only played because his father had forced him to and somehow he thought it would make his father proud. In reality all it did was make things worse. He could never be in the right place at the right time. The big guys bowled him over. He tripped over his own feet. Every time the opposition scored, his father yelled at him. He hated it. Was this the memory she had of him? The geek on ice who she couldn't help but notice because he was such a klutz?

How could he not remember her? What a stupid question. As a teenager he had not noticed most of what was going on around him. That was his problem. He always had his nose in a book and was so intrigued with science that he never really noticed the world around him. He found his satisfaction in delving into the unknown, experimenting with scientific ideas. He supposed to most of his classmates he was considered somewhat of a nerd. That this attractive woman in front of him had noticed him and he had not even been aware of her, made his face turn yet a deeper shade of red. God he *was* a geek.

"We have a large amount of information on the Mi'kmaq history and lots of information on Medicine Wheels too. Come with me up to our research room and I will get you started on your search."

She was pretty, smart and confident.

He ran his hand admiringly along the wood banister as they ascended the steps to the second floor. The feel of the polished wood brought a smile to his face. The solid natural wood, the craftsmanship that molded it, polished it and brought out its natural beauty for the world to see filled him with a sense of appreciation. He revelled in the sensation.

He let his eyes wander around the foyer at the top of the stairs. It was spectacular. Columns of engraved arches dating back to the early 19th century when art was captured in fine wood carvings. He was so engrossed in his thoughts and feelings that he did not see the large supporting column directly in front of him. His collision with the column smacked him into the present. His head flew backwards from the impact. He found himself sitting on the floor in shock.

Francis who was three steps ahead, rushed back to him. "Are you okay?"

She extended her hand to help him up from the floor and with great embarrassment he accepted her help.

"Man, where did that come from? " Simon rubbed his forehead and tried to make light of his clumsiness. He could already feel the bump emerging.

"It is like time stopped still in here," he grinned. "Except for that new post."

"Don't let our historical facade fool you. We are this town's best kept secret. This place has every modern technology available to expedite information transfer. The building is just a cloak. I think you are going to find lots of surprises in this sleepy town you left all those years ago Simon Gallagher," she chided him.

Francis led him into an antique furnished room with two comfortable overstuffed arm chairs, reading lamps and a huge 18th century desk. As they entered the room she flipped a wall switch and two heavy brocaded curtains on the far wall parted to reveal a 80 inch flat screen computer. The screen filled the entire wall. It was like being at a full screen movie theatre.

"It is voice activated," Francis said. "Just touch the screen to start and then you can ask it any questions and it will research your topic. The computer's name is Ranger. She will show you videos, connect you to links around the world, whatever you need. If you need any help, just ask Ranger to page me."

Wow! This was more advanced than his research lab in Boston! Who would have thought this technology was here in this small library in this small backwards town, in *his* home town. Simon touched the start screen. It came to life.

A woman's voice came from the screen. "Welcome. I am Ranger. How may I help you?"

Simon couldn't help but smile. This was his world. It was like Star Trek. "Ranger this is Simon. I need to find information on Mullen Stream Falls, New Brunswick."

"Welcome Simon," the voice replied and instantaneously a live feed satellite video appeared on the screen. Mullen Stream Falls minus the mosquitoes appeared before him.

"Mullen Stream Falls is an uninhabited, isolated area where two converging streams meet and fall over a 30 foot cliff into a round basin at the foot of the falls. It is located 30 miles south and west of Miramichi, New Brunswick."

No new information there. "Ranger what can you tell me about Medicine Wheels?"

Pictures of medicine wheels filled the screen and stopped at Bighorn Medicine Wheel located near Sheridan, Wyoming.

"Most medicine wheels have a basic pattern; a center of stone called a cairn and an outer ring with spokes of stone radiating out from it. The wheel represents the circle of life, the shape of the sun and the moon and the planets. Some of the wheels date back two to four thousand years BC, the time of the Great Egyptian Pyramids. Some archaeologists and geologists have suggested that the Big Horn Medicine Wheel is as old as a few million years. It has been compared to the rock formations of Stonehenge in England."

Overlapping pictures of Stonehenge and the Bighorn medicine wheel then rotated on the massive screen. The images were circumposed on one another showing there was a strong resemblance and fit of the structures.

"There are four cardinal directions and four sacred colors. North and the color blue, represent winter. It is a time for survival and waiting. It is associated with the adult and the achievement of wisdom that should be attained by adulthood. South and the color white represent summer, a time of plenty, of happiness and peace. It is associated with trust and innocence. East and the color yellow represent spring and a time of creation. It is associated with birth and the reawakening and illumination that occurs with the child. West and the color black relates to autumn, a time of harvest, death, the end of life's cycle and the loss of the physical body. The center of the wheel represents balance and harmony in the universe."

Ranger displayed a color graphic overlay emphasizing the directional distinctions with assigned colors and seasons.

"Despite their physical existence, there is great mystery surrounding the Medicine Wheel. No written record of their purpose has ever been found. Many believe that the medicine wheel creates a roadmap to a sacred space. Other theories describe the wheels as containing significant stellar and cosmological alignments. The performance of specific rituals and ceremonies suggests that the wheel is a link between our world and another, but they that have been long forgotten and are no longer practiced. It is speculated that there were over twenty thousand medicine wheel sites in North America prior to settler contact. Theft, vandalism and agriculture have drastically reduced those numbers."

"Thank you Ranger." Simon was about to touch the screen to sign off when he had another idea. "Ranger, can you superimpose the overhead image of Mullen Stream Falls with one of the Medicine Wheels?"

Instantly, two images were superimposed and displayed on the big screen in front of him. The similarities were astounding. When the pool at the bottom of the waterfalls was lined up with the circle in the center of the Medicine wheel, it was easy to see the four quadrants that were created by the two incoming streams, the outgoing river and the canyon wall.

He left the research room feeling like it was the best 15 minutes he had spent since he got home. Francis was waiting for him at the bottom of the stairs.

She smiled up at him "So did you find what you needed? Are you off to make your own medicine wheel?"

Simon laughed "Yes I think I am ready to heal the world now." For some reason, he felt himself blushing again. She was so beautiful. Her light brown hair pulled off her face in a knot at the back of her head had long straggling wisps of hair that framed her delicate features and made her dark brown eyes even more penetrating. Before he knew what he was saying, before he let his nervousness and ever present self doubt overcome his instinct, he asked her to join him for supper. To his astonishment she accepted.

She suggested a local restaurant and he was immediately glad he left the choice up to her. The quaint restaurant with its red chequered table cloths catered to the local clientele's budget in an atmosphere that was friendly and comfortable. When she ordered a Donaire and an Alpine beer, he quickly indicated he would have the same. He savoured the garlicky taste of the meat filled flat bread, sweet sauce and mozzarella cheese. There was no place in Boston that could match this!

"So what do you do, Simon Gallagher?" She asked between bites.

Simon felt blood rushing to his face and wished he could control this basic physiological sign of his discomfort that always seemed to belie his feelings. How could he explain his line of work without her thinking he was a complete weirdo? There was no way he could tell her that he was trying to figure out where one's life energy went after death. That if he could track the energy he could answer the biggest questions of all time. What happens after you die? Is there life after death? Is there a God? She would think he was a kook and run screaming out of the restaurant.

He thought carefully before answering: "I am a physicist. Quantum physics is my specialty." He grinned. "Right now I am working with a woman named Henrietta Storm doing some research on free floating energy." That seemed safe enough.

He found himself rattling off the main principles behind quantum theory before he checked himself. He had to get control of his tongue before he either bored her to death or scared her off. He decided to change the conversation to get the attention off of him.

"Tell me about the library. How does a small town like Miramichi afford such an elaborate place?"

Francis flashed him another beautiful smile. "The library is one of the few things given to this town instead of being taken away. A man named Alfred Innis, a multimillionaire who made his millions by selling off most of the natural resources here to outside companies had a pang of guilt or remorse or something and out of the blue decided to develop the resources in the library. He wanted it state of the art with nothing held back, and it is. He spent a pretty penny doing it."

"Why would he focus on improving the library instead of something that would increase employment?"

"No one is sure really. There is one doctor in town who uses the library a great deal, but other than him honestly the library is mostly used by school kids and stay at home moms who don't have a clue about the potential for information, research and telecommunications that it offers. It was great to see you come in today because it finally gave me a chance to show it off."

"What does the doctor do there?"

"There is a research lab in the lower level of the library that Dr. Thomas uses, but it is off limits to the public. I have only been

51

there once during the grand opening. It was a big deal how old man Innis wanted to show the town how supportive he was by partnering with this company to donate all this money to the library. Celebrities from all around the country came. Anyway, no one has access to the basement but Dr. Thomas and housekeeping staff. He is often there early in the morning before he makes his morning rounds at the hospital. He is a really good guy. Everyone likes him."

Simon noticed the flush on her cheeks as she spoke. He wondered if there was more than a librarian and patron relationship between Francis and Dr. Thomas.

"Dr. Thomas. What is he working on?" Simon asked.

"He is researching life energy too. He has a number of published articles in the Annals of Medicine and they are always about living energy. That is kind of coincidental isn't it? That you are both interested in energy?"

Simon agreed. "What is in the research lab?"

"The lower level of the library is phenomenal. It is truly state of the art; hard core science, physics and engineering stuff. There is even a 3-D Z printer and copier we call Zeddy12. Ever heard of that?"

"No"

"Zeddy12 isn't just a photocopier or printer, it is a replicator that creates fully functioning objects from a graphic design you create on the computer using a particular software program. It works just like a photocopier, only the copies are not just images on paper they are the real thing. It is amazing. At the grand opening, Dr. Thomas put his coffee cup in the copier machine and within 10 minutes an exact replica right down to the color and graphics on it was created. Then he took an ultrasound of a baby, downloaded it into the computer and the replicator created a "baby" that matched every detail of the ultrasound! Of course it was not a live baby. It was just a doll, but none the less he showed how it could be used to let expectant parents know what their baby actually looked like before it was born. Then as a grand finale, he sent the machine a graphic design of a toy airplane through his computer and within 30 minutes, the machine had actually created the real thing. An actual airplane that you could hold and it had all the parts working! The capabilities are amazing and scary all at the same time."

"I can see why that kind of equipment is kept under lock and key. It has to be very expensive and very delicate, so you would not want everyone in the public messing with it. If the opportunity ever arises I would love to meet this Dr. Thomas. I am guessing we might have a few things in common."

"Sure. I would be happy to introduce you." Francis flushed. "I think you both come from the genius strain."

This time Simon blushed. He was not good at handling compliments. It was time to change the topic.

"Tell me about you. Besides being a librarian what else do you do?"

Francis told him about her passion for animals especially horses. She lived on a small farm just outside the town limits. She spent most of her free time riding in the bush with her favourite horse Mike and a border collie named Ben. She talked about how after a day at work there was something about the animals and being with Mother Nature that rejuvenated her. Throughout her life, on her darkest, saddest days, a ride in the bush on her favourite horse would always push the sadness away and leave her feeling good. They talked about the aura that all living things exude, about the energy transfer that just naturally occurs between people and animals. In many ways she was intrigued with the exact thing that Simon was; energy flow and how and where it travels.

He never talked so much about his work to anyone other than Henrietta. Francis was easy to be around and easy to talk to. She genuinely listened and showed interested in his work and his research. She didn't seem to think he was a geek at all. They talked for hours, long after the food and beer was finished.

By the time Simon got home he was feeling exhilarated. His first day in town and he had been nearly crushed by a falling tree, devoured by mosquitoes, overrun by a giant moose, shot at by a mad man and dined with a beautiful girl. Not bad for his first day at home. He was smiling when his father met him at the door.

"Where the hell have you been Simon?" Marcus growled at him, the smell of alcohol strong on his breath.

The smile on Simons' face dropped. He shook his head in dismay at the half empty whiskey bottle on the kitchen table.

"Sheriff Donavan called me and told me you were nosing around up at Mullin falls and damn near got yourself killed. Then no one has seen you for hours."

The syllables at the end of each word were thick and slurred. Simon shook his head in disgust. His father always did this. His enthusiasm deflated in a gush. Without answering, he turned abruptly away and headed up the stairs to his room. He was not going to let his father ruin this wonderful feeling he had.

Chapter 7

The parking lot was already filled with an assortment of pickup trucks when Simon pulled up to the Lucky Lucy. There were two categories of people who came to Lucky Lucy's at 7 am, those who were heading off to work and needed breakfast to sustain them for the day and those who were the old timers who came for coffee and to partake in the most recent gossip.

Michael Lifesong was not a gossiper. He was sitting at the counter waiting for his breakfast of bacon, eggs, toast and hash browns that he had every morning before setting out to work at the county tourist interpretative center.

Simon hesitated. Social situations like this were definitely not in his comfort zone. He had to think about how he would proceed. He took a slow breath. He mentally rehearsed the approach he had planned.

He walked over to the man at the counter feeling subconsciously that everyone in the diner was staring at him. No turning back now.

"Michael Lifesong?" Simon started.

There was no response from the man. He did not even look in his direction.

Feeling like a fool now, his face beat red, Simon forced himself to continue. "I am Simon Gallagher. Marcus Gallagher's son. I think you may also have known my mother, AnnaMae."

Michael slowly turned his head and eyed Simon suspiciously.

In recognition of native tradition, Simon placed an unopened pack of cigarettes on the counter in front of Michael.

"Can I buy you a coffee?"

After what seemed an eternity, in which he felt he was being sized up and analyzed by the man with the long braided hair, Michael reached for the cigarettes and put them in his shirt pocket.

"I knew your mother. I know your father too. He is a hard worker. A man of his word. He gave my son a job once before the mill closed down. What do you want?"

"I hoped to talk to you about Mullen Stream Falls."

'What about it?"

"I work for a university in Boston. " Simon stumbled. "My boss and I are doing research on energy flow. Mullen Stream Falls has the highest free flow energy ratings on the east side of North America. We would like to take some special readings and try to track where the energy is coming from and if lucky where it is going. Sherriff Donavan tells me that the area is sacred to your people. I didn't know this. Yesterday I took a trip out to the falls. It is one of the most beautiful places I have ever seen."

"Yes, you got that part right."

"I would like to go out there again, but I think your son might feel different about that so I wanted to ask your permission to go back"

He knew Michael was sizing him up, weighing his words for honesty.

"Why are you asking me for permission?"

"Your son shot at me."

Michael sat for a long minute without speaking. Simon began to think that he was going to ignore him and leave him standing there in the middle of the diner with everyone staring at him. Finally, he motioned to the seat next to him.

Simon accepted the invitation readily and perched on the bar stool thankful to feel the scrutinizing gaze of the other customers wander away from him.

"The legends of my people are many. The town people do not believe them. They think of the stories of the ancients as folklore. They laugh and make fun at the stories. My father and his father before him were great medicine men. They were handed down the secrets of the Wheel from the ancients and then on to me. I have passed them on to my son. He will pass it on to his and so on until the end of times."

"Are the secrets attached to Mullen Falls, is that why you don't want people there?"

Michael ignored Simon's question. His story, what he chose to share would be shared in his own way.

"Our people are Míkmaq. We chose this name because it means we live in harmony with the land. It is what we believe the Creator intended. *"Msɨt No'kmaq* ("Mm-sit Noh-goh-mah") means 'All My Relations'. It acknowledges man's connection with all things. All the land around this town has been destroyed by white man, feeding his greed. My people recognize and accept the living spirit within all things. The living spirit is in the entire animal kingdom, within plants, and even within the rocks and waters of our world. We do not 'worship' these things. We recognize that their spirits and our own are akin to each other, and we treat these spirits with the same respect we wish for ourselves. We will not kill an animal unless we are in danger, or need food. We give humble thanks to the Creator for its offerings and to the animal's spirit for giving its life for us. We will not kill a plant unless we have need of it for some purpose and again we will make an offering to recognize its sacrifice. If we dig a hole, we make an offering to Mother Earth to recognize that we are disturbing her skin. We recognize our place in the world around us. We must never forget that we are surrounded by other beings that were created by the same Supreme Being that created us. They are just as deserving of life as we are. We take nothing we don't need. We waste nothing. We offer thanks for everything we do take. White man does nothing of this sort. There is no *Msit No'kmaq* between white man and the rest of the earth. "

Simon felt the sincerity as well as the sadness in Michael's words. He knew everything Michael said was true. He himself was guilty of the same behaviour. In a way this was what his father was always preaching to him; "waste not".

Michael continued. "Our job is not just to pass on the ancient mysteries; it is also to protect them. To protect the source. To protect the Wheel."

"Wheel. Are you talking about the medicine wheel?" Simon interrupted. "Sherriff Donavan told me that Mullen Falls is considered some kind of a natural medicine wheel by your people. Is that true?"

Michael glared at him for the interruption but continued speaking.

"There are many medicine wheels all around the earth, Some were built by my people, and some by the Creator. Some native tribes actually adopted the name Cree to describe their connection to the Cree-ator. The native people have always known about the wheels and have been protectors of the wheels. Mullen Falls is one of the few natural wheels that I know of. All medicine wheels made are protected by sacred tribes."

"Is your tribe one of these sacred tribes?"

"My tribe as you call it no longer exists. My family alone have kept the sacred oath to protect the Wheel. My son, who you met yesterday, is in touch with all of the spirits and with the energy that surrounds the Wheel. He is a natural Medicine Man. He feels the energy around the Wheel changing, getting smaller. The spirits are at unrest. He is sure that something or someone is affecting it. When he saw you with your little machine he thought that somehow you were doing this. Plants have never died around the Wheel. No one knows the age of the trees, now they are dying.

58

Healthy trees are falling for no apparent reason. Something is wrong with the balance."

"I only plan to study the area. I give you my word that I will not destroy one living thing during my studies; except for maybe a few mosquitoes. I will not cut down trees or put anything into the water. I only wish to study the area. Maybe I can help find out what is going on. At the very least, I may be able to track where the energy is going. If you and your son work with me, maybe we can figure out what is going on."

"It is not up to me. It is up to the power of the Creator."

Oh man, this is getting out there Simon thought but asked the question anyway. "How can I get the Creator's approval?"

"When you visit the falls, the direction by which you approach is chosen for you. It is part of your life journey. Along that path you will encounter difficulties. When you overcome these difficulties you win the trust of the Creator. His spirit may appear to you in many shapes. It may be an animal or a bird. You will know it is the Creator's spirit because you will feel a great inner peace."

Simon thought about his trip to the falls the previous afternoon. When he came upon the great moose, he felt exactly what Michael was describing. He told Michael about his trip; the falling tree, the mosquitoes, and the moose.

Michael nodded knowingly.

"You were on the north side of the Wheel. North represents the place of wisdom. It is about learning to explore new depths of awareness within yourself and your environment. I will talk to my son and tell him you have been visited by the spirit of the great moose. He will not shoot at you again. Perhaps it is your destiny to help one another. Peter lives in a camp up by the falls. If you think of the center of the falls as the center of the wheel, you will find his cabin in the northern quadrant of the wheel. I will tell him to expect you."

Chapter 8

Dr. Galen Thomas always did his best thinking in the early hours before dawn. It was 5:30 am. He was sitting in the lavishly furnished "great knowledge room" as he called it, in the lower level of the Miramichi Library. He loved this place. His creative juices began pumping as soon as he sat in the luxurious leather chair and fired up the computer.

This morning his mind was sorting out the problem of how to transfer energy from a holding cell to a living recipient. Because the energy was free floating it was influenced by the other many energy sources surrounding the holding cell and he needed to find a way to focus and direct it to a precise point. He was close. It was a matter of weeding out the barriers one by one and then introducing new variables into the scheme. He tried many different methods of influencing the direction of the escaping energy including the use of injections, inhalants, and ingestants. None of it worked. As he browsed through research on energy transfer and energy direction techniques, the information on solar panels kept drawing him back. Something called a heliostat was used to re-direct solar energy. A heliostat was really just a mirror or series of mirrors used to re-direct the suns' energy onto a specific target. If a heliostat could re-direct energy captured from the sun, perhaps it could also work for his purposes. The sudden revelation filled him with excitement. He hurriedly jotted down formulas and scribbled designs before the ideas racing through his mind dissolved and disappeared. Getting his ideas on paper, he discovered long ago was half the battle. Once formulated solidly on paper his mind worked out the details, identified the problems and created the solutions until version by version his diagrams formed the perfect structure he needed to create. He fired up his computer and began inputting his design concepts into the Z software.

After many versions he finally came up with a prototype. The prototype was an assembly of heliostats that would allow him to transfer donor energy he had collected in COLTEN to a host. The biggest revelation he had was that the secret wasn`t just the heliostats and redirection and it was not in the process of living, it was in the "process" of dying. The time when energy was leaving the body, the time when the brain stopped sending signals and the heart stopped pumping was also the time when energy could be received by the body. It was so simple. He couldn't wait to test it out.

Next to the Great Knowledge room in the lower level of the library was a small animal research lab. Wearing a white lab coat, face mask and goggles, Galen held a young mouse in his hands. He had just given it an injection that would end its life in just a few seconds. As the mouse drew its last breath, he inserted COLTEN's pen like tip into the mouse's mouth and slid the button on its side backwards into the "collect" position. He placed the dead mouse on the table. He then picked an aged mouse from its cage and gave it the same lethal injection. As it drew its last breath he inserted COLTEN's pen light tip into its mouth and pushed the button on its side forward into the "transfer" position."

He waited with baited breath. The old mouse lay still in his hand.

"Damn."

He opened the cover to the trash can with his foot. A small tremor ran through the lifeless body in his gloved hand and miraculously he felt it take a breath. Galen placed the mouse back on the examining table, pulled a stethoscope out of the drawer and listened for a heartbeat. There it was, strong and steady. A smile lit up his face. He returned the old mouse to its cage and watched it closely over the next two hours. The changes at first were subtle, barely noticeable. He recorded each with video and verbally described the changes that he was observing. It started with the eyes. The cataracts that occluded the old mouse's eyes cleared. Next it was evident in its claws. The curled gnarled broken claws on its feet looked less scaly, less curved, no longer dull. His fur changed. The dry dull coat gained a lustre that had not been there before. Before his very eyes, the old mouse was becoming young. At the end of two hours the mouse awoke and began sniffing the air, looking for food, scurrying around the cage.

Galen was ecstatic. Success! He was on the right track. Before he could transfer energy to a human being however he had to be sure. His time was running out. He knew old man Innis might die any day now. He spent every waking moment further testing the energy collection and transfer devices on every conceivable combination of animals that he could. He was successful transferring energy collected from a mouse to a rabbit, but the effect was not as incredible as with the mouse and the old rabbit only lived a few more days than had been expected without the energy transfusion. When he did the reverse however, and transferred rabbit energy to a mouse, the mouse seemed to become not just younger but smarter. His latest theory therefore was related to the need to transfer energy either between same animals or from more evolved animals to lesser evolved animals. He wasn`t yet sure how this knowledge would help him with his most urgent task with Innis, but he felt it would help in later usages. He even tried transferring combined energies from several lesser evolved animals into more evolved animals but the results were not gratifying. When he transferred the energy from three rabbit donors into a dog host, the dog only lived an additional few days as well. Yet the total energy units were identical. It was not the quantity of energy that made the difference.

Chapter 9

When he stepped out of the Lucky Lucy the rising sun was casting a golden glow over the town. The town park, filled with flowers in bloom looked surreal. What a beautiful day. He felt great!
Thoughts of Francis filled his head and he wanted to share his new found information with her.

At the library he read the sign that said "Open Monday, Wednesday, Friday and Saturday from 9 am till 5 pm". Today was Tuesday. He remembered her telling him that she lived on a farm across from an old public swimming park that he remembered as a child. He decided to take a drive in the country. Maybe he would find her at home.

It was not hard to find. It was the only farm on what used to be known as the old Enclosure Road and he immediately spotted her small yellow Volkswagen beetle in front of a clean white and blue trimmed barn. The driveway was lined with white board fences and fir trees. He parked behind the beetle. There were three horses looking over the paddock fence at him as he stepped out of his car. A black, white and tan colored border collie ran up to greet him. He reached down to pet its head and its whole body wiggled with excitement. He bent down to the dog's level and scratched behind its small floppy ears. He was rewarded with low squeals and moans of delight from the dog. He stood up and reached into his car to bring out two coffee cups. The dog ran in circles around him, seemingly herding him in the direction of the neat white barn. Armed with coffee he succumbed to what seemed to be the dog's wishes.

As they got close to the barn, the dog ran ahead and disappeared into the dark opening created by the sliding barn door. He was back in a second with a beautiful slim woman in tow.

"Hey Stranger". Francis greeted him, face beaming. Her hair was pulled back into a pony tail. She was wearing blue jeans, a t-shirt and riding boots. She was holding a brush in one hand. "What brings you out here?"

He sheepishly handed her a cup of coffee. "Thought you might be ready for a morning coffee break."

"Thank you. I am always ready for a cup of coffee!" She accepted his offer and took a sip of the steaming brew.

"I see you have met Ben." Hearing his name the little dog, looked up at her and wagged his tail. In fact he wagged his whole body. She laughed. A beautiful joy filled sound that made Simon smile too. "He is my official visitor greeter! "

"Well he certainly did a great job at making me feel welcome. That might not be so great if I was a thief or mass murderer." He grinned at her.

She laughed. "Oh you would be surprised. Dogs have amazing instincts, at least Ben does. He can sense when a person means harm or has bad intent. He might be little, but he is a herd dog by nature and is pretty brave at the end of the day. He won't back down from any sheep, ram, cow or bull! And he is tenacious! He will never give up until he gets what he wants or needs. So you see, I would say he has already figured out your basic nature and has invited you into our home!" She scratched the little dog's head again and was silent for a moment.

"You have a beautiful place, here." Simon tried to fill the silence.

"Thank you. Come on, I will show you around" she grabbed his hand and led him into the barn. It smelled like fresh hay and straw mixed with horse. It was a comforting aroma.

"This is the barn". She laughed. He laughed too. "And this is my best friend Mike".

A stout sorrel gelding with a flaxen mane and tail, a narrow white blaze and the softest deepest brown eyes he could imagine was standing quietly in the walkway looking intently at him.

Francis untied the horse and led him over to Simon. "Mike is not just my best friend, he is my therapist." She laughed and rubbed the big sorrels head.

Mike tucked his head into the crook of her shoulder. Simon ran a hand along his muscled neck. He could feel the strength and power in the animal, yet a sense of quiet peace radiated from it as well.

"How many horses do you have here?"

"Four. Two geldings and two mares. Mike is my favourite. Sometimes you really connect with an animal, and for me, that is both Mike and Ben. When I am feeling down or blue or confused or uncared for or alone, these two bring me back. Ben, well he just loves me no matter what. Mike, he makes me see things in a different light. Whether I am just brushing him or riding him, it is almost like there is a transfer of energy between us that always makes me feel better and helps me to see things differently. I know it sounds kooky, but other people who love horses describe it the same way. It is not just any horse; it is the horse you connect with. I hope that I have the same effect on Mike, but somehow I doubt that he gets as much out of our relationship as I do."

She led Simon through the barn.

The barn had 6 box stalls, 3 on either side of a cement walkway with two large sliding doors at each end of the walkway. One door, the one he entered led to the main driveway and front yard of the farm, the back doorway led into a series of paddocks. Each paddock was contained within freshly painted white board fence. The four paddocks each had separate shelters and gates that led out into a lush knee high mixed grass pasture. They were greeted with a soft whinny and several knickers from Mike's paddock mates.

"I was just about to go out for a ride. Want to come?" she stroked the velvety nose of a tall sorrel gelding. "This is Gibson. He would treat you very well and he could sure use the exercise".

Simon vaguely remembered riding a horse at summer camp many years ago. It hadn't gone well. He recalled being tossed into the bush and a really long walk back to camp where he met with the jeers and jokes of his camp mates. In spite of the sudden rush of anxiety that overcame him he agreed.

Half an hour later, Mike and Gibson were brushed, saddled and bridled. Francis handed Simon the big sorrel's reins and told him to mount up. She gave him a brief riding lesson: left rein to go left, right rein to go right, backward pressure to stop, lift the reins to backup, your legs like two walls that your horse is passing between. Left leg pressure will move your horses body to the right, right leg pressure will move your horses body left. It sounded simple enough.

Francis was positive and encouraged him in his attempts to follow her directions. She had him maneuver Gibson first inside the outdoor fenced arena and then out in the field. It did not take long for him to connect with Gibson. In fact he was amazed. It seemed the horse had telepathy. He simply needed to think about where he wanted to go and look in that direction and Gibson headed there. Francis had him take the horse around obstacles and over fallen trees and even through the small brook that ran through the field. He was astonished at how well he was doing but even more impressed with Francis. She was so comfortable and confident with the horses and with him. When she felt he was in good enough control, she led the way to a gate at the far end of the field. She moved Mike up to the fence, had him sidestep to the gate latch, opened the latch, backed Mike up while holding the gate for Simon and Gibson to pass through and then manoeuvred Mike backwards through the gate and reached down and clasped it shut. He was in awe. Horse and rider were truly partners. They communicated as if by ESP. Each one read the others intentions and cues as effortlessly as a long time married couple. No wonder she loved that horse. He was starting to feel the same way about Gibson.

They rode side by side through the field, each horse matching stride, ears perked and attentive. Simon fell into a natural rhythm with the horses stride and felt himself relax and trust the animal beneath his legs. He was in awe at the sense of confidence and power he had with this animal. Ben ran circles around them and Francis pointed out interesting sights as they walked through the trees along a well ridden trail. The little dog serpentined back and forth through the bush, nose to the ground sniffing out new smells but returning every few minutes to herd his wards forward. The sun was warm with just a slight breeze rustling the leaves of the trees. Simon could not think of another time in his life when he had felt so happy.

Eventually they came to a creek with a wooden bridge over it. Francis suggested they stop and let the horses drink and take a break before heading back. They dismounted, let the horses drink and then tied the horses to a hitching post that had been erected next to the brook. This was obviously a common destination for Francis and Mike.

"Come over here", she coaxed him. She led him across the foot bridge and through a small path in the woods and waited for him to follow. "Isn't it beautiful?"

As if from a post card, a beautiful valley surrounded by gentle hills and lush grass awaited them. She sat down on a fallen log and he joined her.

"There are many hidden wonders in the world aren't there?" He asked feeling the genuine honesty of this place.

She breathed in a breath of fresh air. "Yes. You just need to look and be open to possibilities to see the many wondrous things everywhere on this planet."

"I met Michael Lifesong today and we had a great talk about natural wonders too."

She placed a hand on his arm. His skin tingled with the sensation of her touch.

"The Indians believe that the basin at the foot of Mullen Falls is actually a natural Medicine Wheel that was formed by the Creator at the beginning of time on Earth. Apparently there have been some changes happening at the falls that are really worrisome to the Mi'kmaq people, trees falling and plants dying. Michael and his son Peter feel it is their responsibility to protect the wheel. Peter thought I was somehow affecting the change that is happening and that is why he shot at me yesterday. "

"So your theory about energy around the falls is right."

"Maybe. All I had hoped to do was try to track the energy fields around the falls, but maybe I can also help the natives if I can find out if indeed the levels of energy are decreasing around the falls."

He told Francis about ET and what he had been able to accomplish with his energy tracking device. He expected her to be incredulous, but instead she was looking at him with admiration.

"Maybe this is written in your cards, Simon. You were supposed to come here, now to help protect the Wheel."

They sat in silence for a moment enjoying the warmth of the sun, the view in front of them and the gurgling of the babbling brook behind them. The birds were chirping in the trees and all seemed right with the world.

"I see why you like it here" Simon sighed.

"It is a great place. Whatever made you leave, Simon?"

Simon looked deeply into her eyes and knew that he would tell her the true reason he had left. The reason he had not shared with another living soul. The things that tortured him and kept him awake at night, the real reason why he could never be close to his father. He drew a deep breath and laid his guilt and shame before her.

"When I was fifteen I was as crazy about science and quantum physics as I am now, maybe more so. I spent every waking moment working through formulas and hypotheses. I loved it. It was like a major puzzle and I couldn't get enough of it. One morning in January, my mother told me she was going out to get groceries. I was busy on my computer, working out some new theory. I lost track of time. The phone rang a few times throughout the day. My father was at work, so I was home alone. I didn't bother to answer the phone. It was usually sales calls anyway and I did not want to be disturbed. I spent all day on my computer, completely lost in what I was doing. At around 5 o'clock I heard my Father's truck pull into the driveway and realized that it was already dark out. I hadn't heard Mom come back from groceries, but figured I must have been so absorbed in what I was doing that I hadn't noticed. I heard my Dad yell out that he was home and ask where everyone was. When I came into the kitchen, I saw the red light on the phone indicating that someone had called and there was a message. I dialed into the message replay and sure enough there was a message from 1140 in the morning from my Mother's cell phone. I pressed re-play and heard my Mother's voice. She was calling for help. Her message was "Help. I am at the Cove." And then the message ended. That was 5 hours before."

He paused, the emotion of the memory overcoming him. Francis squeezed his hand.

"I hollered at my father that mom was in an accident somewhere near the Mill Cove. We called the police. Both Dad and I drove to the cove and scanned the hillside and banks for Mom's car. It was windy, cold and snowing. It was hard to see anything. After about half an hour of searching I spotted her car at the bottom of the hill. It had rolled over a number of times and was upside down and lodged between two trees. I got to the car first. She was still holding the cell phone in her hand."

"Oh Simon, I am so sorry."

"I couldn't do anything to help her. I froze. I just stood there, staring at her. I couldn't move. I guess the reality that I could have

69

saved her just paralyzed me. When Dad reached the car, he pushed me out of the way and ran to her. He climbed through the window and held her. I can still see him. It is the only time I ever saw him cry. We never really talked to one another after that. He took into heavy drinking. I don't think he could face what happened. I knew he couldn't face looking at me. I know he blames me for Mom's death. If I had just picked up the phone when it rang, she might be alive today." He hung his head in shame.

Francis put her arms around him. She laid her head on his shoulder.

"She called me for help. I never got a chance to say goodbye. Or tell her how much I loved her. Or tell her how sorry I was that I let her down."

His eyes welled with tears.

"I think she knows."

Francis leaned forward and brushed her lips against his cheek. The warmth of her breath, the closeness of her body made him shudder in sudden wanting. He squeezed her hand in response. They stayed like that for a few minutes and then Francis slowly moved away. She looked up at the sky.

"Looks like it might rain. The clouds are starting to roll in from the east."

"Guess we better get back."

They made it back to the barn just as the first raindrops began to fall from the darkening sky. They untracked and groomed the horses in silence. It was a comfortable silence. Simon helped Francis clean the stalls. The manual labor had a soothing effect. As he climbed into his car to head home, he realized that his relentless overpowering sense of guilt about his mother's death was being replaced with a sense of sadness and acceptance.

Chapter 10

Simon lay in bed tossing and turning. Something Francis said the day before was still resonating in his mind. She talked about how animals give energy to you, that somehow their aura of energy can influence your mood. God knows since being home he felt the familiar draining of energy every time he was around his father. Alternately, he felt a surge of energy every time he was around Francis. Maybe there is a constant transfer of energy between living things all the time. Maybe no one entity owns their energy but rather it is moved about. If there is an ebb and flow of energy maybe it could be tracked among living organisms. Why hadn't he thought of this before? He was so excited about the thought that he could barely sleep. He jumped out of bed, grabbed ET, and called for Randi; the golden retriever that never left his father's side.

She wagged her tail and obediently jumped up on Simon's lap. Simon petted her for a while. Now that he was aware of it, he could feel the comfort radiating from the dog. He activated ET. The screen came immediately to life. Sure enough a bright red dot appeared on the graphic display of the room he was in. A soft buzz emitted from the speakers. The dot just moved slightly back and forth in the same general area. There was no doubt; it was picking up the living energy transfer between man and dog.

Simon sat in stunned silence as the realization of this new information sunk in. The conclusion was so obvious. Of course life energy was in the living. If it wasn't it wouldn't be there at death! He pulled up the digital display on ET and closely analyzed the waves that showed his and Randi's energy merging. He could tell by the amplitude which was which. The amplitude of his own energy was quite high signifying he had large quantities of energy. Both he and the dog were benefitting from the merging of energy fields, each one becoming richer. The differences in amplitude made him begin to ponder if there were differing amplitudes within same species or if this was just because it was the difference between man and dog.

Simon hadn't spoken with Henrietta since they arrived in town two days ago. He had the sudden intense urge to talk to her but he forced himself to wait till the sun was just barely above the horizon before phoning her.

***

Henrietta arrived at the Gallagher home just after 9 am. Randi and Marcus met her at the door. The big golden retriever who was quite enjoying all the company and attention she was receiving was quick to welcome her with a wagging tail and an expectant look for acknowledgement and praise. Henrietta immediately fell in love with the golden retriever with the big soft eyes and welcoming heart.

"You must be Marcus," Henrietta extended her hand in introduction. "I am Henrietta Stone, Simon's boss."

Marcus reached out his large calloused hand to welcome her into his home. Her hand felt small and warm in his. He was impressed with the firm confidence her hand shake be told.

"I hear you and my son are working on some interesting theories about energy movement."

"I am not sure if you are aware, but Simon is somewhat of a protégé in the field of quantum physics. I feel very fortunate indeed to have him working alongside of me." A smile lit up her face. "I am happy to finally meet the man who is his father."

Marcus nodded at Henrietta's double compliment. He found himself smiling back at her. Her twinkling blue eyes induced a sense of happiness that was contagious.

"Can I get you something to drink?" he asked.

"I would love a cup of tea if it is not too much trouble."

"Tea. Yes, I was just going to make a pot when you drove up. Come in." He pointed to the living room. "Go make yourself comfortable. Simon will be down in a minute."

When Simon joined Henrietta in the living room, he couldn't help but notice his father's broad smile. His father never smiled.

Humming to himself, Marcus headed to the kitchen to heat water for tea. He returned the unopened can of beer to the refrigerator.

While he was gone, Simon eagerly shared his adventure to the waterfalls and his latest discovery about energy quality with Henrietta. He demonstrated his findings by taking energy readings of both Henrietta and Randi again and then also of himself. The energy waves emitted differed not just between Randi and Simon and Henrietta, it also differed between Simon and Henrietta. Henrietta's amplitude was considerably higher than Simon's.

"What do you make of that? Do you think it is just the difference between male and female genders?" Simon asked.

"Maybe. Let's test it out. Marcus? Could you come in here for a minute," Henrietta called.

Marcus came carrying a tray with a tea pot, mugs, a can of condensed milk, sugar and spoons.

"We need your help. Would you mind us taking an energy reading from you?" Henrietta smiled at him.

"Sure. I guess. What do you need me to do?" He sat down on the sofa beside her. It always felt good to be needed.

Henrietta pointed ET at him and took an energy reading.

"See these red lines and the size of wave they make. This one is yours. She pointed to the thick wavy line in the middle of two others. Mine is on top and Simon's is on the bottom."

"What do you think? Can you think of anything that might play a role in why our levels of energy might be different?" She directed her question to Marcus.

He considered her question for a moment before answering.

"It might have something to do with age as well as gender. Simon and I rate lower than you, so maybe females generally have higher ratings. I am also older than Simon so maybe age has something to do with it. Have you tried it on animals?"

Simon looked at his father curiously. He had forgotten how pragmatic and intuitive he was when he wasn't drunk.

"Just with Randi. The difference between me and the dog was huge. So it is good to know that at least somebody rates lower than me." Simon chuckled. "That is a good idea, Dad. If we could test it between different species and genders of animals it might give us the information we are looking for."

Marcus nodded with a slight grin. Two compliments in less than an hour, he was on a roll.

"Well I do have cats you could try it on. I have a male and female and three kittens in the barn. I also have a couple of rabbits."

Their experiment revealed that indeed, the differences in amplitude were higher between lower and higher species. Human levels were higher than all of the animals. Among the animals, Randi's level was higher than the cats and the cats were higher than the rabbits. There was a male and female cat and three kittens in the barn, they all registered the same energy amplitudes, the same was true of the rabbits. Age and sex did not seem to make a difference in the animals they tested.

The results confirmed the basic tenants of life; the hierarchy from animal to man was more than just evolution of the brain, it was evolution of energy. Yet some animals had a purer form of energy than others that was depicted by the cohesiveness of the energy waves they emitted as well as the volume of energy. The dog had a more cohesive energy wave than the cats or rabbits. They all agreed that they needed to test energy readings on more people. It was Marcus who again came up with the idea.

"The local fair is running at the agriculture park this week. Why don't you two set up a booth? "Come one, come all, step right up and get your free energy reading!" People are suckers for stuff like that. You could test as many people as you need to help you figure out if the differences you are seeing are just a fluke or not."

Simon couldn't help himself from looking at his father with a new sense of appreciation.

"That is a great idea, Dad," he acknowledged.

Marcus gave Simon a quizzical look at yet another unexpected compliment.

***

The following evening, back at the Gallagher house, Marcus was listening intently to the excited conversation that was occurring between his son and Henrietta. He pulled up a chair to the table to join in.

"It was amazing," Henrietta said. "It was such a great idea, Marcus. The people lined up in droves. We tested 800 people; men, women, and children of all ages."

"We were able to rule out our hypothesis about women having higher amplitudes than men. And we also discovered that you do not necessarily develop more cohesive energy as you get older. In fact we found out just the opposite. Children consistently had higher and more cohesive energy levels than adults," Simon added.

"There were a few exceptions. Me, Father Murphy, a nurse named Tirisa who works in the emergency department at the Miramichi Regional Hospital, a farmer from Nordine, a lobster fisherman from Neguac and Francis, the librarian all had exceedingly high energy readings," Henrietta said.

"Want to hear my theory?"

Simon looked at his father with interest. "Let's hear it."

Marcus spoke slowly weighing each word carefully before speaking. "Remember your mother?

Simon's face flushed red. Why would his father bring up his mother now?

"How would you describe her energy level?" Marcus asked, ignoring Simon's discomfort with the question.

"I would make a guess that the quality of her energy was high."

"Do you see the similarities between Henrietta and your mother?"

Simon had never told Henrietta how much she reminded him of his mother, but well here was his father putting it on the table and the similarities in their personalities were driven home by being in this house surrounded by her memories.

"I think she would be very similar to Henrietta. They are both very much alike. Both were positive, both comfortable and content with life, both good people." He smiled at Henrietta as he spoke.

"Well, I think the amplitude of the energy people emit is related to how they are as people, and how they live their life. People who are genuinely good have higher energy levels than people who are not so good."

"You think that people's personalities make the difference?" Henrietta asked.

"Not exactly, I think it is who they are inside that makes the difference," Marcus replied.

He went on to explain. "What if the quality of energy we emit is based on how we live our lives? People who are basically good like your mother, Henrietta and Francis have high levels and those of us who are not so good or who have more to learn have lower levels. Growing old is not just about aging, it is about gaining knowledge and virtue. It is about getting to be a better person; one who is selfless, who cares about others and goes out of their way to not just do things right, but to *make* things right. Children have not yet been corrupted, by the very nature of being young, they are virtuous. As we grow old, we need to find ways to overcome the corruptions, to not be influenced or sucked into them. If we can do that, then the quality of our energy is more pure, cohesive."

Simon thought about this for a while before answering. As always when baffled, he needed to read, to research and to think through the theories in a pragmatic way. Right now he was thinking about correlations.

"I need to go to the library. I think I can get the computer there to take all of our findings from today's tests and cross reference peoples jobs, religions, backgrounds, education, community involvement and anything else we can think of into a chart that might help us to test Dad's theory. Maybe I can come up with some common themes among the people we tested."

"I am going to hang out with your father for a while. I want to get his take on the background work I am doing on the other sites where energy ratings have diminished over time. If that is okay with you, Marcus?" Henrietta asked.

Simon noticed a slight flush to his father's cheeks and a light in his eye he had not seen since before his mother had died. He also realized that he had not seen his father with a drink in his hand all day.

"Ok. We will connect later this week once I have something to tell you," Simon said.

Simon phoned Francis to enlist her help. She agreed to meet him at the library.

Chapter 11

It was nearly four in the morning when blaring sirens and flashing lights announced the arrival of the ambulance to the emergency bay. The triage team quickly joined the EMS attendants to evaluate and stabilize the victims while they waited for Dr. Thomas to arrive.

Two teenage boys, brothers, were the victims of a motor vehicle accident. A quick assessment told Tirisa that the younger of the two brothers, the 15 year old who had been the passenger was in critical condition. Raspy breathing indicating a collapsed lung and broken ribs, extreme internal abdominal injuries from the amount of pain he was in, as well as a head injury from where his head hit the windshield. It was not looking good.

His older brother was stable but tears streamed down his face and he kept repeating: "Please let him be all right, I am sorry, I am so sorry, oh God, please help him."

"Hi Tirisa," Dr Thomas acknowledged the young nurse with a familiar nod. "What have we got?"

"Glad you are here," Tirisa replied. She matched his rapid stride down the long ER corridor to where the teenager waited, filling him on the details of the accident and the boy's condition as they walked.

Before he stepped behind the curtain she placed a hand on his arm. "If anyone can help this boy, I know it is you," she told him quietly.

He felt a soft glow from her words of confidence and jumped into action.

"Start oxygen, an IV of Ringers Lactate wide open and 2 units of packed cells."

Tirisa began slapping cardiac monitor electrodes on the boy's chest while another nurse threaded an intravenous needle into the collapsing vein in the boy's left arm.

"Pulse 160, R 60, BP 80/60. Not looking good," Tirisa reported.

"Call respiratory, we are going to need a ventilator here."

Tirisa, already anticipating his needs had a chest tube tray open and set up on the examining table.

Gowned, masked and gloved, he expertly inserted the large bore needle into the chest wall. He needed to re-inflate the lung if the boy was going to survive. The nurse connected the tubing to the suction vacutainer and as expected, the water began bubbling indicating air being removed from the plural space and the re-inflation of his lungs.

"He has stopped breathing." Tirisa's voice was sharp and anxious.

"Okay...give me the laryngoscope and a size 7 ET tube."

Galen Thomas expertly inserted the laryngoscope in the boy's mouth and visualizing the trachea, he slowly guided the ET tube into the boy's airway. He connected the Jackson Reese bagging unit to the end of the ET tube and began forcing oxygen into the boy's lungs.

"No pulse."

"Start compressions."

"It's not working. We are losing him."

"Adrenaline"

"It's not working"

"Stop compressions on my count."

"1, 2, 3 stop."

Dr. Thomas disconnected the bagging unit from the ET tube, reached in his pocket for his examining light, inserted it into the opening of the endotracheal tube and slid the button on its side into the forward position. He quickly re- attached the bagging unit and inflated the boys lungs with 3 breaths.

"Begin compressions."

The cardiac monitor straight line a moment ago abruptly flashed and sprung to life.

"Stop compressions. We've got him back!!"

The boy's pulse jumped to 90 beats per minute and stayed there.

"Good work team. Let's get him connected to the ventilator. This boy has a long road to go yet."

Everyone on the team broke out into smiles. This was what it was all about. Saving lives. Galen winked at Tirisa and patted her on the back. She beamed from ear to ear. They were a good team. The trust and connection and same mindedness between nurse and physician in a critical situation like this were far greater than any hormone rush. It was a soul connection. He felt the admiration in her eyes and an inner glow warmed him and made him smile too.

Galen put the energy transfer device that looked like an examining pen back in his pocket.

"My God, it worked," he thought to himself.

It was too early to know how well or if the energy transfusion from Sara Dickson to Todd Adair was going to be enough to keep him alive or what the long term effect might be but the empty collection chamber that once held the energy of Sara Dickson was now empty and the boy who should have died just moments ago was now alive.

It was exciting beyond belief. Saving lives, this was his purpose.

Chapter 12

Standing in front of the library, the feeling of exhilaration he felt when Todd's heart resumed its powerful beat was now overshadowed by the realization of what he had done. He pulled out his energy transfer pen and looked at the digital display indicating remaining energy cells and volume. The only energy remaining in COLTENs storage cells was that of a wife abuser, an alcoholic, a homeless man and a variety of small lab animals. The total amount of energy was less than 3200 units. He wasn't sure how much he needed but his best guess suggested he needed about 6000 units to be successful. He should have *taken* the energy from the boy, not given him energy but he was caught up in the moment, in the opportunity to save a young man's life. In the expectations of young blond charge nurse who looked at him with faith and belief in his abilities. She believed he could save that boy.

He would just need to find another donor. At least he now knew that it worked. He could actually transfer life energy collected from a one person who was dying without hope of cure to another who was dying and actually save a life. His research was successful!

Entering the library he noticed that the lights on the second floor were on. He looked at his watch. It was six am. He was always the first one in and always first to open up so he was surprised that there was someone else already here. Instead of going directly to his basement oasis, he ascended the stairs to the upper library where he heard the big computer, Ranger hard at work. Long lists of names, descriptors and figures were scrolling across her screen. She was comparing and cross referencing names into categories.

The work table in the room was scattered with books and pages with scrawled notes and hypotheses. He stood in front of the large digital display and tried to decipher what was being worked on. The names were listed under four column headings. The headings were: Temperance, Justice, Wisdom and Fortitude. He scanned the names that were listed under each column. He recognized a few of them. They were people from the town and surrounding communities. Many he knew because they were personal patients of his. Some names were listed under more than one column, and a very few were listed under all four.

He was not surprised to see Tirisa, the charge nurse from ER with check marks under all four categories. In addition to her work as a nurse, he knew she spent countless hours volunteering at the local soup kitchen and homeless centers in the town. She was always fund raising for charities that would help those in need and he had bought many a box of candy to support her causes. The other name that he knew was Francis Simpson. Just seeing her name here made him grin. He has a special place for her in his heart. She genuinely cared about people and went out of her way to make everyone's day better. When he had a really bad shift in the ER, she seemed to sense it somehow and would make a comment about an article he had written or provide a story with a moral about overcoming struggles and the greater good. He always felt better after a visit with her. He had heard somewhere that she spent a lot of time at a wildlife rehabilitation center that looked after wild animals that were injured or ill. Everyone knew her as the librarian who loved animals. He had even laughingly nicknamed her Francis of Assisi one day after the kindly saint who cared for all animals. Yes, he could see why she had check marks under all categories.

He flipped through the pages on the desk trying to figure out what the meaning of this work was about.

"Dr. Thomas." Francis's voice startled him. He turned abruptly to see Francis and a young man he didn't recognize standing in the doorway. They were holding steaming cups of coffee. They had obviously been at the library all night but the flushed look on their faces was one of excitement not fatigue. A lump formed in the pit of his stomach.

"Dr. Thomas. You are here early this morning. "Francis smiled, a big beaming smile full of sunshine and happiness. "Can I help you with something?"

"No, I just heard Ranger humming away up here and thought I should check it out. Looks like you two are pretty mired in some project."

He shifted his gaze from Francis to the man next to her.

Noticing his line of sight, Francis smiled broadly and made introductions.

"I am sorry Dr. Thomas, this is Simon Gallagher. Simon is a quantum physicist with Boston University. I have been helping him with some research. Simon, this is the brilliant Dr. Galen Thomas that I told you about. I think Dr. Thomas spends more time at the library than I do!"

It wasn't hard to tell that Francis was quite smitten with the young physicist. For a physicist he didn't look that bookish. He actually had a slightly rugged air about him that Galen could appreciate. He reached out to shake Simons' hand. His grip was firm, confident. His gaze was steady. The strength of his hand clasp created an aura of instant acknowledgement and mutual appreciation.

"You must be doing some pretty interesting work to keep you here working all night."

Galen invited conversation, shrugging off the initial feeling of contempt or was it jealousy that had started to singe the corners of his mind.

"My area of research is in the field of energy. I am mostly interested in living energy, the energy that keeps living things alive. I know it sounds kind of kooky but I started out trying to determine where living energy goes after death. I have taken a bit of a side track here as I discovered that not every person carries the same level or quality of energy."

Galen couldn't believe what he was hearing. Right here in front of him, was a man who had the same interest as he did. It was incredible. Head tilted, eyebrows raised in interest, he pushed the feelings of jealousy that were clouding his vision aside and encouraged Simon to continue.

"Today we did a small research project at the County fair. We set up a booth and tested energy levels of 800 people; men, women and children to see if there were trends or commonalities that could suggest why individual levels may be different. It actually has nothing to do with the real reason why I am here, but was an interesting side bar. Sometimes when those side bars present, it is for a reason and I have always found that I need to follow my intuition and when opportunity or an idea presents itself, I can't help but follow it through."

"I know what you mean. Some of the greatest break throughs in science occur by "luck" or "accident", but in reality it is like there is some other force or influence that leads us down that track and to a discovery that otherwise never would be made. I have had it happen myself many times." He looked at Simon with sincere appreciation and acknowledgment. They seemed to have a few things in common.

"How did you measure the energy levels?" Galen asked.

Simon picked up the small handheld electronic device. "I created an energy tracking application. There is a built in device that senses, quantifies and tracks energy particles in any living being. Today we used that to measure both the quantity and quality of energy of each person that agreed to participate in our study at the fair. Each person filled in a small survey first that gave us some of their personal context as well."

Simon handed Galen the handheld computer. Galen couldn't help but smile as he looked at the application logo of the little ET alien with the pointing finger. Simon was a man with a sense of humor.

"Ranger has been amazing." Francis jumped in. Her face was flushed with excitement.

Galen couldn't help but notice how she glowed.

"She has pulled information from energy readings we took and the survey that people completed and then paired it with any known characteristics about that person. She linked into things like police reports, hospital visits, registrations and program enrollments, school records, donations, subscriptions, even the most commonly visited Google sites to create a personal profile for each person in our study. Who would know that anyone can access all of this information about any one of us at any time?"

"So much for protection of privacy legislation," Galen commented.

"Isn't it a sham?" Simon interjected. "There is no protection of privacy in this age of computers. Anyway it is working out in our favor, because Ranger is able to cross reference all of this data for the 800 names we put into the data base. She created four major themes for the characteristics she has uncovered and linked them to the energy readings we took. Come here and you can see what she has come up with."

Simon pointed to the screen. "Do these four categories: Temperance, Justice, Wisdom and Fortitude sound vaguely familiar? "

"Weird choice of words in today's society. I haven't been to church in a while, but this brings me back to my early catechism days. Aren't these the original virtues described in the bible? I seem to recall that there were more than four though. Wasn't there also Faith, Hope and Charity?"

"Yes, but those three were not added until later, in the New Testament. These four were the first cardinal virtues described in the Old Testament. I think it is astonishing that out of all the possible theme titles that could have been chosen, Ranger pulled these four."

"What characteristics would make Ranger place people in the categories she has?"

"We have been trying to figure that out." Francis spoke up. "See how Simon here has check marks under Temperance and Justice? We think the rating for temperance is based on the fact that Simon owns a very modest car, has few possessions, does not own a house, and has no bad habits. " she winked at Simon " We are not sure what led Ranger to place him under Justice except that he has signed several petitions over the years and gone to court once to defend a victim of a hit and run accident that he had witnessed. So based on what is considered public knowledge, Ranger has made some assumptions about people and placed them accordingly."

"From the small group of people listed in all four characteristics, it looks like there are only a few people who hold the coveted designation of saint except for Francis of Assisi here and maybe Mother Tirisa!" Galen observed with a laugh.

"As I said, I am not sure what the relevance of all of this is; it was just a point of interest. It does not really help me in the work I am doing, but interesting none the less. Maybe I can write an article for a religious magazine some time."

Back in the Great Knowledge Room, Galen's mind began to race. The answer to his dilemma was staring him right in the face. Simon was right. When things presented themselves to you, it was for a reason. He had a feeling that Simon's research and his ET application would come in handy in his own work. After all patience is a subset of fortitude and he possessed an abundance of that virtue. He seemed to remember a famous biblical quote that "All good things come to those who wait."

Of course he couldn't wait too long.

Chapter 13

The climb to Peter's cabin was not an easy one. Simon headed due north of the falls as Michael instructed but quickly came to a dead end. There was no direct path that he could find. Before him lay a variety of intersecting wild life trails, if you could call them trails. In some cases the brush was so dense that the only animals he could think of that might have created the trails were coyotes or rabbits. He bent under leaning willows, crawled through underbrush, climbed over fallen trees. Thistles and rose bush thorns tugged at his pants and threatened to trip him on more than one occasion. None the less, he was not deterred and continued working his way, this way and that always aiming to a point somewhere north of the falls. At last he entered a small clearing surrounded on three sides by differing levels of bush. Sitting cross legged facing a rapid flowing brook was the man who had shot at him just two days ago.

Without turning to look at him or acknowledge that he had heard him coming, the man spoke. His voice was slow and each word carefully chosen.

"You are Simon. My father told me you would come. He told me you are trying to track the movement of life energy. He told me that you came upon the moose at your last visit." a smile formed at corner of his lips "He told me I shouldn't shoot at you again".

"I would appreciate that." Simon smiled. "I kind of like my life at the moment and wouldn't mind having it a little longer. You must be Peter."

Peter nodded and motioned to the ground next to where he was sitting.

Simon accepted the invitation and sat down next to the tan skinned native. He silently handed the man a package of tobacco. Peter looked at him, accepted the tobacco and placed the package in his jacket pocket without a word.

Simon stared down at the fast flowing brook watching it gain momentum as it made its way down the sloping bank over rocks and boulders toward the falls ahead.

After a long silence, Peter began. "There is a great balance in life. Life comes and life goes. It all meets here at this Wheel." He pointed in the direction of the water falls. "For thousands of years my family has protected this place. We have watched. For three months now something has changed. The flow of energy is not the same. There is less energy coming into the wheel and less energy leaving. Look around you".

Simon obediently looked in each direction trying to understand what it was that Peter was expecting him to notice.

"What do you see?"

"Well other than that cabin tucked up there in the trees that I am guessing is where you live, I see a place that has not been greatly touched by man. I see lots of trees of every kind, shrubs, grass, rocks, water. The air smells clean and fresh. There are lots of mosquitoes, but not as many as the last time I was here." Simon made an attempt at humour.

"Is there anything unusual about what you see and hear and feel?" Peter was serious.

Simon took another look. A slow realization of what Peter was talking about dawned on him.

He had not really noticed before, but the trees and shrubs surrounding the cabin, looked like they were about to lose their leaves. They were yellow not the brilliant shade of green that they should be at the end of June. If he didn't know where he was, he would have guessed that there must be a huge factory sending out massive pollutants to affect the plants in this way so early in the season. As he looked around he began to notice other signs of death as well. Wild flowers, lupines and daisies which should be in full bloom were withered; in fact there was little of the color that the area should have at this time of year. The difference here at the northern end of the falls was in sharp contrast to what he had experienced on his first visit and on the south side of the falls.

"So if this is a wheel, a medicine wheel, and we are on the north end of the wheel, this is the area that should be associated with adulthood, with winter. Is that why the trees all look so aged and things look like they are dying instead of blooming as they are at the south end of the falls?"

Peter shot him a look of surprise and continued on "You have done some homework and I can see how you might think that, but that is not the case. The lack of life in the plants here is not because they are on the north side of the wheel. This is the change that I have been noticing. To understand what is happening I am going to share with you the secret that our people have been protecting."

"My people call the Creator, *Kisu'lk* ("gee-soolg"). *Kisu'lk* created Earth. Earth is a growing place. It is like a factory. In fact the ancients first called it the "earth factory". Over time the name shortened to the "earth plant" and finally man called it *"planet"* earth. To understand the purpose of the Wheel you must first realize that the Ancients are not of earth. They are from another place. They come here from the center of a great Wheel. The center of the Wheel is here."

He pointed toward the falls into the bottomless pond at its base that Simon had observed on his previous visit. Indeed it did look like a wheel. Sitting here Simon could see the converging streams of water that gurgled and swirled and made their way toward the great pond below. The streams entering along with the river leaving divided the pool at the bottom into natural quadrants just as Ranger had shown him.

Simon was unsure of how to respond so he remained quiet; focusing his attention on the words he was hearing.

" *Kisu'lk* created the earth plant to replenish life in his world; the world of the Ancients. The world of the Ancients is not like this. It is a world of pure energy. The people of that world are highly evolved. They do not have a physical form, to hold their energy and because of that they are unable to reproduce. Earth is one of a number of plants in the universe that provides them with new life. Humans whose spirits have evolved and achieved the highest possible level of energy here are able to transition to the Ancient's world. This process of growing pure life energy takes a very long time but the Ancients are patient. In their world time may not seem as long as it does in ours."

Simon was speechless. He was not sure what he had expected Peter to tell him but this was certainly not it.

"How are people on earth supposed to achieve this level of pure energy that you are talking about?" he finally asked.

"Man's evolution to purity of spirit takes many births and re-births. With each birth the spirit of man must achieve new goals. These goals are directed by *Kisu'lk*. The experiences you need to achieve those goals are presented to you throughout life's journey. You will meet certain people, or be present at a certain place and time to witness a certain event. You can choose to benefit from your experiences or not. You can resist the urges that try to steer you in the right direction or go there willingly. If you make it through an entire lifetime without accomplishing the things you need to accomplish, you come back in a new body to try again."

The idea of reincarnation was not new. It has been around for centuries. As he listened to Peter, Simon began to make connections with the work that he, Henrietta and Francis had done on quantifying the levels of energy from the people they tested at the fair. Could this be true? Since the dawn of time man has questioned the purpose of life, sought to understand it and figure it out. Could it really be this? The purpose of man's life on earth is to achieve the purest level of energy possible so that his energy may be transferred to another world to keep the inhabitants there alive? It was pretty incredulous.

"What happens if someone dives into the pool at the base of the falls, the center of the wheel...do they cross over to this other world?" Simon struggled to keep skepticism out of his voice.

"No. Only the purest spirit energy can cross over. The local kids come here to jump off the cliffs and dive into the bottomless pool below all the time. They love the rush it gives them. I think they get a feeling of exhilaration, but they cannot cross over."

Peter paused. He seemed lost in thought. Reaching into his jacket pocket, he withdrew a pipe and the tobacco Simon had given him. He slowly filled the pipe bowl, struck a match and lit the tobacco. Soft gentle puffs of smoke rose into the morning air. He handed the pipe to Simon. Simon took a shallow puff and handed the pipe back.

"For each of us, the human experience is different. For some, destiny may require that they be a Chief, while others will be an ordinary member of the village. In either case, these are the best possible destinies for these spirits, and to turn aside from their paths means that they will not be doing what is required to accomplish whatever it is they need. In all cases it is possible to find that preferred road again. If a person realizes that they are off-track and wishes to return to their path, help is provided by the spirits to make that happen. The right person will show up, or another opportunity will arise to offer a particular learning experience that was missed previously. Once you are walking the intended path, all things you need will be made available. When you have achieved the goals you need to, your time on earth comes to an end. Your energy enters the center of the wheel and does not return. For those who have not achieved purity of spirit their energy also enters the wheel, but it is re-routed back to earth in another form. Maybe a tree, maybe a dog, maybe a new baby."

Simon sat in silence and disbelief throughout Peters' monologue. He knew Peter truly believed what he spoke. He felt the sincerity in his words. His brain quickly began synthesizing the information Peter told him. He made connections and assumptions and linkages within his knowledge of religion, physics and the paranormal sciences. Peter was not an educated man, and yet the stories he told and the parallels described were undeniable. How could he ever prove this though?

"Why do you think the energy here is decreasing?" Simon asked.

Peter took another puff on the pipe before continuing.

"For the past year, things have been changing. The balance is wrong. There is no longer the same energy entering or leaving the Wheel. The death of the plants you see is one sign. There is not enough energy coming out of the wheel to keep the plants alive here. On the east side of the falls, it is still plentiful because that is the first place of exit. The south side of the falls is also green with growth, but the north side of the falls is not. It is being depleted of energy. It is as if there is not enough entering from normal causes and so it is being drawn from everything in the area to somehow make up for the overall loss of incoming energy into the wheel."

He paused and was silent, lost in thought for a long moment before finally continuing.

"In the old days, our people only took from mother earth what was required for survival. There was a natural balance. Today that is not so. Every man wants more and more. There is no moderation. Because he can have it, he takes it. He hunts but does not eat his kill. He fishes but leaves the fish to rot. He cuts trees but does not re-plant. He covers the earth with pavement. He builds concrete jungles taking more and more land. He even takes over the waste land, filling sloughs with garbage. No one practices restraint. Greed is everywhere. It is depleting the balance of this world."

"What if this is a sign that more people are achieving the level of pure energy they need to pass through the Wheel and so there is less energy returning?"

Even as the words left his mouth, Simon knew this could not be true, not if his survey of the 800 people was correct. If it were, there would have been more than a handful of people with check marks in all four boxes. He reached into his back pack and removed the small electronic computer that housed ET. He held it out for Peter to see.

"This device is designed to pick up on individual and cohesive streams of energy that leave the body of any living animal when it dies. So far I have only used it in a laboratory setting. I have never been able to track energy further than the walls of the lab. I have never tracked the energy leaving a human's body, just animals so far."

Simon pressed the ET logo and the screen lit up. A bright red dot appeared on the screen and a soft hum emitted from the speakers. Excitement flushed through his veins. ET had picked up a life energy source! Almost immediately it was accompanied by a second dot, then a third and fourth. All were moving toward the falls. He activated the digital display and a hologram projected in front of them. He pointed out the four dots each representing separate energy streams heading toward the falls to Peter.

"The image you are seeing is the movement of four separate life energies. According to this graphic, there are four separate streams of energy heading this way. They are coming from that west stream right now. Because the energy waves are so cohesive, or so closely knitted, I am guessing that these energy streams are from people who have just died, or rather whose energy has just left their body. I am not picking up on any signal indicating that any energy is coming from the falls."

"Energy is received from the west of the wheel." Peter confirmed the information being transmitted by ET.

Simon remembered what he had learned from Ranger in the library resource room. The medicine wheel is divided into four directions: East, South, North and West. West is for fall, a time of death. East is for spring; new life, South is summer, a time for growing and happiness, and North is winter, a time for waiting.

"And it leaves from the east side."

"How did your people get to know this?"

"It has been handed down father to son. Stories were told to me by my father and his before him. The stories tell of a great ball of fire that that rose up from the center of the pool." Peter pointed to the pool at the base of the falls. "The fire brought a man and a woman. The man and the woman were to populate the earth. The fire comes back from time to time. Although I have never seen it, many of my people have. It is the Great Spirit *Nisgam*. The messenger of *Kisu'lk*. He has spoken in the minds of many people and has had many messengers on earth throughout time. His messages and stories are always about how to live a good life. Sometimes he gives directions telling the person what to do next. It is through living a good live that you gain the kind of energy that is needed in his world. There are lots of books that tell his stories but my people pass them on by word of mouth.

"What kind of books?"

"The Bible. The Torah. The Qur'an. The spiritual books of rules. The rules were told in commandments and then later in stories describing the results of good behaviours and the results of bad behaviors. The books tell stories about floods and plagues. They also describe what awaits in the other world if man lives a good life. The rules seem simple, but we all have a hard time following them."

Simon's mind was racing. Peter was talking about heaven.

Could this be Heaven's Gate?

"Nisgam comes less and less," Peter sighed. "I think he is giving up on the earth plant."

Chapter 14

"Heaven's Gate! My God, Henrietta, I think Mullen Stream Falls is Heaven's Gate!"

Simon was talking to Henrietta in the big farm kitchen of his family home. Steaming cups of freshly brewed tea, compliments of Marcus, sat in front of them on the polished oak table that once belonged to his grandmother.

"The water falls, the converging streams and the pool at the base of the falls create a natural medicine wheel. The center of the wheel is the pool. It acts as a portal. I know this sounds crazy but the Mi'qmak think it goes to another dimension outside the realm of earth. When a person dies, their energy enters the wheel. If their energy is acceptable it moves onto another dimension forever. If the energy is not acceptable it is re-routed back to earth to be reused. I think what people have always called "Heaven" is through that portal. Heaven is another world with its own race of beings. Henrietta, Heaven actually exists! It is real."

"Only Heaven is not what we thought it was." Henrietta stated matter of factly. "If we find a way to prove that your theory is true, it will confirm that Heaven actually exists, but it will destroy Man's image of God and the afterlife forever. It will shake the foundation of religion."

Henrietta began to think about the energy map she had created back in her office. Perhaps there was more than one Gate to Heaven. Mullen Stream Falls was just one of the areas on her map in which the converging energy lines met. She phoned her assistant back at Boston U.

"Melissa, can you look at the map in my office and name off all the spots where the lines seem to converge into one area and tell me if there are any significant landmarks in those areas?"

Henrietta could hear Melissa typing in the coordinates of the other sites she had circled on the maps on her office wall. In just a few minutes she was back on the line.

"The areas that have the highest energy recordings are in Egypt, Tibet, Africa, England, Mexico, Wyoming, British Columbia, and where you are in Eastern Canada."

Henrietta was already considering the landmarks that she knew of in those areas: there were the pyramids of Giza in Egypt, the Porta Palace in Tibet, Victoria Falls in Africa, Stonehenge in England, the Mayan ruins in Mexico, the Big Horn Medicine Wheel in Wyoming, and a place termed Center of the Universe by some Tibetan monks that existed high on Mount Revelstoke in British Columbia.

She thanked Melissa for her help, terminated the call and passed on the information to Simon.

"Simon, remember the maps of energy I showed you in my office?"

He gave her a quizzical look.

"What if there are more gates?"

After a moment of consideration he answered. "Good question. Why would Mullen Falls be the only one?"

"Exactly. But what is bothering me is the idea that some of the sites on the map like Victoria Falls and Mount Revelstoke are lush with life, but others like the pyramids in Egypt, the Mayan ruins and even Stonehenge are not. Think about the wars and unrest in Egypt for centuries, the loss of civilization around the Mayan ruins, the early wars in England, man's loss of virtue if you will. Yet areas like Victoria Falls and Porta Palace are not highly populated, literally untouched by man. I have a feeling there is an important message in the differences. But that is for later. Right now we have some pretty farfetched theories here. If we are to win respect in the scientific community about your theory we have a great deal of work to do to get acceptable proof. Think you can come up with a way to do that?"

The readings coming into the falls picked up by ET could arguably be from any number of sources. He needed an analytical approach to this. The first thing to do was prove that indeed the energy waves entering the falls were in reality from people who had just died. If he could track energy actually leaving a person at the moment of death to this very spot, his theory would begin to hold weight. But how? Dying people were not just hanging around waiting for him to come and track their energy. There had to be a way that was ethically acceptable to him.

Henrietta broke into his thoughts. "I know what you are thinking. How do we find a dying person who will let us track their energy, right?"

Simon raised his eyebrows. "You know me too well. Know anyone who fits that category?"

"I have an idea."

They had forgotten that Marcus was still in the room.

"Put an advertisement in the paper."

"What?" both Simon and Henrietta asked in unison.

"Put an advertisement in the paper. You might be surprised to find out that there are people just like you, who want to know where their energy goes after they die".

They both stared at him in amazement. His simple solution, as kooky as it sounded, was worth a try. The rest of the afternoon was spent drafting the advertisement. It had to be just right, not too much information, but just enough to intrigue someone to respond. The finished advertisement read:

Are you or a loved one dying?
Do you wonder where life energy goes after death?
We may be able to answer this question.
Call 555-555-5523

Chapter 15

Two days after the advertisement went into the local newspaper, Henrietta received a call. It was from a young woman who said her father was dying and she was calling on his behalf. He had read the article. He had always been intrigued with the notion of life after death as had she. They felt compelled to answer the advertisement.

The woman's name was Sally Sandstrom. She told Henrietta that her father was dying of cancer. Although he was coherent at the moment he was not expected to live longer than another day or two. Cancer had invaded his entire body and slowly each system had shut down; first his liver, then his kidneys now his lungs. Every day she read to him from the newspaper and when the advertisement came out two days ago and she read it to him, he insisted that she call. He thought he had nothing to lose and maybe his death could provide some answers for others. He would like this to be part of his legacy.

Simon and Henrietta arranged to meet Sally so they could explain their research more fully to her. They met in the cafeteria of the local hospital where her father was a patient. Sally was a small girl no older than 20 at most. She had snapping brown eyes and in spite of the weariness in her shoulders and a sluggish walk that suggested she was spending many hours with her dying father and very few sleeping, she smiled and reached out her hand in welcome.

Henrietta took her hand in hers and felt the compassion, warmth and caring spread from this young woman to her.

"If you and your father agree, we will use this small computer and a program that is inside it to track your father's energy as he dies. We do not want to interfere with your last moments with your father. If you like, we can leave this computer with you. As he draws his last breaths you will just need to touch this little ET logo on the screen and it will activate the program. The program has a GPS tracking system in it that identifies life energy streams and tracks its movement. It may not tell us anything. The energy may just dissipate into the air or it may travel in a stream. In the research we have done so far, it seems that life energy mostly travels in streams at least for a little distance." Henrietta's voice was soft and comforting.

"I know my Dad would like you to do this and so would I. I would like to know what happens to our energy when it leaves our body. It is worth a try. "

She led them to her father's room. Mr. Sandstrom was sleeping fitfully. Although an IV was dripping constant sedative into his veins his face was tight with pain. Sally took a seat at his bedside, held his hand and gently massaged it. He did not open his eyes, but the tension in his face relaxed.

"Hi Dad. I am here," she whispered in his ear. "I brought two people with me; Simon and Henrietta. They are the people who put the ad in the paper. Dad they have a device that will track your energy when it leaves your body. I trust them. They seem like really good people." Tears began to roll down her face. "Do you want them to try it Dad?"

She felt him lightly squeeze her had. She turned her tear stained face to Simon and nodded.

Simon handed Sally the computer tablet. She placed it on the mattress next to her sleeping father.

"You can call us just by touching the "Phone Home" icon on the screen."

Simon and Henrietta left the girl with her father.

***

When Sally called Simon three hours later, a slight lift in her voice overshadowed the sadness.

"Dad died just a few minutes ago." The loneliness in her voice was tangible

"Sally I am so sorry." Simon had to choke back the emotion as he remembered how he felt when his mother died. The deep emptiness and sense of loss that over rode all other emotion. To lose a parent is the hardest thing. He hadn't even asked Sally if she had other family. She had been at the hospital all alone.

"I activated ET."

"Thank you, Sally. That must have been very hard for you to do."

"It made me feel like I was helping him somehow."

"Do you think it worked?"

"I don't know. A red dot came on the screen right away when I touched the logo so I think it must have picked up on Dad's energy."

"Would you like us to come to the hospital?"

"No, I can come to your place. The nurses are just taking Dad's body away now. I need to get away from here. I need to be with people."

"I will meet you at the library in 10 minutes."

****

Francis had Ranger booted up and ready to go when they arrived.

"I hope it works." Sally handed Simon the handheld computer.

"Thank you, Sally". Simon placed a gentle hand on her elbow. He felt the exhaustion she felt. He pulled her into a hug.

Sally sobbed heart wrenching sobs into his shoulder. He did not move until she pulled away and wiping the tears from her eyes told him to get started.

Simon gave the command for Ranger to connect to his laptop, selected the spaceship logo and immediately a map was displayed on screen. He clicked "recent activity" and a red dot appeared on the screen plotting a journey along the map. The energy depicted was cohesive and in a single stream. It did not dissipate. It moved in a straight line. Simon switched the map type to geographical and zoomed out from the image to see if he could pre-determine the direction in which the energy was headed. It appeared to be heading straight for Mullen Stream Falls!

The three sat in wonder as they watched the scene unfold.

ET captured the video of the dying Mr. Sandstrom. As he drew his last breath the red dot that appeared on the handheld computer transformed into visible waves that lifted from his body. The wave hovered in the room for almost 20 minutes before beginning a journey that took it straight through the walls of the building and out. On screen before them now was an overhead view of the town, the surrounding communities and the forest that stretched for a hundred mile radius around the town. They watched as the cohesive energy wave made its way above the tree line and slowly progressed north of the town. It seemed to stop here and there for periods of time before continuing on its journey. After an hour, the energy flow began to take on a straight line of direction. It headed over the trees in a north westerly direction. Simon, Francis and Sally watched in awe as the energy stream hovered directly over Mullen Falls and then descended into the bottomless pool below.

They sat in silence for a moment. No one dared to believe what they just witnessed.

Sally reached out and grabbed Simon's hand. Tears were flowing freely down her cheeks. "Where is it? Where did he go?"

Simon smiled gently back at her. "I would say he has gone to Heaven."

Chapter 16

"Old man Innis was admitted to the palliative care unit at your hospital this morning. Are you ready?" Devlin was on the phone with Galen.

"No, I still don't have an appropriate donor."

Galen could feel the anger his response evoked before Devlin replied.

"Well you better damn well get one."

"How do you suggest I do that?"

"Find a suitable donor and take what you need. You work in a hospital for Christ's sake. Make it happen."

Galen kept his emotion in check. He would not rise to the bait. Devlin was a cold heartless bastard who thought he could control the world and everyone in it. Well he could not control him, not completely anyway. It made his blood boil. What he was implying in his backhanded way, was murder.

"My job is to preserve life not take it." Galen replied. "I may have helped to speed up the process, but only when there is no other hope and death is inevitable. The kind of energy that I need to find to keep that old man alive is energy from the pure of heart. It is not the energy you get from the usual run of the mill alcoholic, wife abuser, sociopath, drug addict or criminal that shows up in the Emergency department about to draw their last breath. I need energy from either a "saint" or child who has not yet been corrupted by the world. It is not possible. And it is not justifiable."

Devlin's irritating voice broke into his thoughts. "If you don't make it happen soon, I will make it happen. Trust me. You won't like it."

The dial tone told him that Devlin disconnected the call.

"There has to be another way," Galen thought to himself.

Maybe he could combine energies from a number of unworthy donors together and work on a quantity not quality option. It worked for a little while with the mouse. Maybe that could buy some time if the old man decided to croak before he found the perfect donor. May be it wouldn't work at all. With Innis in the last stages of lung cancer he did not have enough time to experiment or test theories.

***

It was quiet in the library. Francis had already locked up for the day. Galen was about to leave as well, but a niggling thought told him to go up to the Research room and see what she and her new found friend were working on.

The work station in the room was still spread out with the papers that Francis and Simon had been working on earlier. Simon's back pack was sitting on the floor under the table. The handheld computer he had shown him earlier was sticking out of the top of the pack.

He touched Ranger's large computer screen. "Start program."

Ranger sprang to life "How can I help, Dr. Thomas?"

"Give history of last three weeks".

The screen filled with images. Medicine wheels, waterfalls, Stonehenge, the Bible. Ranger displayed town census documents and energy graphs. The last entry was a video. Galen watched an old man die, a young woman at his side. He saw what had to be a depiction of the man's energy actually leaving his body. He watched as the energy traveled beyond the walls of the hospital room to a place on the map called Mullen Stream Falls.

He sat in stunned amazement for a moment, letting the information settle into his brain. Simon had managed to capture energy leaving the human body at the time of death on video. More than that, he tracked it to a real location. A real location here on earth. A location that was not far away. If the energy from everyone who died went to that location, this might be the answer to his problem. Perhaps he could find a way to capture the energy before it entered the water falls. If he could find a way to do that, he would not need to take life from anyone. He could capture life energy on its way to this common place.

But how to do it? There was no way COLTEN, his little collection pen could capture that much free floating energy. If this was in any way possible, he would need more collecting and holding cells and a method of directing the energy to the cells to be captured. He needed a device that would incorporate the functions of COLTEN into a large scale design.

He rushed down to his basement lab taking two steps at a time. Ideas were formulating in his head and he needed to put pen to paper and computer to task. The new device would need to be big enough to collect and re-direct multiple streams of energy into one large holding cell. He used Zeddy's design program to bring his ideas into reality. Diagrams whirled on the screen and he made corrections to angles and spheres until all of the formulas added up equally. It was the perfect mathematical number so he knew it must be correct. There was no time to test it. The end result would be a perfect circular object with a radius of a 4.96 foot satellite dish. It was similar to a TV or computer dish only it had a reflective surface with many cells and mirrors each angled perfectly to direct, capture and re-direct energy. It would be fragile. He designed a handle on the back side that held a large attaching clamp so that it could be attached to a tree or a stand and be quite mobile. It would open and close like an umbrella for easy transport.

He filled Zeddy's cartridges with carbon and initiated the start sequence. It was a large prototype so would take some time to build.

Chapter 17

It was 0830 and most of the breakfast crowd at Lucky Lucy's had already left. Simon and Francis scanned the room for a quiet booth where they could spread out their papers and talk privately.

Immediately Simon spotted his father and Henrietta sitting at a sunny window table, deeply engrossed in conversation. His face flushed with embarrassment as he realized he had not spoken with Henrietta in days. He had been too deeply involved in his work and findings and because Francis had been with him sharing in the excitement, he had completely forgotten about keeping Henrietta in the loop. He had so much to tell her.

"Hey you two, what brings you here?" Simon asked.

"Do you mean besides breakfast?" Henrietta smiled. "It turns out your father and I have some friends in common and we were just swapping memories. Care to join us?"

Simon and Francis pulled up chairs to the table. It was weird seeing his father and Henrietta together. He had never seen his father with any woman other than his mother. He looked at his father for any tell tale signs of alcohol intoxication. He seemed sober.

They ordered coffee, bacon, eggs, toast and hash browns. After the waitress put two steaming cups of coffee in front of them, Simon filled them in on the events of the past several days.

He started with the story of Mr. Sandstrom trying hard to keep the excitement out of his voice and give the man's death the respect deserved.

"Sally was able to activate ET before her father died." He stated matter of factly. He could see Francis nodding enthusiastically out of the corner of his eye, encouraging him to jump to the exciting part.

"So what happened? Was ET able to track the energy beyond the walls of the hospital room?"

Simon couldn't keep the smile back any longer. "Yes! It did! "

Henrietta clapped her hands together in excitement "Yes! Fantastic! How far did it track it?"

"A long way." Simon was being sheepish. "Guess."

"To Mullen Stream Falls?"

"Yes! Using the hologram feature we were able to play back the entire sequence of events and watched his energy which was one strong cohesive stream of energy travel from the bed where he died to its descent into the pond at the bottom of the falls. After that it was gone."

"Oh my God." Henrietta said.

"Exactly. God. Heaven's Gate. We found it." Simon grinned. "I have more to tell you."

"More?"

"Yes, remember our survey at the county fair? Well we had Ranger, the computer at the library cross referencing people and known characteristics with their individual energy readings and she came up with four major themes that you are going to find fascinating."

"You are telling us that instead of the good and not so good categories we had roughly thought about there are actually four themes or sub groupings that Ranger has come up with?" Henrietta asked.

"Yes. The interesting thing is that the themes she chose to classify the descriptors under are: Temperance, Justice, Wisdom and Fortitude. Do they sound familiar?" Simon asked.

"Aren't those the first four of the seven virtues outlined in the bible?" Marcus who had been sitting quietly, listening to the conversation until now interjected.

"Yes! And that's the thing, faith, hope and charity were added in the New Testament, but in the Old Testament it was just these four. The other interesting thing is that when I talked to Peter earlier this week, he said the Ancients gave man directions to follow. Directions that would lead man to everlasting life. In order to achieve everlasting life, man just needs to follow the directions or teachings given to us in many great books throughout time. Books like the Bible, the Torah, the Quran and the Tip taka. Christian, Jew, Islamic or Muslim, there are more similarities than there are differences. The major teachings are the same in all. Even the natives, who we thought were godless before Christianity was brought here, were definitely not godless. In fact they followed perhaps the truest form of religion and respect for the Creator. The natives gave true meaning to the word temperance-only using what they need to survive and nothing more." Simon explained.

Their chatter was excited and exhilarating all at the same time. They finished breakfast together and made plans for the rest of the day. Francis needed to work at the library, Simon and Henrietta were going to spend some time writing up their theory and latest evidence and Marcus had a day of fishing planned.

While Simon paid the bill, Francis stepped outside to enjoy the early morning sun and fresh air. The birds were chirping, the sun shining. She was exhausted, but she felt great. She closed her eyes, stretched her neck back and let the sun warm her face. In spite of the many mysteries of life they seemed to be unravelling she felt relaxed and happy. She revelled in the moment. She was so lost in her thoughts that she did not hear the oncoming car headed straight for her.

Marcus, who was just leaving the restaurant, reacted instinctively. Arm extended, he reached and dove for Francis. In one fluid movement, he pushed her out of the way of the oncoming vehicle.

The body of the car brushed his shoulder as it flew by and he landed on top of Francis in a heap on the side of the road.

Breathing hard, he straightened his arms and pressed against the hard pavement to lift himself off of Francis. "Are you okay?"

People poured out of the restaurant to see what had happened.

A young blond man who Marcus had never seen before identified himself as a doctor and pushed the mob away. Seeing Francis struggling to sit up, he gave her a hand, smiled and spoke briefly to her.

"That was close. I thought you were a goner." He offered a calming smile. "Are you all right?"

"Dr Thomas. Where did you come from?" Francis asked, relief flooding her face. "I think I am okay. Just a little shook up."

"Sit here for a moment and let me check you out for any broken bones or ribs." Galen directed her.

The knees of her jeans were ripped and torn and she had abrasions on her right elbow from where she hit the ground but other than that she seemed to be fine.

"My verdict is - you will live." He smiled at her and helped her to her feet.

He turned to Marcus and extended his hand in a welcome. "I am Galen Thomas. I am a doctor at the hospital and a part time researcher at the library. Are you okay? If it were not for your quick thinking Francis might not be smiling at us right now."

Marcus brushed off his hands on his pants and accepted the handshake.

Simon came out of the restaurant just in time to see Dr. Thomas and his father shaking hands. There was a crowd gathered around

112

and Francis was looking dishevelled, her hair falling down around her face and torn jeans.

"What happened?" His heart was in his throat as he searched her eyes and then ran his gaze from head to toe to make sure she was indeed all right.

"Your father just saved my life." She managed a slight smile. Adrenaline tremors overcame her. She leaned into him and his arms instinctively engulfed her. She laid her head on his chest. Comforted by the steady beat of his heart, her tremors began to subside.

"You are a brave man." Galen was talking to his father." Did you see who did it?"

Marcus shrugged. "I just acted on instinct. I have never seen that car before. I don't think it is from around here."

Marcus looked to see where Henrietta had gone and spotted her talking to some of the restaurant patrons trying to get a description of the vehicle and any other information any one might have that would help them to determine why Francis had just been the target of a hit and run. She looked confident and sure of herself and he admired how she had immediately won the respect of the people in the community who were talking to her like she was a local. It was never easy for a newcomer to fit in with the locals and he watched her in amazement.

In this small town where everyone knew everyone, no one recognized the car. A number of people did see the car coming directly at Francis and said that the car actually seemed to swerve from its course in what looked like an intentional run down attempt. Everyone agreed that if it had not been for Marcus's quick reaction, Francis would be dead.

"Why would anyone want to hurt you? Do you have a jealous boyfriend? Unpaid debts? Really pissed someone off with a late library book charge?" Marcus asked Francis, trying to make light of the situation.

"No. I don't know. I have lived here all of my life. I don't think I have any enemies. Maybe he just didn't see me. I can't believe he would intentionally try to run me down. But then I can't believe he didn't stop either."

Now that the adrenaline rush had subsided she felt exhausted and drained.

Marcus was already on the phone to the police. "No one recognizes the car. I did get the first couple of numbers of the license plate. 69. But that was all I got. It was a black sedan. That's about all I know."

Sherriff Donavan told Marcus they would talk to the rental companies in town to see if that would help them to trace it down.

Chapter 18

Devlin Matthews parked on a side street next to the library and waited. After talking with Galen the evening before about theories around pure energy he was certain he had the solution to their problem. The main library door was locked. Finding the back entrance to the library locked as well, but certain that someone like Galen would hide a key somewhere, he searched all the usual places, under the mat, under the flower pot and above the door. He smiled briefly when he spotted the shiny reflection in the window and found the key hanging on a small nail on the inside of the window frame.

The Library was quiet. The door to the basement was open. He flipped on the light switch. This was his first time in Galen's office. The room was furnished with a large antique maple desk, lazy boy chairs, a leather sofa, side chairs and tables and a fully stocked bar along the far wall. The space was well organized and clean. He noticed that there was a wide hallway leading into what looked like at least 4 other rooms.

He moved down the hallway opening each door as he went. The first room was a full bathroom with shower and sauna all impeccably decorated and sterile clean, with chrome and mirrors and white tile.

The second room looked very much like an operating room complete with a large overhead light, anesthetic equipment, stretcher, intravenous pumps, a cardiac monitor, a ventilator and glassed in shelves stocked with surgical supplies.

The third room he entered was a research lab. The room was white and bright. It held six cages lined up in a row on a long table that extended the length of the room. Five of the six cages had an inhabitant. There were two rabbits and three mice. The mouse in the last cage seemed extremely agitated. He continually circled his cage and sniffed the air hunting for a smell or an escape. Surprisingly there was no odor in the room. Feeling a cool breeze on his cheek, Devlin looked up to the ceiling. A large overhead air exchange system was exchanging the air in the room, eliminating any odor that might be created by the animals.

The last room he entered was a technological marvel. The three walls were lined with multiple computer screens. The screens held different images of an item in differing stages of development. In the center of the room was a gigantic piece of equipment that took up most of the room. It was at least 10 feet long and 5 feet wide and reached about 6 feet in height. The machine was humming and buzzing. It sounded like a gigantic printer. Devlin approached the machine and peered into one of the two large observational windows on the right side of the machine. The machine was blowing a fine layer of material into the center of the cabinet and Devlin could actually see a shape forming with each added layer. His eyes moved to the computer screens and he realized what was happening. The machine was creating the object that was shown on the screens. Each screen was giving the machine messages about what exact layers of carbon to lie down and the machine was actually creating the object that was displayed on the screens. The object did not look like the energy collection pen that Galen coveted, it was something different. It looked like a satellite dish.

"What is that brainy bugger working on now?" he wondered.

Prepared to wait for Galen, he returned to the Great room. He pulled up the luxurious black leather office chair and rolled over to Galen's desk. There was a neat stack of papers sitting on the corner of the desk.

The cover page read:

"COLTEN"
Collecting and Transferring Energy

A research project

Author: Dr. Galen Thomas, MD

He flipped through the pages noting the diagrams and theories used to develop and create what looked like an ordinary physician's examination penlight. No wonder it was taking Galen so damned long to collect the energy they needed. He was too damn busy trying to make himself famous. In addition to whatever it was he was creating in the Zed replicator in the next room, he was writing a book for Christ's sake. A book that would give all their trade secrets to anyone who wanted to duplicate what they were doing. Once people read this, there would be no reason for anyone to sign a contract with them. The rich sons of bitches that would have paid their fortunes for eternal life would just hire their own geniuses and re-create the miracle that they had invented. He felt his blood pressure rising. Galen was an arrogant ass and was going to ruin everything.

As he read through the papers he heard the main library door open.

Finally Galen was here.

***

Francis pulled into the library parking lot and into her usual spot. It was no surprise that hers was the only car in the lot. Dr. Thomas had probably headed to the hospital. Few people actually drove to the library. Readers were walkers. She grabbed her purse and satchel out of the front seat and humming happily, headed toward the front door looking for her door keys in her purse as she walked. As she approached the front steps, she found her keys, stopped and looked around. On the side street next to the Library she noted a number of cars parked; the usual array of vehicles from people shopping in the surrounding stores. One of the cars caught her attention. It was shiny and black. A twinge of anxiety made her draw in a sharp breath and walk slowly over to the parked vehicle.

It was an Audi. It was empty. There was nothing on the seats or anything to say who or what kind of person owned the vehicle. There are a million black cars she told herself. You are just being paranoid. Just because it is black does not mean it was the car that almost hit her earlier. Besides there was no way that near miss could have been intended for her. She just happened to be in the wrong place, day dreaming and should have been paying attention. If anything, it was no one's fault but her own. Still, she pulled out her cell phone and dialed Simon's number.

It rang three times and went to his voice mail. She let out a sigh. She had hoped he would pick up.

"Hi, Simon. It's Francis. This is probably nothing but I am at the library and there is a black car parked on the side street just to the south of the library. It probably just belongs to one of the neighbors, but just thought I should let you know."

She returned to the library steps and put the key in the door lock. It did not disengage the locking mechanism. The door was already open. That was strange. She must not have locked it when she and Simon left for breakfast this morning. She opened the door and entered the library. She threw her jacket on the coat tree at the back entrance and reached out to flip on the "library open sign".

A large strong arm wrapped around her arms and shoulders and yanked her backwards. Before she could scream, a soft damp cloth was held over her nose and mouth. The cloth was drenched with something and the fumes burned her nostrils. She struggled to turn around; to free herself. She was held fast. She felt herself fading, losing conciousness.

Her purse dropped to the floor and its contents spilled out everywhere.

She tried not to inhale. She couldn't help herself.

Everything went black.

Chapter 19

Dr. Galen Thomas turned off his pager. It was from the oncology unit at the hospital. He did not need to return the call. His instruction to the nursing staff was to page him when the aging millionaire dying of lung cancer in room 3201 was close to death. He made sure he had COLTEN in his lab coat pocket and took the elevator from the Emergency Department to the third floor of the hospital.

The oncology suite was quiet. An expectant hush prevailed over the unit. It was the revered silence that preceded death. Quiet solitude. The realm that was open to only those who were about to pass through. Alfred Innis was a rich eccentric with no family and really no friends. He was not a well liked man. In this community he was considered a traitor; a man who sold out the town for his own benefit. He had made his millions by pillaging the natural resources in the town, selling off all that was valuable to the community and leaving an ecological mess in its place. No one would mourn his last hours. Galen did not expect there to be any grieving relatives or friends at his side so his work should be easy to do. He shook his head morosely. He was not looking forward to this.

Innis's raspy and irregular breathing reached his ears before he even entered the room. He took a deep breath, held it for a minute, building his fortitude for what he was about to do and then slowly exhaled. The time had come. The old man lying in the hospital bed was pale, his cheeks slack. It was as he had suspected. Unlike other patients dying who were surrounded by family and friends, the billionaire was alone.

Galen went to the old man's bedside. He placed a gentle hand on his.

"Mr. Innis. I am Dr. Galen Thomas. I am here with you."

The old man looked at him through jaundiced eyes, nodded and squeezed his hand. Galen could sense it took all of his energy. The cardiac monitor showed a slow sinus rhythm of less than 50 beats per minute. His BP was 70 on 30. Galen sat on the side of the bed and waited.

A nurse stuck her head in the door. "Is there anything you need Dr. Thomas?"

"No, thank you, Claire," he replied. Claire was a caring nurse who he had worked with on many occasions. She turned and softly pulled the door shut behind her.

He sat alone with the dying man. As he held his hand, instead of feeling sorrow and a sense of loss or even a sense of completion, Galen felt only anguish. What was he doing? Was this man worthy of what he was about to offer him? In eighty years he had done nothing to advance the community, nothing to demonstrate caring or compassion. His life was based on dishonesty and greed. He had no friends. No family that cared to spend his last moments on earth with him. He shook his head in disgust.

Innis shuddered. Galen took COLTEN from his pocket. He had a job to do.

As Innis drew his last breath, Galen inserted the light into the old man's mouth, slid the activate button to the forward position and held it there, transferring all its contents into the dying man just as the cardiac tracing straight lined on the monitor.

A long minute passed. He waited. Would it work? He continued to hold the wizened wrinkled old hand in his as he stared at the cardiac monitor. The signal flickered than turned into a solid green illuminated glow as it began to trace a regular sinus rhythm pattern on the monitor. Galen let out a long breath not realizing he had been holding his breath while he waited. The heart rate steadily climbed from 15 to 25 to 60 beats per minute, steady and regular. His BP climbed to 120/70.

Innis was sleeping. His breathing was no longer irregular.

Galen got up and left the room. He knew it would not last long. He had bought maybe a few more days for the old man at most. The energy he had transferred would not be enough to sustain and change a life that had been lived without an ounce of virtue.

Chapter 20

After leaving the Lucky Lucy, Marcus returned home and Simon and Henrietta spent several hours at her hotel room, transferring their theories, observations and findings into electronic text. In their field, it was not just the collection of information; it was the documenting of it that often helped to create new assumptions and knowledge. Knowledge is only valuable if it can be transferred or shared with others and getting it on paper was the first step in that transfer process. The task left him feeling exhilarated. It was 3:30 and he decided to return to the library and check up on Francis. The thought of seeing her filled him with happy anticipation.

He pulled up next to her yellow Volkswagen in the otherwise vacant parking lot and did a half skip to the front door of the library. He grabbed the big brass door handle and pulled, expecting it to open with ease. The door did not budge. It was locked. He looked at his watch in bewilderment. The library should be open for another hour and a half. The Library Open sign was not lit up. That was strange. His mind took a minute to absorb this conflicting information. Francis would not just lock up and leave without a sign on the door. Maybe she just stepped out for a minute. He looked around to see if perhaps a sign had blown off the door into the surrounding bushes. There was no evidence of a sign anywhere. Her car was still here so she must not be far.

He wandered around to the back of the library and banged the large brass door knock against its metal receiving plate. Maybe she was filing books in another room. He waited.

Only silence answered.

He looked at his watch again. Something was not right.

He reached into his side pocket for his phone. It was missing.

Damn. He must have left it at the Lucky Lucy in all the confusion this morning. He jumped into his rusted car and sped back to the restaurant. He parked on the curb, jumped out of his car and was met at the door by Tara the waitress who had served them this morning. She was holding his cell phone in her hand.

"I am guessing you must be the owner of this thing?" She waved it at him.

"Thank you, Tara. Glad you found it. Hey have you seen Francis since we were here this morning?" He tried not to let his rising anxiety show.

"No, but your phone did ring a couple of hours ago. Maybe there is a message".

Simon flipped open his phone. There were 2 messages.

0930: "Hi Simon. It's Francis. This is probably nothing but I am at the library and there is a black car parked on the side street just to the south of the library. It is an Audi. It probably just belongs to one of the neighbors, but just thought I should let you know."

1130: "Simon" It was his father's voice. "The police found out that the black car that hit Francis this morning was an Audi. It was rented to someone named Evan Billard. He works for a company called Living Energy in New York. I wondered if you ever heard of them, or if they have anything to do with your research."

With his heart racing, he selected Francis's phone number from his contact list and pressed the call button. His anxiety rose with each unanswered ring tone. Panicked now, he called a number that he hadn't used since he was a child. He expected the phone to ring the usual three times before his father picked up but was amazed when it was answered on the first ring.

"Simon. Are you okay?" He was relieved that his father's voice sounded worried, not slurred.

"No Dad. Something's wrong. I had a message six hours ago from Francis saying she was at the library and there was a black car parked nearby. Her car is at the library but she isn't. The black car is not there either. I am worried Dad. Something is going on. I don't know what to do."

"Meet me at the library. I will be right there." His father replied.

Simon jumped back into the Ford and slammed the little car into gear. Spinning tires, the car jumped into action and sped back to the library.

Familiar paralyzing fear threatened to overpower him.

"Please don't let this happen again." he pleaded out loud.

On the library steps, breaking free of fear's hold, he feverishly dialed Francis's number again.

Nothing.

He tried again.

A faint ringing from behind the library door reached his ears. Her phone was inside the library. Maybe she had fallen and was hurt, lying on the floor unable to call for help. His mind raced with images of possibilities. He peered into the windows on the ground floor, but it was dark inside and he could only make out the outlines of the book shelves. He ran to the back of the library and tried that door. It was locked too. He searched for something he could open the door with or break a window with. Surely there must be a rock or something he could use. In desperation he scanned the ground and walkway for something to break the window with. Relief flooded over him as he saw, peeking out from under the rose bushes a row of large gardening stones. He selected one the size of a grapefruit. He hurled it through the door window. Glass shattered. The alarm rang. He didn't care. He reached in through the jagged fragments and turned the knob to open the door. He rushed into the library.

"Francis? Francis?" His cries echoed in the silence.

There was no sign of her. Her desk was empty. Her computer was not logged on.

He climbed the stairs two at a time and rushed to the Research Room panting, short of breath.

"Ranger, last entry, please," he gasped.

Ranger's screen lit up with an image of both Simon and Francis working at the research table. The time of the entry was 0500h this morning.

Panicked, he raced down the stairs to the lower level of the library where Dr. Thomas' lab was. The door was ajar. He pushed it open quietly, expecting someone to jump out at him. He edged his way into the room wishing he had some weapon. He could hear a soft hum of equipment in a back room and made his way quietly to the room. Other than the large copier that Dr. Thomas had shown him before, the room was empty.

He pressed Francis's number on his cell phone again. He could hear it ringing on the main floor. He rushed up the steps following the sound.

It was coming from under the hallway desk. She must have dropped it when she came in. But where was she?

He grabbed the phone at the same instant that he heard the sound of a key disengaging the door lock. With a wave of excitement, soundlessly praying it was Francis, he reached out and opened the door.

Sherriff Donavan was holding a key in his hand. Standing next to him was his father.

"The rental company was able to track that black car using their GPS anti-theft equipment that was installed in the car and it is located west of town up on an old electric tower cutline by the provincial park. My men checked it out. It was empty. They did find this in the back seat though. He held up the key chain."

The words Lord Beaverbrook Library were embossed in white stitching on the leather key fob.

The Sherriff looked at his watch. "5:30; that message you got was at 9:30. That was 8 hours ago. They could have travelled in any direction and gotten into another vehicle or flown to another country by now. I am going back to the detachment to organize a search party. It will take a lot of men to search those woods. I suggest you two stay here in case she comes back."

Simon wanted to pull his hair out. The frustration, the sense of helplessness was overwhelming. He had to do something. Every minute wasted was another minute he could be searching for Francis.

"Where they found the car, you said it was by an old provincial park. Is that the park they used to call the Enclosure?"

The sheriff confirmed that it was. He told Simon and Marcus that he would keep them informed of any progress, then turned and left the library.

Simon turned to his father, "The Enclosure is out by where Francis lives. If we go there maybe we could use her dog, Ben. I am guessing he could track her scent and he could help us to find her. Will you help me Dad?"

He had never asked his father for help before. He needed him now.

Marcus nodded in agreement.

They jumped into Marcus' truck, a ¾ ton 4X4 and lost no time getting to Francis's ranch.

Ben jogged down the driveway to greet him. Simon took a minute to reach down to rub his ears and scratch his chin then told him to jump in the truck. The little dog sensing the anxiety and concern in the air jumped willingly into the truck box.

They drove to the coordinates of where the black sedan had been found. The car was still there, somewhat hidden in the trees.

"Ben, find Francis." Simon gave the dog the command.

Hearing his master's name, the little dog whimpered and immediately began sniffing a circumference around the car. He latched onto a scent and bolted forward through the trees. Simon and Marcus did their best to keep up. Every few minutes, Ben emerged from the trees to check that he was still being followed.

Finally the little dog ran ahead and disappeared from view. They could hear him ahead, whining and barking. Pushing under some overgrown bushes they found the reason why. In front of them was a metal page wire fence. High Voltage and Keep Out signs were posted at eye level all along the perimeter. Electricity hummed through the wire.

Simon and Marcus ran down opposite ends of the fence looking for a gate or an entrance of some kind. It took 10 minutes for them to arrive back at the same spot.

"Anything?" Simon asked breathing hard.

"There is a gate at the east end but it is padlocked with a keyless entry code. The whole fence is electrified. Did you find anything?" Marcus asked.

"No. The fence at the west end stops at a cliff leading into the river. There is no way down the cliff without climbing gear. The shoreline at the bottom looks really rocky...we could never jump and hope to survive."

Simon who had been rubbing his head furiously dropped his arms in frustration and let out a cry of anguish.

"Where is Ben?" Marcus asked. They had not heard the little dog in a while.

"I thought he was just behind me." They backtracked along the west end of the fence. Stopped and listened intently. The sound of scratching and digging directed them down a small incline just south of where they were standing.

Ben was about three feet away from where the electric fence touched the ground. He was digging furiously, dirt flying backwards from the lightening quickness of his front paws.

"Hey. I think he is on to something. Maybe we can dig under."

"I have a shovel in the truck". Marcus ran back to the truck and Simon was already on his hands and knees helping the little dog pull the dirt away from the fence.

Marcus was back in minutes and joined in the furious digging to carve a tunnel under the fence. Perspiration soaked his shirt and ran down his face as he dug.

They took turns on the shovel; one digging the other pulling the dirt away. When they could see light on the other side of the tunnel Ben pawed relentlessly at the soft dirt until he could fit his body into the tight hole. He wiggled through the opening, darted through the brush and disappeared.

The hole was not big enough for either Simon or Marcus to fit. They kept digging praying that precious minutes were not being wasted.

Finally, there was enough space for each to wiggle through. Simon went first and then reached out to grab his father's hands to help drag him through the small opening.

"God, Dad I hope we are not too late."

Marcus placed a hand on his shoulder but said nothing.

Beyond the perimeter of the fence, the forest was lush and dense. They were surrounded by a combination of evergreen, birch and willow. They stood still for a minute trying to determine which direction to go. The woods were enveloped in an unusual quiet. Not a bird was chirping, not a leaf cracking.

All of a sudden the little dog bounded out of the bush and ran to Simon, circling him and running forward.

"He wants you to follow him," Marcus said. "Let's go."

Crouching low to the ground, Marcus edged forward. Simon followed in his shadow. Within minutes a large sprawling log building came into view. It was a chalet style of building with a massive wrap around deck that faced out to the river.

Marcus lifted a finger to his lips signalling Simon to be quiet.

They edged their way slowly up to the house. Ben crept forward, belly to the ground. When they reached the outside of the building, they stood, flattening their bodies tight to the wall. Slowly and quietly they made their way around the perimeter of the house until they came to the large floor to roof window that overlooked the river. Simon peeked in at the edge of the window, thankful for the lengthening shadows of evening.

A man dressed in a business suit, looking strangely out of place in this wilderness setting was pacing back and forth in the center of the room. He looked at his watch every few seconds. There was no sign of Francis in the room.

Simon felt a soft touch on his elbow.

"I found something," Marcus whispered. He pointed to a window at the side of the house. It was just slightly above shoulder height. The window was open. Most likely a bathroom window.

Marcus knotted his hands together and lowered them for Simon to step up to the window.

Simon carefully pushed the window further ajar, praying that the hinges were as well maintained as the house and would not betray their presence.

Inside it was dark. He could make out the shadow of what looked like a sink and a toilet. He gave his father the thumbs up sign signaling him to lift higher. Grabbing onto the window ledge, he hoisted himself upwards and through the window. Once inside, he signalled a silent okay with his thumb and forefinger to his father.

He tiptoed to the door and slowly, quietly turned the knob.

He peered through the narrow crack between door and jamb. There was a hallway with several doors on either side. The hallway led into the main room that they had seen from the window. He could hear a man's voice. It sounded as though he was talking on the phone. He was angry and talking loud.

"Stop being such a high society wimp. You want all of the glory but none of the pain". The voice said.

There was a pause and when the male voice spoke again. He seemed less angry.

"Okay. You bought some time but your job is not over. It is just starting. I expect action and I expect it now. I have the girl. Today was a lucky day for her, but it won't be so lucky if you don't come through. She is here and she has what we need. I will do it myself if need be."

Silence as the man listened to the response. Then, "I will meet you at the dock."

Simon tiptoed back into the bathroom and silently closed the door. With his ear pressed against the jamb, he heard the main door open to the outside. The man who had been on the phone had gone out. Standing on the rim of the bathtub, Simon could see him heading down to the shore line. He could see Ben lying perfectly still in the bushes. At the shore line, there was a wooden dock with a 16 foot motor boat tied to it. The man with the slicked back silver hair was climbing into the boat. He turned toward the house and looked toward the bushes where Ben was lying. Simon said a silent prayer hoping that the dog would go unnoticed. He did not know where Marcus was. He let out a slow sigh of relief when finally after what seemed an eternity, the boat motor sprung to life and the boat edged away from the dock and moved slowly down the river.

Not knowing where the man was going or for how long he would be gone, Simon moved down the hallway listening for any other sounds that might indicate that he was not alone.

Hearing silence, he cautiously proceeded down the hallway opening one door at a time.

In the main room of the cabin he quickly took note of the furnishings and two doors. One led to the outside and the other perhaps to a stairwell or closet. He crept toward it. Grabbed the door knob and slowly turned it. He pushed the door open with his foot.

There were stairs leading into a basement.

With flashlight in hand, he descended the steps. Feeling along the wall, his fingers searched for a light switch. Finding it, he flipped the switch and the dark basement was immediately flushed with light.

In the middle of the room tied to a chair was Francis. Her mouth was taped shut and her eyes were closed. She did not respond to the light.

"Francis! Oh my God." his eyes filled with tears. "Please, not again," he moaned, as he rushed to her.

She was breathing. He could see the steady rise and fall of her chest.

He ripped the tape from her mouth with one quick movement.

Francis's eyes fluttered open as the sudden stinging pain of the tape ripping from skin reached her drugged senses.

"Simon? Simon, is that you?" She whispered.

"Oh my God, Francis. Thank God you are alive," he cried. "We need to hurry."

His fingers struggled with the knots securing her to the chair.

The rope jumbled in his hands. The more he pulled, the tighter the knot became.

"I am so stupid. Why don't I carry a knife, like my father always told me to do." He silently berated himself.

A rush of anxiety washed over him.

Fear constricted his throat, made it hard to breathe, and threatened to paralyze thought and action. He willed himself to be calm, to focus on the task at hand.

Every fibre of his being told him to abandon the task and search for a knife. He fought the urge. There was not enough time. He had to focus.

"Please," he silently prayed.

Miraculously, he felt some give in the rope. His fingers working faster now, loosening the knot first from one side and then the other, all the while willing himself to be calm. Finally the slight slipping of the rope gave way to the release of the knot.

Francis was free.

She collapsed into his arms. Sobbing.

"Are you okay?"

"He is crazy! I heard him talking to someone. I think he plans to kill me! I don't know what is going on! What did I do? Who is he?"

He hugged her to him closely for an instant. "Let's get out of here."

Grabbing her hand, he pulled her to the door and up the steps. They reached the front door of the cabin at the same time as they saw the boat motoring up to the dock. There were now two people on board.

Simon pulled Francis back into the house and down the hallway to the bathroom.

Forefinger to lips, he motioned for her to be quiet. He pointed to the open window above the tub and silently signalled that he would lift her up to it.

Hearts pounding, they listened.

A door opening.

The men were in the house.

Simon clenched his hands into a foot hold. He nodded his head at Francis. She placed one foot into Simon's clenched hands and he hoisted her up to the window opening. She swung a leg over and slowly descended down the outside wall of the house.

Terror seized her as she felt hands grasp her waist and pull her to the ground.
Her face was unexpectedly wet with dog licks. Marcus's strong arms pulled her over to the brush.

Inside the small bathroom Simon prayed that the noise outside the window was covered by the men entering the room.

"What the… "He heard a deep voice registering surprise. It was the voice of the man he heard on the phone earlier.

Simon immediately realized that in his rush to get Francis out, he left the basement door open. There was no time to waste. He heard the thump, thump of loud footsteps descending the stairs.

Now or never. Heart pounding, he hoisted himself up to the bathroom window. His sweaty palms could not get a hold on the window sill to allow him to noiselessly lower to the ground. His body fell to the ground with a loud thump. He stifled a yell as he felt his ankle twist under him.

Loud footsteps running into the bathroom, Voices. No time to run. He needed to hide. He rolled his body tight to the house prayed the foundation shrubs would serve to conceal him and remained still.

Two voices above him, in the bathroom were speaking loud. He guessed they were looking out the window. They did not look directly beneath the window or they would have seen him there. He did not know where Francis, Marcus or Ben was, but prayed they were in safe hiding.

When the voices stopped, he slowly crawled forward toward the thick bush that surrounded the property. When he reached the edge of the lawn strong hands reached out and pulled him under the brush.

Arms circled one another. Marcus led the way back to the hole under the fence where they entered the compound. Simon was now wishing they had not parked there. Surely that would be the first place that the kidnappers would rush to, and not needing to hide, they would make it there first. Hearing no noise behind them they made their way as quickly as possible. The truck came into sight. Francis wiggled through the hole followed by Simon, Marcus and Ben. They made a dash to the truck. Francis still unsteady from her ordeal and the sedative they had given her fell several times along the way.

Hearts pounding, they scrambled madly into the cab of the truck; Ben hopped into the box of the trunk in one flying leap.

Marcus threw the gear shift into reverse. The truck pealed out of the road, spraying the Audi with gravel just as the two men emerged from the trees.

Chapter 21

Sitting in the safety of the police station with steaming mugs of dark coffee in hand, it felt surreal. Like a bad dream that could not have possibly happened but they had the muddy jeans to prove it did. Francis's face was still excoriated from the tape that had been used to keep her quiet.

The aging policeman was speechless as he listened to their incredible story. Nothing like this had ever happened in his 30 year career on the Miramichi. This was a small town. People were not kidnapped in his town! What was going on? And why?

Francis felt like she was in a fog. She could hear Sherriff Donavan asking her to describe the kidnapper. He wanted to know why anyone would want to hurt her, or kidnap her. Nothing made sense. There had been no request for ransom, and Francis's family did not have any money or great property investment that could be sold to put up for a ransom. It had to be something different.

Finally Marcus spoke. "All of this has happened since Simon came home. Simon maybe this is somehow connected to you and your work. Maybe someone is trying to get at you through Francis."

Simon looked at his father in astonishment. It was just like his father to think that somehow he was to blame. His face flushed crimson. He was speechless. He was thankful that Francis did not look at him.

Henrietta, who had arrived at the police station just moments after they did, gave Marcus a look of disappointment. "That seems unlikely," she commented.

It was Marcus' turn to flush as Henrietta's words made him realize the cutting quality of his comment. "Well maybe not you specifically Simon, maybe that ET tracker gadget of yours."

"What could anyone want with an energy tracker? Even if anyone knew what to do with it, why not just steal it from *me*? Why involve Francis? It does not make sense. Besides whom besides us in this room even know about ET?"

Marcus spoke in a softer voice than normal. "Anyone who was at the county fair last week would know."

Simon slumped in his chair as the realization that maybe his father was correct hit him. Once again he had allowed harm to happen to someone he cared about because he was too enthralled with his own business to think about others, or the impact it would have or damage it could cause. He hung his head in resignation.

Francis reached out and put her hand on Simon's arm. She squeezed. He looked up. She was looking into his eyes with as much emotion and compassion as he had ever encountered. He placed his hand on top of hers and returned the squeeze. She was beautiful inside and out.

"Look folks, first things first," Donavan interrupted. "I need to find out who owns that building that you were taken to Francis and I need to do a background search on this Evan Billard. I already have an APB out on him and the car. We will find him, and we will get to the bottom of this. Francis, I don't want you to be alone tonight. Are your parents in town?"

"No, they are on vacation right now." Her voice was flat, drained of all emotion. She looked exhausted.

Simon looked to his father for silent approval and at the barely perceptible nod, put his arm around Francis's shoulders. "You are going to stay at our place."

Back at the Gallagher residence, Simon made a bed for her on the sofa.

"Can you stay with me for a while Simon?"

The aftermath of exhaustion overcame her and her eyes were already closed before he could answer.

"Yes, I will be right here," he whispered.

In minutes her breathing had slowed to the steady rhythm of sleep. He watched the silent rise and fall of her chest, noticed how angelic she looked in sleep. His heart ached with the need to protect her, to keep her safe.

Chapter 22

Staring down at the set of tire tracks next to the Audi. It was pretty certain that whoever had made them had the girl. She had not escaped on her own. Someone had tracked her here and managed to get her out of the basement in the short time he had been away from the lodge.

Devlin grabbed his head and let out a cry of anguish. There would be no conceivable way to re-capture Francis now. Any thought to do so would lead the law right to them. Thankfully he had used a fake name to rent the car. Still it might not take the police long to make the connection. He needed to ditch the car. If the police somehow linked it to his company, he would deny any knowledge of Evan Billard, or why he might have used Living Energy as his place of employment. He didn't think Francis could identify him. He had drugged her pretty good and she really hadn't been conscious at any time he was near her. Still, he needed to lay low, not be seen. With the energy Galen had already transferred to Innis, the old man must have at least another 72 hours. Surely they could come up with a solution in that time.

"Well, Brains, got any ideas?"

"You figure out how you are going to clean up the mess you created with your attempted murder and kidnapping. I will worry about how to get more energy for Alfred." Galen snarled in return.

Devlin drove the Audi to the secluded dock further down the river where Galen had left his Jeep. He followed Galen to a roadside cafe where he abandoned the rented car. They drove together in silence.

Devlin couldn't believe his misfortune. He had it all right in his grasp. He shook his head in silent anger.

It was all because of that damned physicist. If that kid hadn't gotten mixed up in this, Francis would be dead and he would have the kind of energy he needed to keep Alfred alive. Now he had to rely upon Galen to find another source of energy. A source of energy that apparently couldn't just come from any low living scum bag. It had to come from someone who was supposedly "pure of heart", who had enough virtue that the energy harvested would be enough to sustain a heartless bastard like Innis. Getting another chance at the librarian was unlikely. He needed to get the energy tracking device that the physicist had created to help them to identify who would be an acceptable donor.

A plan began to formulate in his mind.

If he could get his hands on this energy tracker application on the kid's hand held gadget, he could test who had the appropriate energy levels and then plan a better strategy. He had been rushed with this Innis thing, it had him acting in ways he never would normally. He hated this pressure. This was not usually how he operated. It was throwing everything off. He would find a way to get the ET application. In the meantime he would work out a way to either get the Energy Collection and Transfer Pen from Galen or re-create it. Then he would not need Galen anymore. He could run this thing on his own. The brains had created the tools. He would use their tools and get rid of them. Damn brainy people. They always got their genius mixed up with some stupid thought that they could do good. Well the only good he cared for was getting good and rich. He laughed to himself.

By the time they pulled into the roadside motel in Boiestown, Devlin had a plan formulated. He was back in the driver's seat.

"Lay low for a couple of days." Galen advised him as he headed to the hotel.

Like he would take advice from him. "Yeah. I will be in touch".

"I need three things" he told the motel clerk. "A room, a liquor store and a drug store."

"I can help you with all three," the clerk laughed handing Devlin the registration forms. Under the request for name, Devlin thought for a minute and then wrote down: Jim Beam. He always liked that whiskey and he sure felt like a drink now. It was as good a name as any and even though he had just been through a disaster, he felt like celebrating.

The clerk indicated that both the liquor store and the pharmacy were just a short walk down the street.

With motel room keys in hand, he walked down the street with a swagger of confidence in his stride.

Chapter 23

Devlin had been using Francis to blackmail him. To force him into action. His blood boiled. He had been played like a violin. He shook his head in disgust at the situation and at himself. He had to find a way to get the energy needed in another way. He rubbed his forehead, trying to will anger out of his mind and bring creativity into it.

If Simon's theory was correct and his new collection device worked, he might be able to capture great volumes of energy without needing to harvest it from any living person. He might be able to capture enough to not just keep Alfred alive but if he was lucky, enough to infuse many people with new life. Simon was intelligent, a genius. If Simon really believed that all energy entered the falls through some sort of a medicine wheel, then he needed to pay attention to that detail. If Mullen Stream Falls is the portal or gateway that Simon and Francis think it is, maybe there is a way to pull energy trying to enter the portal into his collection device. If there was a way to prevent the energy from flowing into the falls and he could capture it, well the opportunities were limitless. It would allow him to save the lives of many people, people who deserved to live. The energy was from people who were already dead after all, so what harm could it do? It was worth a try. He needed to get back to the library to do some research.

Excitement flushed through his veins. He was already forgetting about Devlin.

He drove directly to the library. With a sigh of relief he saw that the building was in darkness. He parked his car several blocks away and walked back to the library, entering through the back door and leaving the lights off. He did not want to have to entertain any questions about his whereabouts for the past couple of hours and he needed time alone to work.

The next several hours flew by as he assembled his new prototype. The replicator had done an amazing job. The energy collection satellite dish was a thing of beauty. It was almost 5 feet in diameter

142

when extended and was covered with millions of tiny reflective collection cells. They glimmered as if in anticipation of being filled. He carefully and gently folded it and placed it in a fabric sleeve with a shoulder strap for easy transportation. Then hoping that Simon's backpack with the handheld energy tracker in it was still in Ranger's room where he last saw it, he hurried up the stairs. He let out a sigh of relief when he saw that it was right where he remembered. Simon had not come back to retrieve it after all the excitement earlier in the day. He looked at his watch. It was 3 AM. My God, it was hard to believe all that had transpired since this time last night.

He asked Ranger for directions to Mullen Stream Falls and plugged the directions into his smart phone. He threw Simon's backpack over his shoulder along with the shoulder bag holding his new energy collection device and left the library.

The street was dark and deserted. He needed some additional supplies. The stores wouldn't open for a few hours yet. Just as well, he was overcome with exhaustion and needed to sleep. He had a lot to do and he needed to be fresh and alert to do it. He reclined the driver's seat as flat as it would go. He closed his eyes. In a minute he was asleep.

He didn't see the vehicle or its occupant pull into the library parking lot, enter the library and leave a short time later.

***

Bright sun warming up the inside of the jeep along with the sounds of early morning awakening seeped into his consciousness. He looked at this watch. 8AM. He had slept for six hours. In spite of the cramped position he had been in for the last several hours, he felt surprisingly refreshed. He straightened the seat, stretched, and peered into the back seat to make sure the shoulder bag and back pack were there before starting the jeep and driving off.

"First breakfast, then supplies, then on to the falls." He had a suspicion that his planned adventure would not be without complications and he needed to be prepared.

The jeep bumped and manoeuvred over the rough trail to the falls. He came to an abrupt stop in front of a massive tree that blocked the road and prevented any further progression by vehicle. He parked the jeep, climbed over the tree and headed out on foot. Looking left and right, he listened to determine which direction the sound of falling water was coming from. With Simon's bag containing ET and the other supplies he had picked up at the local hardware store and the bag containing his new satellite energy collecting device, slung over his shoulder, he followed the sound of falling water. Bending under low lying branches and swatting mosquitoes, he made his way toward the increasing roar of water falling from a great height. The path wound down a steep slope. There were towering canyon walls on either side. He forged ahead, hanging on to branches to keep from sliding down the path. At last he entered a clearing.

He was at the bottom of the falls, standing in front of the most brilliant green pond he had ever seen. Water was rushing down the canyon walls creating a mystical ethereal mist that enveloped everything. His face was covered in a fine spray and the roar of the water drowned out all other sound. He was mesmerized by the beauty here and a feeling of reverence overcame him.

A flicker of movement captured in his peripheral vision dispelled the hypnotic state he was in. Someone was up above on the ridge overlooking the pond. He scampered behind a willow bush to avoid being seen. The man had long black hair pulled into a ponytail and he wore a brown denim jacket. He was too far away for Galen to make out any other features. He was not anyone Galen recognized from his medical practice. A feeling of hunter vs. prey tingled at his senses. He remained perfectly still. After what seemed an eternity the man turned and walked away. Galen breathed a slow silent sigh of relief. His chances of doing this unnoticed he realized were slim.

He took the hunting knife out of his back pack and tucked it under his belt. He removed the ET tracker he had stolen from Simon's pack, pointed it toward the falls and pressed the alien logo on the touch screen. A shimmery hologram of the area he was standing in appeared before him. It was filled with red dots, at least a hundred of them! They were headed toward the pond cascading down the falls on three sides of the canyon.

He scanned the periphery. In order to capture the incoming energy streams he needed to get closer to the walls of the canyon. Any hopes he had for a bridge or a ledge that he could set up the satellite collector on were dashed. Except for the path he was standing on, the pond was encased on all sides by steep canyon walls. A rather large fallen tree that he climbed over to get to the edge of the pond was the only option he saw. If he could somehow position it to allow him to crawl out under the water fall he might be able to collect the incoming energy as it entered the pond. He pressed his shoulder to the rough trunk of the tree and pushed. It would not budge. There had to be another way.

He took the collapsed satellite dish that he had coined "HELEN" out of its sleeve and extended the arms to open it.

"Hello HELEN."

The many translucent segments containing thousands of collecting cells shimmered in the morning sun. It was light in his hands. No more than five pounds at the most. If he could secure it to a long rod or pole, perhaps he could just extend it out to the middle of the pond and collect the energy that was entering the pool.

In his back pack he had a roll of duct tape. He hid the satellite under some tall ferns and walked back along the path he just descended in search of a long sturdy branch that he could use as an extension arm for the floppy disk. He walked cautiously, trying not to make any noise that would alert his presence to the man above the falls.

A twig snapped. It was followed by the sound of soft foot falls on the spongy earth. Galen slipped behind a fir tree. The man from above the falls was coming down the path toward him. He was less than 50 feet away. At this close range there was no mistaking that he was Indian. There was also no mistaking that he was carrying a rifle and that it looked comfortable in his grasp.

Galen froze; his hand on the butt of his hunting knife, just in case. He watched as the tan skinned man knelt down and touched his fingers to the damp ground and then stood and looked around. He was afraid to take a breath for fear it would alert the seasoned hunter to his position. He watched as the Indian made his way to the base of the pond. The mist created from the rushing water connected with the early morning sun to create a halo around him. Galen was transfixed. If he were a religious man he may have taken this as a sign. The man stood there for many minutes overlooking the water.

When at last he turned and made his way back up the path, away from the pond, Galen could finally breathe. He was thankful he hid HELEN under the tall ferns. From his hiding place he could see a 6 foot high poplar sapling that could possibly work as an extension arm for the satellite dish. Wary now, he crawled over the damp moss laden ground toward it. He used his hunting knife to slowly saw at the base. Once felled, he stripped the young tree of its branches. He weighed it in his hands. It was sturdy enough. It should work.

In silence, he made his way back to the pool, extracted the dish from its hiding place and secured it to the sapling with duct tape. Laying flat on the ground he extended the makeshift pole with its attached floppy dish out into the center of the pool. He depressed the start button. HELEN was beautiful but flimsy. It fluttered and waved amidst the moving air caused by the rush of the water down the steep banks. The mist and the foam from the water encompassed the satellite. He could not keep it still. Exasperated and arms heavy from holding the makeshift rod out over the surface of the pond, Galen pulled it to shore and laid still for a moment. It was not going to work.

A new plan was needed. Picking up his stuff, he spotted Simon's energy tracker on the ground at the edge of the pond. It must have fallen out of his pocket. Stooping down to pick it up, he noticed something he had not seen before. In addition to the steady stream of dots entering the pool, there was also a steady stream leaving the pool. Frowning in confusion, he did not know what to make of this. ...how could there be energy coming out of the pool? It did not make sense. Maybe it was not the same kind of living energy that was going into the pond. Regardless, it was right here happening in front of him and he had a collecting device that he could capture it with. He would figure out what it was later. He extended the legs of the dish into the dirt next to the energy tracker and switched it on. HELEN's floppy crystalline fabric began to flutter and wave and within minutes a soft tone emitted from the control indicating that the collecting cells were filling. The digital display on the handle indicated that 50 cells were filled with energy. He depressed the switch to the off position and looked auspiciously around to see if his activity had created any disturbance or alerted the Indian to his presence.

There was no other sound than that of birds chirping. He folded HELEN up and put it back into the shoulder bag, grabbed Simon's bag and made his way back up the path and out to the jeep unseen. He couldn't wait to get back to the library. He needed to work out how to now transfer the captive energy held in HELEN to COLTEN so it could be specifically directed and used.

Chapter 24

"Where the hell have you been?" Devlin Matthews yelled into the phone. "I have been hiding out here in this hotel for the past two weeks. I had to shave my head, grow a mustache, change my name and get a fake ID. The police are crawling all over my company."

Galen's kept his voice calm. "I knew it would be hot, that is why I left you alone. We both need to lie low, and I cannot be seen with you. The police have been to see me too."

"Luckily I was able to get to my secretary before the police did. She covered for me. She told them I was missing and she was worried that maybe something happened to me. She told the cops that there was no such person as Evan Billard who worked for Living Energy Corporation. From what I gather they also figured out that the cabin where I kept Francis belonged to Alfred and I am guessing they are at the hospital visiting him now."

"Well, no worries there. They won't find him. Alfred Innis is gone."

"Gone? What do you mean gone? Dead? You mean all of this was for nothing? He died?" The exasperation in Devlin's voice brought a smile to Galen's face.

"Yes the Alfred Innis that we knew is dead," Galen stated flatly. He reveled in the silence on the other end of the phone. Pay back. He loved it. He let Devlin soak in his own despair for a few more minutes.

"*Allen* Innis, long lost great nephew of Alfred who is 25 years old and has been living in South America has just inherited a 50 billion dollar estate."

The groan from Devlin had Galen grinning from ear to ear. He was glad Devlin couldn't see him, but he couldn't keep it up.

"After I infused Alfred with energy that I collected from a new found source, he turned younger right before my eyes. I could hardly believe it. He sat up in the hospital bed, took off his heart monitor electrodes, got dressed and walked out. He said the 50 million would be in your bank account by morning. I signed his death certificate and told the nursing staff that I arranged for a private burial so there was no need for his body to go to the morgue. Alfred wrote up a will leaving his entire fortune to his fictitious nephew Allen, alias himself and no one is the wiser."

"You bastard," Devlin let out a bottled breath. "I thought my life was over! How did you do it? Where did you get the energy?"

"Remember what I told you about coincidences and how there are none? Everything, every encounter you have is for a reason. Well, when I met Francis's friend the young physicist from Boston U., he shared his work with me and I followed up with a little research of my own. Let's say I got lucky with finding another energy source that did not require kidnapping or murder to attain." He couldn't help but rub some salt into the wound of Devlin's stupidity.

Galen was not about to tell Devlin about his road trip to what he now thought of as the "Fountain of Life" and the fact that he had been able to collect enough energy for Alfred and another 30 or 40 people as well. Devlin did not need to know that real life energy was literally flowing out of the falls, just waiting to be contained! His face flushed with excitement. He could already see his name on the Nobel Prize for the invention of the century. His discovery would do more for the health of mankind than anyone in history. Not even the invention of penicillin or insulin could top his discovery and the impact he would have on human illness and suffering. He would be able to heal anyone. He would be famous beyond belief.

On the other end of the phone line, Devlin bristled at Galen's hesitation to tell him where he had found the alternate source of energy. He suspected that Galen was not telling him everything. That was okay. He had his own ways to find out what Galen knew and if Galen couldn't be trusted, well he was working on a way to look after that too.

"Galen, you cannot breathe a word of this to anyone. Not anyone, you understand? This find is not about being famous; it is about being powerful and rich beyond your wildest imagination. Just lay low for a while till I figure out our next steps."

Galen did not bother to reply. There it was. As expected, Devlin jostling for control, wanting to take over and steal the glory. Well he had fulfilled his end of the bargain. He had transfused Innis with enough energy to keep him alive for another 10 lifetimes. He would not be told what to do by a low life cheat like Devlin. He did not trust Devlin and he would not be denied his discovery. He would collect energy from the falls whenever he needed it. He would control who got the benefit of extended life and for damn certain it would not be given to low life scum bags like wife abusers and crooked millionaires. Like Devlin suggested, he would keep the whole thing quiet. Devlin would never know about the fountain of life he had discovered.

Chapter 25

Sherriff Donavan tucked in his shirt and straightened his tie before pressing the door bell. He felt out of place here. The house was intimidating- a three story mansion set back on 5 acres and surrounded by manicured lawns and gardens. He knew the man was intimidating, although he must be old by now. His last memories of him were as a child and the man was old then. He remembered how mean he was. He never smiled. He would come into his father's store and demand attention. He held the mortgages on almost everyone's business in the town and never cut anyone any slack. Billionaires with their air of superiority, their idea that they were above the law, above questioning were not the type of person he was accustomed to dealing with.

A young man, well groomed and in his mid twenties opened the door.

"Sherriff." With one word, the man acknowledged him and created an air of superiority at the same time.

"I am looking for Alfred Innis."

"Well I am afraid you are a bit late. Alfred died today."

Donavan was taken aback. "I am sorry." He had not expected this. "Is there a next of kin, or an estate lawyer that I can talk to?"

"I guess that would be me. I am Allen Innis," he hesitated for a second before continuing "Alfred's great nephew."

The sheriff felt scrutinized and looked down upon.

"What can I do for you, Sherriff?" Allen asked in a condescending tone.

Sherriff Donavan eyed the young well dressed man suspiciously. To be so young and already have such airs of superiority seemed out of context somehow. Guess that was what having money did to you.

"I didn't know that Alfred had a nephew. I didn't know he had any family at all." He blurted out.

"Yes, well I am afraid you don't know much now do you?" The young Innis sneered at him.

Donavan glared at him without saying a word but did not move from his spot on the step. He would be damned if he would be intimidated by this young whelp.

Allen continued with a sigh "No one really spoke much of my mother. She was Alfred's illegitimate sister."

"So I guess you stand to inherit quite a sizable fortune then," Donavan stated matter of fact.

"Yes," Allen surveyed the yard, "I guess you could say I landed under a lucky star, but don't let me keep you from your reason for coming here."

"There was a kidnapping and the hostage was kept at a secluded fishing lodge on the north side of the Miramichi River. The building and surrounding land is owned by your uncle."

"I hardly believe that my uncle could have had anything to do with this." Allen's tone was immediately defensive. "He has been in the hospital for the past month attached to life support systems. He certainly could not have coerced a young woman into his cabin and held her hostage there."

The sheriff eyed him suspiciously. "I am looking into all connections that your uncle may have had. I am not saying *he* was the kidnapper. Perhaps he loaned his cabin or gave the security information to someone else who used the cabin. Would he have a list of people who he would have provided access to?"

"I vaguely recall that he had a fishing lodge that he took his company investors to periodically but I don't really know where it is. I believe he used it for entertainment purposes and to give his investors and supporters who like to salmon fish a token of appreciation."

Fair enough. "Do you know if he worked with a company called Living Energy?"

"No I don't know. Look Sheriff, he was in the business of Energy. I would guess that he has dealt with every company that deals with energy at some time or other."

"We believe your uncle may have been involved with some shady business."

"Well that would not be like my uncle now would it?" Allen did not try to conceal his impatience. "Sherriff. I hardly know the answers to your questions, but it would seem to me that you are on a wild goose chase here. I just arrived in town today and really did not know the old man at all. I do know that he was rather peculiar." A hint of a smile crossed his face. "Now I am sorry, but I have funeral arrangements to make."

With that Allen Innis turned and closed the door. Sherriff Donavan was left standing on the step.

***

Francis and Simon were waiting at the police station when Sherriff Donavan returned to work. Simon's arm was encircled around the librarian's shoulders and her head was resting on his shoulder. In unison, they stood up when he walked in.

He took off his hat and gestured for them to follow him into his office. He knew they wanted answers but he did not have the answers they sought. His initial excitement at finding out that the building in which Andria had been held captive was owned by the town's billionaire was squashed when he found out that the old man had been in the hospital and had since died. He told Simon and Francis what he knew.

"Alfred Innis is dead. His entire estate was willed to a long lost nephew named Allen Innis. Not a pleasant individual, I might add."

"What about the Audi? Have your men found it yet?" Simon asked

"Yes. It was abandoned at a roadside cafe not far from the fishing lodge. My men have impounded it and dusted it for finger prints. Nothing came up."

"I thought you found out that it was a rental car that was rented to someone named Evan Billard?

"Yes, that was a dead end too. There is no Evan Billard that we can find. No social security number, no license, no record of him at all. I talked to the guy at the rental agency that did the paper work. He didn't really remember anything about him or what he looked like. Said they rent so many cars that all the customers' faces just blur into one for him. Since neither of you can provide much of a description either, we are not able to get a composite sketch of him."

"What about the company he listed as his place of employment?" Simon asked.

"We did call Living Energy Corporation. They denied having an employee by the name of Evan Billard. The secretary I spoke with thought the name sounded familiar. That maybe somebody by that name had worked there several years ago for a short period of time and left on bad terms. There might be an angle there. I have one of my officers working on it but other than that we are really at a dead end here."

Francis looked at him, her dark brown eyes brimming with tears. "I don't believe it. This cannot be a dead end. There has to be a way that we can track down the man that kidnapped me. I can't just

154

forget it and pretend that it didn't happen. I am afraid to be alone. I am afraid to walk down the street alone, to go to the library, even to go home. I don't know why people want me dead."

Simon squeezed her hand and drew her close. They could be brother and sister with their tanned complexions, dark hair and eyes, but Donavan could tell that Simon was smitten with the librarian. His drive to protect the woman he loved was easy to read.

"What *can* we do Sherriff?" Simon was vibrating with pent up frustration at the helplessness of the situation.

"We just have to wait and take the proper steps. I will get a search warrant for Innis's house and work offices and set up a meeting with the estate lawyers. It will take some time but we will find out who may have had access to the cabin and work it through one step at a time. Clues will emerge. We will find out who did this to you Francis and what it is they want but it is going to take some time. Now you kids go home and leave this up to us."

***

The hot afternoon sun did little to remove the dark chill that enveloped them. Simon's heart ached as he saw the defeat reflected in Francis's eyes.

"Simon, I can't go on like this. I am afraid. Afraid of everything."

He was not accustomed to playing the hero role. He was a thinker not a leader. Infuriation crawled from the tips of his toes to the top of his spine. He wanted to punch someone, to scream, to shake his fists in fury at the sky. Instead he took a deep breath and exhaled it slowly, gaining control of his emotions and his thoughts. This was not a dead end. There was a way to find out who was doing this and why.

"I am with you, Francis," he squeezed her hand in encouragement. "We can't just wait and do nothing. We are going to need to tackle this - logically just as we would any scientific problem. I have an idea on how to start."

The look of trust and belief in her eyes sent waves of pleasure through his body. She was placing her confidence in him. His determination solidified.

"More brains are always better than one- or even two," he smiled at her. "I am going to phone Dad and Henrietta and ask them to meet us. Can we use the library and maybe make use of Ranger to start working out a plan?"

Chapter 26

Francis opened the door to the library with the same key that the Sherriff had recovered from the car that she had been transported to the cabin in. She looked at the key in her hand and memories of her ordeal flooded her mind. An uncontrollable sob escaped her lips. She felt a comforting hand on her shoulder and reached up and gave Simon's hand a squeeze. It was hard to believe that she had known him for only a few weeks. She already relied upon him, trusted him; needed him.

The library with its heavy brocaded window drapes blocked the heat of the day. It was dark and cool and inviting. It offered no intent to harm, only to help. Francis placed her hand in Simon's. Their fingers entwined naturally. Together they would tackle this. Together they would find out who was at the bottom of this and why.

Marcus and Henrietta joined them in the great room where they already had Ranger working.

Simon led the discussion. "Okay...let's go over what we know. Ranger, take note."

At Simon's command, Ranger sprung into life. The words "Things we know," magically appeared on the wall sized monitor.

"We know that someone tried to run over Francis," Henrietta started.

"We know that the same car that tried to run me down was used to take me to a cabin owned by Alfred Innis, the same billionaire who donated a ton of money to the library."

All heads turned to Francis. Other than Simon no one else knew about Innis's involvement with the library.

"We also know that Alfred Innis is dead," Francis sighed. "That rules Innis out of the equation."

"We know that the car was a rental and was billed to a man named Evan Billard who used a credit card from a company called Living Energy Corporation to pay for his rental," Marcus continued.

"We know that Living Energy Corporation denies that he is employed there," Simon added. "And apparently a corporate credit card was missing".

"We also know that Dr. Thomas has had a lot of contact with Living Energy Corporation for some work he was doing," Francis stated.

All eyes turned to her.

"How do you know that?" Simon asked.

"Well I get all of the phone bills for the library and that name is usually on the bill many times every month."

The group was silent for a minute letting this new information sink in.

Finally Henrietta spoke "However we also know that Dr. Thomas was at the scene of the hit and run so he was not directly involved in that."

Everyone nodded, absolving the doctor of blame.

The small group looked at the items listed under "The things we know" on the computer screen.

"Living Energy Corporation would seem to be our most likely answer," Simon said rubbing his brow. "It just didn't make sense. Why would an international energy company want to kill or kidnap Francis, a lowly librarian in a small town? No offense, Francis."

"None taken, Simon. I want to know that too," Francis smiled in response. Her smile warmed him to the core.

"Let's keep thinking about possible connections." Henrietta prompted the group to stay on task.

"Well another obvious connection is energy," Simon started. "Dr. Thomas is doing research on energy. I am doing research on energy. I am guessing a company called Living Energy must be doing research on energy too."

Marcus contributed: "Dr.Thomas works in the library and so does Simon."

"The library is a common theme. Not only do Simon and Dr. Thomas work here but Alfred Innis donated the money that bought the equipment in the library. Maybe the connection is that I am the librarian or the library itself?" Francis added.

"So the two common themes are: "Energy and the Library."

"Ranger start new list: Things we don't know".

"We don't know *who* the man was that kidnapped me or *why*."

"We know the car was rented to an Evan Billard but we don't know anything about him."

"We don't know if there is any connection between Billard and anyone else we know."

"We don't know the main business of Living Energy Corporation."

"We don't know why Dr. Thomas has been communicating with Living Energy Corporation."

"We don't know if there is a connection between Dr. Thomas's research and Simon's."

"We don't know why Innis donated money to the library."

"We don't know if there is a connection between Living Energy and Innis or Innis and Dr. Galen for that matter."

"I wonder who this long lost nephew Allen is. Who is he and what has he been doing until now?"

Everyone nodded in agreement. There was a lot they did not know.

Having exhausted additional ideas, Henrietta continued "Let's jump to the possible whys."

"Maybe someone thinks I know something that is top secret or classified or something," Francis stated flatly.

"What could you possibly know that would warrant your attempted murder?" Simon placed his hand on Francis's shoulder.

"Maybe from Ranger. Maybe there is information that Ranger holds that they are afraid I might be privy to?"

"That does not make sense. It would be easier to delete Ranger's memory, then to delete you," Simon commented.

"Maybe it is like your Dad said; maybe it is because of your research." Francis looked at Simon. "But that doesn't make sense, because nobody really knows about your research except us"

"As I said before, except for the 800 people you tested at the fair." Marcus stated the obvious but had another thought. "Maybe it has nothing to do with Simon or *what* you might know Francis, maybe it has to do with *who* you know. Maybe you are being used as a bargaining chip."

All eyes turned to Marcus.

"Well. Think about it. Dr. Thomas has communications with a company, someone from whom rented a car that tried to run you over and then kidnapped you. I am not saying that Dr. Thomas was involved, but maybe this person whoever he is, is using the potential of harming you to influence Thomas to produce whatever it is that he is working on. May be you are a bargaining chip."

The group stared in silence, letting the enormity of Marcus' observation sink in. Indeed it sounded like a plausible theory. Francis could be a pawn being used to blackmail Dr. Thomas into doing something that perhaps he did not want to do. The doctor could not have been directly involved because he had been at the scene of the accident when the car had attempted to run Francis over. At the time of the kidnapping he was working at the hospital.

Simon found himself unconsciously taking control. His mind was filled with the problem at hand and possible solutions. The steps were clear. Get Ranger working on background information on Living Energy Corporation and its owner, find out who all of Alfred Innes's major clients and partners were, do a reference check on Allen Innis and talk to Dr. Thomas about his research and connections with Life Energy Corporation. They needed to continue to logically and methodically work through their suspicions to get the proof they needed to catch this criminal. They needed to test and validate their theories just like he would for any research project. This was no different. He was good at this. He could do this. He would find out who was targeting Francis. He would protect her.

Chapter 27

The man who greeted Devlin at the door indeed looked like a younger Alfred. He could not help but stare at him in amazement.

"Alfred?" Devlin began.

"I am afraid you are looking for my elderly uncle who has just passed away." The man was dismissive and about to close the door in his face.

Devlin remembered that he had shaved his head, grown a mustache and beard and changed his style of dress so of course he would not look familiar. He quickly blurted out. "I am Devlin Matthews."

A look of faint recognition crossed the young man's face. "Devlin?" he extended his hand for a firm handshake. "I didn't recognize you. You look different."

"Not as different as you," Devlin grinned. "Looks like it worked!"

"Allen Innis at your service." The young Alfred bowed and gestured with a wide arm sweep toward the entrance foyer, welcoming Devlin into his home.

Devlin had never been inside the billionaire's home. It was as lavish on the inside as it was on the outside. The foyer was massive with marble flooring, a central stone fountain and a dazzling crystal chandelier that must have been six feet in circumference. The sitting area that he was directed to was as equally lavish as the entryway, open beam ceiling, field stone fireplace, leather chairs and sofa, floor to ceiling windows overlooking the entire river valley.

Devlin took a seat. He could not take his eyes off of the exuberant young Alfred who was pacing back and forth in front of him. God, it really was a miracle.

"How are you feeling?"

Allen laughed. "I feel great. I feel young. I feel alive." He spread his arms in a wide open gesture in the air. "I have so much energy, I can't sit still! Look at me!"

He posed, hands on hips, in front of the massive wall mirror and admired the reflection staring back at him.

"I am young. I am young and I am rich! I have no signs of cancer. How could I feel anything but great?" His voice was exuberant.

Devlin did not know Alfred as a young man, but as an old man he was as calm and emotionless as a stone. This young Alfred was nothing like his senior self. He was in constant motion, his voice accelerated and high pitched. He was not still for more than a minute at a time; sitting one second, standing the next, pacing back and forth and making wild arm gestures. He supposed it was to be expected, after all the man had just experienced a miracle that dropped 60 years off of his life.

"I have a million thoughts racing through my head." Allen said, pacing in front of Devlin. "We need to start marketing this. Everlasting life. My God the power we will have! Where did Galen get the energy from anyway? I know the thing with the girl did not work out, so where did he find the alternate source? I realize I put some pressure on with my deadly timing." He smirked at his own joke and continued rambling. "As a doctor he must have a ready supply of dying victims that can serve as energy donors. There is going to be a phenomenal market for this Devlin. Maybe we can get people working in every hospital in the country collecting energy from the dying. Hell maybe we need to create a store house to store all the energy we collect. I mean how many people die every day in the world? Millions? The beauty in this is that new people are also born every day, so it is an endless supply!"

Devlin was having difficulty keeping up with the flight of ideas that were flowing from Innis. "Slow down Alfred, I mean Allen. We need to go slowly here. I am not sure that I have the doctor completely on side. He is pretty hung up on the need for recognition and some altruistic notion that he can heal the world. He has the God complex going on. We need to get him on side. If we can't do that, we need to get the information he has, duplicate what he has invented and then get rid of him."

"Money has a way of convincing everyone to come on side, but on side or out; that is my philosophy. It doesn't matter much to me. We don't really need him, we need his devices. Doctors and scientists are a dime a dozen". The man in front of him might look and sound different, but he was just as ruthless at 25 as he was at 75. This was the Innis that Devlin knew. Cold hearted, emotionless, all about the dollar and the power, the kind of partner he needed.

"I am still not out of the woods on the thing with the girl. The cops are all over my company. You could get linked to this too, if they dig deep enough."

"The sheriff was here just before you came. He was trying to link my 'uncle" to this unfortunate kidnapping. Alfred's timely death got him out of that one! "He laughed. "But none the less, these police officers, sometimes they get pretty cocky and go after a lead like a dog with a bone. They are jealous of people with money and are always looking for any excuse to bring us down. So we cannot be too careful. I suspect he will be getting a subpoena to go through *Uncle's* books. If he does it won't take him long to find out the connection between you, me and Dr.Thomas. You have not been very tidy with this ordeal Devlin. You left a lot of loose strings. I don't usually work with people who are so careless. I expected more of you." He glowered at Devlin with an abrupt turn in emotion.

Devlin's cheeks burned with the berating.

"Well, things got a little dicey, what with you threatening to die at any moment and with Galen so reluctant to do anything risky. I found out that he really only needed the energy from one person as long as that person was considered to be *pure of heart*. When I discovered that the little librarian that he is so smitten with fit the bill, it put me into a situation where I realized I could speed things up a bit. There was no more time to wait for an opportune moment, so I made one. You should be thanking me, for acting in your best interests." Devlin defended his actions.

"Okay, I will give you that, but next time, put more thought into it. Your recklessness does not instill confidence and I need to be confident in my partners."

From careless to partner, from a berating to a compliment in 30 seconds; Devlin was not sure how to react. It was good to know that Innis was on side with him even if he was upset with him. Admittedly he had made some blunders recently. Alfred or Allen whatever the name, he could be a phenomenal ally but there was no doubt, he could also be a formidable foe.

"The police are looking for a man named Evan Billard who rented the car that was used to kidnap the girl. Evan does not exist. He was a figment of my imagination. I screwed up though, as I used a Corporate Visa to rent the car and the police have linked it to my company. My secretary confirmed that there was no such person as Evan Billard working for our company and that a corporate credit card had been reported missing by one of our employees, so hopefully that throws them off the track. But if they link my company with you and your fishing lodge, the wolves will close in."

"Pretty weak, Devlin," Allen let out a sigh of exasperation that in no uncertain terms indicated that he again thought he was working with an incompetent.

"I will destroy all records that I have of our transactions or should I say, the transactions that you had with my uncle," Allen's expression changed from one of irritation to one of humor. "I would suggest that you do the same, as quickly as you can. It will only take the police a couple of days to get a judge to sign a search warrant. Can the girl recognize you?"

"No, I don't think so. She was pretty drugged and I kept her blindfolded the whole time."

"Well then get rid of that foolish disguise and go back to being Devlin Matthews, CEO of Living Energy Corporation. Do not act like you have anything to hide. The best cover is in the confident bluff. Have you never played poker?" he chastised Devlin.

Devlin resented the air of superiority that Innis, this *very young* Innis displayed. It was hard to think of him as the old Innis and it was hard to take direction from a kid. He needed to keep telling himself that this man was Alfred in a young body. He did not like being treated like an imbecile. After all he was the one that found Thomas and convinced Alfred to invest money in the research. If it was not for him, Alfred would be truly dead right now and not standing here in front of him giving him shit. It was the arrogance that came with being wealthy beyond belief. He would be there soon. He would be the one lording power over others.

"I have some things to do now to help clean up your mess. Call me on a line that is not connected to you or your company in the next day or two."

Allen stood up and walked to the door. Devlin was dismissed.

Chapter 28

It was 2:30 am. Simon waited. The doctor would come to the library eventually. According to Francis, he spent the better part of every night here when he was on call. Eventually he would turn up and Simon would talk to him about his research. While he waited, he kept himself busy researching Living Energy Corporation. The company web page was quite informative. It described the company as having a fresh approach to meeting the energy demands of the people of the world, rising from traditional energy sources like oil and gas to more evolved systems of capturing wind and solar power. The company mission statement talked about fresh approaches to renewable energy sources. He was able to access their profit loss statements and saw at a glance that the company was in financial trouble. They made huge investments in research with no return on their investments in the last year. A bank account that once had millions in profits was looking like it was now in the red. The company byline was that their investments would soon see huge returns and encouraged investor confidence in a new source of energy. Before he could get to the tab about leadership he heard the back door to the library open. Dr. Galen Thomas had arrived. Simon logged off of the computer. He moved to the work station where he had staged a show of books and open journals, a coffee cup, pen and paper with numerous equations and scribbled notes.

He stood up, stretched, yawned and walked to the door to greet the doctor.

"Dr. Thomas." He looked at his watch. "Man, is it really 2:30? I lost track of time. Looks like you did too!"

"Simon." Galen extended his hand to greet him. "You can call me Galen. I am on call at the hospital and sometimes it just makes more sense to stay up all night rather than go to bed and be roused from a deep sleep by an alarming beeper and then be expected to perform in a crisis. Never could do that. I just come here between calls instead. What are you doing here at this late hour?"

"Oh, just doing more research on my theory about the quality of life energy. Sometimes I get so engrossed in what I am doing that I lose track of time."

"I do the same, in fact, sometimes I lose track of reality too." Galen laughed a good hearted and honest laugh.

"I was thinking about our discussion the other day. You told me you were working on some research related to life's energy too, and I never got a chance to ask you about that. Maybe we have some things in common that we could mutually benefit from by sharing."

Galen passed a scrutinizing look at Simon and for a moment he thought he would refuse. He forced his face to remain open with what he hoped was a look of innocence.

After a moment, Galen nodded."You know that would be good. Come on downstairs with me to the Library's inner sanctum where I do most of my work. I will put on a pot of Java."

Sitting in the luxurious leather recliners and with the fortitude of freshly brewed Columbian coffee beans, Simon and Galen got lost in each other's research. The hours flew by as they shared theories about energy sources, transfer of energy and the creation of energy. Simon was so engrossed and enthralled with the discussion that he almost forgot the reason he had waited for Galen.

Galen's pride in his work was evident in the way he spoke and the euphemisms he used. He was a genius and he knew it. Simon fed into his pride by complimenting and acknowledging his work. When the doctor began telling him about his theories around the collection of life energy, Simon sat up straighter. He couldn't believe what he was hearing.

"What are you saying? You think you can collect life energy at the time of death?"

"Yes. " Galen's face was lit up with an ear to ear smile of self pride. "That is exactly what I am saying. Of course it is just a theory at this time. Think about it. You have already confirmed that energy leaves the body at the time of death and have been able to actually track it. I am just taking your work one step further by finding a way to collect it. My theory is that energy collected from a person whose death is inevitable can be collected and re-directed to save the life of someone else."

As Galen talked, he continuously and subconsciously played with a shiny silver penlight on his desk. He held it, turned it, placed it on his desk, picked it up, turned it his hands, and stroked it. It was probably a nervous habit, but the motion kept pulling Simon's attention to the pen.

Simon pulled his eyes away from the pen. "How would you do that?"

"It is all just conjecturing at this point- games to keep my mind interested in the wee hours of the morning, but it could work like any energy collection device. The theory is similar to that of solar panels and batteries. First you collect the energy, then you transfer it into a holding device and then you transfer it into the device that needs energy to function. In this case the device that needs the energy to function or operate is a human whose life battery is running out."

Simon couldn't believe his ears. He highly suspected that what Galen was describing was not mere conjecture, it was already a reality.

"Have you made any prototypes to try to capture the energy?" he asked.

Simon acknowledged Galen's eyes dart to the silver penlight now lying on the coffee table. He shook his head.

"No, I have tried a few things, but nothing concrete yet."

Simon decided to press a little "It is hard to develop prototypes without financial backing and technical support. I am lucky that the University of Boston is interested in my research and so has provided a great deal of support with my research especially with technology development support. I never could have developed the ET application without that support. You need to find a company to sponsor your work."

Galen gestured around the room they were sitting in. "Well this library is already pretty well equipped with the finest and latest in technology I am pretty fortunate that the town has allowed me to do my research here so I guess you could say in a way I do have a sponsor. I am also lucky to have the finest research assistant in the land."

"You mean Francis?" Simon asked, sweat beads breaking out on his forehead.

"Yes. Francis has been an unbelievable support to me."

Simon was sure he saw Galen's face flush. Was he subtly letting him know that Francis was his territory? Simon decided to ignore the statement about Francis and push Galen a little further along the sponsorship angle.

"Yes, you do have it pretty good. This is a pretty impressive library. I understand some aging billionaire sponsored all of this in a moment of guilt over everything he stole from the community."

"That's right. The heartless old bastard died yesterday." Galen stated flatly.

"Have you ever heard of a company called Living Energy Corporation?" Simon pushed.

There was a slight hesitation before Galen answered. Simon sensed that he was becoming suspicious of the conversation.

"Yes. I have done some work for them as a consultant, working on theories related to free floating energy transfer. My work was not really what they were interested in though. They are a company that mostly deals with oil and gas and energy that is related to supporting our living practices, not living energy as you and I think of it."

Simon weighed Galen's words. He felt Galen was not being completely forthcoming but he sensed an honest dislike of the company of which they spoke. Why?

It was six in the morning when Simon and Galen finally said good night and left the library. As much as he didn't want to, Simon could not help but like the man. They were kindred spirits in a way, both sharing the same interests and beliefs and passion for science. He sensed they also shared an attraction to the same girl and he could not believe that Galen could be involved in any activity that would threaten Francis. Still the link to Living Energy Corporation seemed a little too coincidental and he was certain that Galen was hiding something. That coupled with the fact that he was convinced that Galen had found a way to collect energy from a dying person was alarming. Science had a way of getting in the way of humanity. He was starting to sound like his father.

Chapter 29

"Alfred, I mean Allen," Devlin corrected himself.

"Are you calling from a secure line?"

Allen Innis was relaxing by the inside pool in his mansion. He had just finished swimming 50 laps. He hadn't done that since he was a boy. The thought made him chuckle. I am a boy! A boy with endless energy! He rose from the lounge chair and paced the perimeter of the pool with the phone to his ear.

"Yes I picked up a disposable phone," Devlin answered.

"I trust payment for services has been received into your account?" Allen had to force himself to focus on the conversation at hand, his mind wanted to jump in ten different directions.

"Yes. It is good to be back in the black. I am ready to get started with the next stages of the project. I have a plan that will make us the most powerful men in the world."

Allen felt himself bristle slightly. He did not need Devlin Matthews to make him one of the most powerful men in the world.

"I already am one of the most powerful men in the world."

Devlin ignored Allen's comment. "I don't trust Galen. He is writing a book. A book revealing not just his thesis but also the methodology he used to create his energy collection and transfer device. The book is complete with formulas and diagrams. Any fool with half a brain could read the book and duplicate his work. Galen is full of pomp. He thrives on recognition. No matter what we do, he will end up talking about or trying to publish his work or sharing it with some brainy colleagues. We might need to eliminate him."

Allen stopped mid stride. He was renowned for taking what he needed, for capitalizing on others weaknesses. Some might say he was a thief, a manipulator and a scam artist, but he had never killed anyone nor had he had anyone killed. He cleared his throat providing Devlin with the impetus to continue.

"I went to the library and took the book. I tapped the library phone lines and Galen's office phones. I copied all of the computer files onto a portable memory drive and then deleted them from the main drive of his computer. I don't know if he has other copies saved. I couldn't find the actual devices. He must have them with him, but we could recreate the devices using his diagrams. If we make our own copies of the collection and transfer devices, we won't need Galen's but it would be better if we could get them away from him. Do you have access to the same type of technology that is in the library?"

Allen smirked and made his first comment in the conversation.

"I am not an idiot. When I had those computers installed in the library, I not only had duplicates installed here, they are all connected. You could have saved yourself some work by talking to me first. I have access to any information that Galen or anyone else for that matter, may have put into the library computers. I can monitor every key stroke he makes. I can deny him access to his own files or I can delete the files from his computer. I can also tell if he made any backup copies and I can "run" his program here into my own Zed replicator."

"Great, do that right then." Devlin ordered "There is also a visiting researcher in town that has some kind of a pocket GPS system that tracks life energy. If we could get our hands on that it would make our work easy."

Irritation clouded Allen's senses. What made Devlin think he could give him an order? He was the one who gave the orders. So far, the doctor had not caused him any grief while Devlin seemed to be nothing but trouble with his demands and screw ups. He was reconsidering Devlin's assessment of Galen. After all it was the doctor who saved his life. He owed him some piece of trust. Galen Thomas was a man of science, of extreme intelligence. He was not sure what kind of a man Devlin was. He chuckled to himself. That was not true. Devlin was like him but there was only room for one man to be in power.

"Demands. Demands." Allen's mind was wandering.

"Allen, don't you see?" Devlin tried to keep Allen's attention. "If we had Galen's energy transfer device, we would have endless access to energy. We could sell it to whoever was willing to pay for it. I have an idea for a new company called "Forever Young". It will double as a vitamin and natural herb business but the real business will be the bottling and selling of life energy. We don't need Galen for this. Even if we can't get our hands on his pen, we have all the information in his book and computer files to replicate his work. We can build on your idea to hire people in every hospital to start collecting energy for us. I will start developing a marketing campaign and you can start linking up with your "uncles" rich contacts."

Devlin was still rambling. God the man was tiresome. Computers, devices, tracking, vitamins and herbs, I need this, I need that. It was all too much. He needed to burn off some energy, go for a run, climb some trees, Hell, go sky diving! He hung up the phone without saying goodbye.

Chapter 30

Thank you for coming in, Dr. Thomas," Sheriff Donavan extended a hand of welcome to Galen Thomas and gestured for him to have a seat in the solitary wood chair next to his desk.

Galen shook his hand and sat in the Spartan styled chair, feeling very much like he was about to be interrogated.

"I have a few questions for you related to the kidnapping of Francis." The Sherriff peered at him over the rim of his glasses. Galen suspected that the Sherriff was smarter than he appeared.

"I am happy to help in any way, but I am not sure I know much."

"You were there at the scene of the hit and run when someone tried to hit Francis, and because you work so much at the library with Francis, I wondered if you might have any suspicions of who might do this."

Galen appreciated that the Sherriff got directly to the point of the interview. He hated making small talk and beating around the bush.

"No, no-one. Francis is a wonderful girl; always positive, optimistic, happy. As far as I know everyone likes her. I can't imagine why someone might not."

"There are a few coincidences in this case that are troubling me. Like the fishing lodge she was held captive in belonged to Alfred Innis, the same Alfred Innis who donated so much money to the library and who you pronounced dead earlier this week. Doesn't that seem strange to you?"

Galen calmly controlled his emotions not allowing his face to belie signs of his discomfort. Medical school taught him how to hide any expression. The sheriff was just fishing; he didn't have any suspicions about his part in this.

"Well no, not really. This is a small town. Everyone and what they do is connected in lots of ways. Alfred Innis was a billionaire. He had lots of connections. He was old and dying. I understand he was a miserable bastard in life and probably had a guilt complex in his aging years that made him donate money to the library. I rent the office space in the basement of the library from the town. As for me signing his death certificate; I was the doctor on call when he died. I don't know what to tell you about the fishing lodge, but since he used it as a perk for his investors, I would guess that the people who have access to the security code are numerous. Unless Innis had the security code changed every month or so, almost anyone who knew anyone would have access. The way you describe it, it sounds like the perfect hideaway for any criminal."

"Yes, I was thinking those same thoughts but I need to follow every possible lead. You are a smart man, Doctor. What are your thoughts on why someone would want to harm Francis, or why she might be a target?"

"My thoughts? I am afraid, I am not smart in the way you suggest Sheriff. Now if your question had to do with how to diagnosis an illness or determine a treatment or a cure for an illness, I might be better able to help you. This situation baffles me."

Jealousy. The word presented itself to Galen's mind. He felt his confidence return as he formulated a plausible explanation for the Sherriff. It was an explanation that wasn't too far off the mark. He just had to describe his own feelings about Francis. Jealousy and the drive to protect those you love are one and the same. At the end of the day both motives were about selfishness; keeping the thing you love for yourself.

"Does Francis have a scorned lover who is pissed off because of this new man who seems to have entered her life? It could very easily be an injured heart that is at the root of all of this. God knows in my line of business I have seen lots of bad situations caused by a jealous boyfriend."

"That would make sense except that Francis says she does not have a boyfriend. Even if it was some secret admirer, wouldn't you expect the kidnapper to show himself to Francis?"

"What if some sick sociopath has been stalking Francis and the introduction of Simon on the scene escalated his anxiety to be with her. He may have had plans for abuse or even murder or maybe just to protect her from this new man on the scene. The hit and run could have been his first flash of anger, but his second more calculated strategy was to kidnap her and keep her for himself."

The Sherriff listened intently to Galen's theory. He had to agree, it was plausible. This was small town New Brunswick. There was no corporate crime involving a librarian. What was he thinking? He needed to take his investigation down a new road; connections to Francis. He could pull the lists of people who regularly borrowed library books, or who accessed computers in the library. He didn't know if the library had security cameras, but perhaps it did.

Chapter 31

Simon spent all day on the computer. He was trying to find information about Allen Innis. The man had no history, or at least none that he could track down. He seemed to have come into existence out of thin air. Giving up on Allen, he began to research Alfred.

Alfred was all over the internet. The rich billionaire with no scruples. There were multitudes of pictures of the man as he rose in riches in fame. He was a tall thin man with a long slender face. He had a pointy nose and chin, small eyes and thin grey hair. There was not one picture of the man smiling. Every pose captured the shrewd business man, with cold mirthless eyes and a rigid posture. There was no sense of warmth about the man. His family history was scant. He outlived his brother and sister, neither of who had made anything of themselves. He never married and had no children. He was ranked as one of the top ten richest men in the world, making most of his money from the exploitation of the province's natural resources. The last entry about him was that at 85 he was residing in his home community on the Miramichi River. There were numerous pictures of the fishing resort where he entertained "business associates". Smiling faces, holding up their trophies- the famous Atlantic salmon for which the area was renowned. Simon scrolled through the digital images. There was a familiarity about one of the faces that re-occurred in several pictures; a stocky man with greying hair. He had only seen Francis's kidnapper briefly and had not gotten a clear look at his face, but the man in the photo shared some resemblance. He drew a selection around the digital display of the man's face on the monitor and asked Ranger to run a face recognition scan. In seconds, Ranger matched the face with a photo of the man identified as the CEO of Living Energy Corporation! His name was Devlin Matthews.

Simon printed the picture.

Chapter 32

Peering over the architectural drawings of the library the Sherriff mentally berated himself. Why hadn't he thought of this earlier? He slapped his forehead in disgust. He was soft. He worked in a town that with the exception of a few DUIs and speeding tickets to reckless teenagers who occasionally needed their wings clipped was essentially crime free. He had not exercised any criminal investigations since his training days 30 years ago. Of course the library had security cameras. They were located not just at the front and back entrances; they were also located throughout the library, in the big research room with the fancy computer and at the reception desk. They ran continuously. The cameras did a steady digital video capture record for two weeks and then downloaded the data into memory banks of the computer main drive. As far as he knew no one ever reviewed the recordings. Hell he was pretty sure that even Francis didn't realize that the cameras were there. They were masterfully hidden. Maybe there would be an actual digital display of the kidnapper that would help them to identify and nail the bastard.

***

At the library he was surprised to see Francis sitting behind the reception desk.

"What are you doing here? I thought I told you to lie low?" he admonished her.

"Yes, you did. But I can't run scared. This is what I do. I am the librarian and I need to be here. Besides, I am not alone. Simon is upstairs in the reading room." Her eyes twinkled with fun.

Donavan nodded. "Did you know that the library has security cameras?"

"No." She was incredulous. "Where?"

"Well from the diagrams, there should be one," he looked around her desk, at the ceiling, the heavy brocaded curtains that framed the great panelled windows, "right there."

He pointed to the curtain rod. Sure enough the end of the curtain rod was a reflective lens!

"Oh my God. Is it running? Where does the video go?" Francis asked.

"Well, my dear that is what I came to find out. I think it must download to that fancy computer you have on the second floor."

"Well who checks it?"

"I don't know, if you don't, I am guessing nobody does. When the renovations were made to the library the cameras were installed and put into operation. I don't think the town ever hired a security agency to do anything with it, the money for the renovations were for the capital costs not for operations so I think the tapes just go into memory. The renovations were done almost two years ago, so I am guessing there is 2 years worth of video feed stored in the computer's memory banks. Do you know how we can access the information?"

Francis flashed him a smile. "Have you ever met Ranger?"

The sheriff looked at her in puzzlement.

Francis laughed, "Come with me."

She led him up the great oak staircase. Simon met them at the top of the landing.

"I thought I heard voices. What's up Sheriff?"

Francis jumped in. "The sheriff discovered that there are security cameras in the library. At both entrances. At my desk. Even up here. We are hoping that Ranger has the information that they record stored in her memory. Maybe we can actually see who my kidnapper was!" Her voice was excited with hopeful anticipation.

Ranger was already lit up and working on Simon's project.

"Sherriff, meet Ranger." Francis pointed to the large monitor that filled the entire wall of the room. "Ranger, this is Sherriff Donavan."

Donavan was taken aback when a voice emitted from the walls in the room.

"Good morning, Sherriff Donavan. How may I help you?" the voice asked.

Gaining his composure, he asked, "Is information from the security cameras located in the library downloaded to your memory banks?"

"Affirmative. That is correct."

"Can you please show the files for July 6?"

The video feed immediately began to play. The time was documented in the right upper corner of the screen. 1410h on July 6. Large as life on the full wall screen they watched Simon breaking the window next to the back entrance of the library, they watched him run to the reception desk, and pick up Francis's phone from under the desk. They heard him shouting her name. Next they watched the door open and saw the Sherriff and Marcus Gallagher enter.

"Ranger, please play earlier recording. Start from 0900h on July 6," the Sherriff requested, quickly getting the hang of how the computer worked.

"I am sorry. There is no earlier recording for July 6."

Chapter 33

Allen Innis had been watching Galen for the past week. The library security cameras were now directly downloading to his home office computer. His office resembled what he imagined an FBI investigative unit might look like with a number of computers, monitors, recorders, video and audio enhancers providing a steady stream of input from every electronic device that Galen Thomas possessed. Holding a place of honor on the central table was an umbrella shaped object. It was extended in its open position with its reflective fabric stretched between aluminum holding rods. Each segment of fabric held taught by the metal skeleton, held thousands of tiny small discs. Each disc was no bigger than the head of a pin. From reading the in-progress book that Galen was writing, Allen knew that each pin head was actually a holding cell. Right now the cells were empty, waiting to be filled. He was unable to find the energy transfer device that Galen described in his book. From its description it looked like a penlight and was used to both extract and infuse energy from and to animals and people. Galen probably kept it on his person. If he could just stay focused he knew he could re-invent the penlight from Galen's notes and diagrams, but the diagrams were not quite as explicit as needed and the measurements or at least one of the measurements must have been off. Galen was probably smarter than Devlin gave him credit for. In all likelihood, the doctor had put in one incorrect measurement on purpose.

His team of engineering technologists had created a stand for the dish that emitted an electric protective shield around it. Once the dish was placed in the position Galen so nicely outlined in his book at the base of the falls, no one would be able to move it. The switch was controlled remotely. They just needed to develop the pen so they could move the energy they collected in the dish into a device that could transfer it to a person.

Staying focused. That seemed to be the thing he was struggling with the most these days. His mind wanted to run in a million directions at once. He tried his damndest to keep it in check. He supposed it was understandable. After all he had just undergone an unbelievable transformation. From elderly and dying to young and healthy in a matter of minutes. Surely that would shock any brain. He probably just needed to do some brain exercises. He tried doing Sudoku puzzles, but couldn't stay focused because he couldn't force himself to sit still. He wanted to move, move, move. This afternoon he played tennis, swam 50 lengths in the pool, and jogged 5 miles.

It wasn't just the need to be in constant movement that had him worried. It was also the constant moving of his mind, a swing of ideas and emotions that would overcome him unpredictably at any moment. He supposed he should see a doctor, but what would he tell him? He had to ride it out, hope his mind and body acclimatized soon. If not maybe there were some drugs that could slow him down.

Right now he was waiting on that stupid bumbling idiot - Devlin Matthews to come and take the dish to the falls. He was supposed to have been here an hour ago and he was tired of waiting. He decided go for a bike ride. A ride through the town and down along the shore line would be nice. Maybe he could skip some rocks. He was sure there were some nice flat rocks that would really skip. He bet he could get one to skip at least eight times.

Chapter 34

Finally things were going his way. Galen had not heard from Devlin in over a week. He hoped that meant that the man was happy with this fifty million and was gone from his life forever. He just finished what should have been a horrendous shift at the hospital, but because of the stored up energy held within COLTEN, he had miraculously saved a motor vehicle accident victim who otherwise would have died. His entire team looked at him like he was God. The use of Simon's ET application helped him to determine which energy levels were a higher quality than others and as a result, he felt confident that he was providing the 10 people he "saved" in the last week with renewed life to last a lifetime. He smiled at the thought. It was hard to keep the discovery of the millennium a secret. He was on top of the world and wanted desperately to share it with the world.

He was standing at the nursing station writing some final orders on the young MVA victim's medical chart but lost in his thoughts when he felt a hand on his shoulder.

"You did a great job today, Dr. Thomas. Hope you have a great evening."

Before he had time to respond, to thank Tirisa for the compliment, she was gone. He turned just in time to see her enter the staff locker room.

He couldn't help but smile. Tirisa made him feel good. She was the kind of person who noticed, recognized effort, and cared. She appreciated and valued people. Somewhere he heard that her boyfriend dumped her as soon as he discovered she was pregnant. What a loser. Why would anyone dump a girl like Tirisa? In fact why would any man shirk fatherhood responsibility? He shook his head in disgust at the number of worthless beings in the world. So many selfish people existed; people without any moral obligation to others or society. He was overcome by an impulse. Since Francis was most likely with Simon and the library would be vacant, maybe Tirisa would like to go out for supper. He felt like celebrating, like sharing life with someone tonight and who better than Tirisa? He finished writing his orders, grabbed his jacket and left the unit. He waited outside of the Emergency Department staff exit, deliberating the right approach to use.

When he saw her come out the exit door 10 minutes later, she was no longer a nurse. Jeans, sweater, sneakers, rosy cheeks, blond hair down around her shoulders, she was really quite pretty. He would have forgotten what he was going to ask if she hadn't interrupted him.

"Hey Dr. Thomas, what are you still doing here?"

"I was waiting for you. It was a draining shift and I don't feel like cooking tonight. I wondered if you might like to grab a bite to eat with me."

Tirisa eyed the doctor suspiciously. She blushed from ear to ear. He could tell she did not know how to answer.

"I just didn't feel like eating alone tonight," he shrugged.

Her face melted into a smile, her kind blue eyes twinkled. "A bite to eat sounds like a great idea. On one condition."

"What's that?"

"We can't talk shop. When I leave this place, I try to leave it behind."

"You are on."

***

It was Friday night and the Steak House was hopping. Galen and Tirisa were told it would be a twenty minute wait for a seat. They looked at each other and simultaneously shook their heads. As they turned to leave, Tirisa waved to someone seated at the window who beckoned them over. Galen felt his heart speed up when he recognized that the couple that called to them was Francis and

Simon. It appeared that Tirisa and Francis were friends. Who knew?

The two girls hugged. Galen willed his face to remain emotionless.

"Hey do you two want to join us?" Francis gestured to the two empty seats at their table.

"Sure." Tirisa looked to Galen for agreement. He could not deny the look of anticipated expectancy.

"That would be great, thank you," Galen replied while pulling out a chair for Tirisa. So much for his evening of celebration. Still he did get to spend it with three people that he did respect and like, so it could be worse.

Tirisa and Francis knew each other from volunteering at the soup kitchen. They fell into an easy conversation about the homeless, the status of the food bank and of course society and the world in which we live. The gentle ebb and flow of the conversation, the positive energy and easy acceptance of one another the group created provided the sense of enjoyment Galen wanted after all. He couldn't remember the last time he had done this with a group of friends.

"Simon and I were just talking about the latest news story about miscarriages. You two are probably the right ones to ask. What do you think is causing it?" Francis's question broke into his reverie.

"What's the story?" Galen asked, embarrassed that he was not aware of what must be a news breaking story on every local and national news channel and newspaper. He was too preoccupied with his own work; too excited by what was happening in his own world to take note of what was happening in the world around him.

Tirisa jumped in to help him out. "The news is painting the story of the number of miscarriages and fetal demises in the province as a pandemic."

"Pandemic? I don't think there has been a rise in flu or other viral agents, at least not that I have seen with my on-call shifts."

"No it is not viral in that sense. You probably haven't tuned into this, Galen because the cases have all been obstetrical. All pregnancies bypass the Emergency Department and go directly to the obstetrical unit."

Galen caught that she used his first name and not Doctor Thomas. He liked it. Tonight he was a person not a role.

"The press is calling it a silent pandemic that is causing pregnant women to have intrauterine deaths. This week, on every shift I worked there was at least one woman who was in labor and delivered a stillbirth." Tirisa took a deep breath. "It is not just here either. There has not been a new live baby born in New Brunswick in over a week."

Francis chimed in. "No one knows what is going on. There are usually at least 3 babies born every day at the Miramichi Hospital alone. The Moncton and Saint John hospitals usually have at least 7 a day. We are talking no babies born alive anywhere in New Brunswick in 8 days! There have been lots of deliveries, but all the babies have been still born. There is a worry that New Brunswick is the victim of some type of biologic warfare, or that there has been a nuclear leak somewhere."

"The phone lines in the ER have been ringing non-stop. Pregnant women who are afraid and wanting to know what they should do. No one knows what to tell them. The Medical Officer of Health is involved and there is a major review of all of the cases to see if they have anything in common," Tirisa added.

"You mean like what they ate, places they visited, immunization status, that sort of thing?" Galen asked.

"Yes, exactly. So far they have not come up with anything in common that this could be attributed to."

Galen's analytical mind kicked in. "Have there been studies on the placenta and umbilical cord bloods?"

"Yes, so far all autopsy, lab, toxicology and pathological reports are normal on all of the women and their babies. It does not make sense. Women who are close to their due dates are asking if they should leave the province. What do you think?"

Galen stared at the pretty blond nurse who was looking at him like he should have the answer. She expected him to have the ability to fix this, whatever it was. The worry in her voice was hard to miss. He knew she was worried for others, but he also knew her condition and didn't miss seeing her hand resting on her abdomen. Logically she was afraid for her own unborn baby too.

"When did it start?"

"Well no one is certain for sure, but the first miscarriage that we are aware of happened here at the Miramichi Hospital two weeks ago."

Galen thought back through the past eventful weeks. Two weeks ago. That was about the time that he went to Mullen Falls with his energy collector. Surely the two things could not be related. Consideration of the intended purpose of energy leaving the falls never crossed his mind. His mind raced. Could the energy he collected from the falls somehow have an impact on these miscarriages? Was he responsible for this?

As if entering into his thoughts, Simon said; "I have been here for almost a month now. When I first came I noticed that there were parts of the town that didn't seem as vibrant as I thought they should. My research focuses on tracking energy and the highest recorded energy levels in the country are listed at Mullen Stream Falls. When I visited there, there were areas that were vibrant, breath taking in fact, but there were other areas at the north side of the falls that seemed out of sync. The leaves on the trees were not as green, some already turning yellow and red. Flowers that should have been in full bloom were not blooming, that sort of thing.

Peter, the aboriginal man that lives there told me it has been deteriorating like that for a few months. He and his people believe that something is causing an imbalance in the energy that sustains the planet. They have strong spiritual beliefs about the area and its role in the continuance of the circle of life."

"Simon is right. The Miramichi historically has always been vibrant with life, all kinds of life. Of course some of that was before all the natural resources were stripped away and the river polluted. But even since those big industries left, the area has recuperated, regenerated and has been thriving. Now, I see what you are describing too. It feels like our town is dying." Tirisa said flatly.

A surge of emotion coupled with a paternalistic desire to protect Tirisa and her unborn baby rose from the pit of Galen's stomach and filled his mind with a sense of urgency. He needed to get back to the library.

"Don't worry Tirisa. If everyone is working on this problem, the cause will be determined. Once the cause is discovered, it will be corrected. I will start doing some research into this too; phone some friends and get some opinions."

***

Supper finished, Galen walked Tirisa home. She lived in a condo overlooking the river valley that was only a few blocks away from the Steak House and not far from the library. There was an awkward moment at her door. Should he kiss her goodnight? He wanted to. An internal urge flooded his senses, telling him to envelope her in his arms, protect her, to tell her that he would look after her and her baby, not to worry. He suppressed the urge. They were colleagues; colleagues who worked together to save lives. He couldn't jeopardize that relationship for what was surely just a testosterone rush.

"Thank you for coming out to supper with me Tirisa. It was just what the doctor ordered." He placed a hand on her elbow in a parting gesture. "See you tomorrow."

It was still early. The sun would not set for another two hours. He made his way back to the library processing ideas as he walked. Could the energy he diverted from the falls have been intended for the birth of babies? He ceased the collection of energy units into the satellite at 50. That number would not account for what Tirisa was describing. Not a single live baby born anywhere in New Brunswick in two weeks. If there were usually 20 babies born in the province each day that would mean that 280 babies were born dead. It did not add up. There had to be something else going on.

He subconsciously became aware of subtle differences in the town. It was the end of July. The town should be in the height of its season with flowers in full bloom, trees in their deep green foliage, birds singing, and dogs barking. There was none of that. There was a dullness that enveloped the town. The summer colors were subdued, leaves were withered and flowers were dropping their blooms. The air actually felt heavy now that he was aware of it. Maybe there *was* a virulent pandemic of some sort going on that had nothing to do with his work.

Back at the library, he fired up his computer. He had a lot of work to do. He needed to do research on possible causes of these miscarriages. It had been a long time since he had worked obstetrics. He also needed to get busy duplicating Simon's ET application so that he could sneak it back into his backpack before it was noticed missing. He also needed to start testing the remaining energy he had transferred from HELEN to COLTEN.

Sitting at his computer, he typed in his usual password.

The words: "Incorrect Password. Access denied." flashed across the screen.

He stared at the screen in disbelief. He couldn't remember the last time his fingers had mistyped his password. He re-entered it slowly this time, making sure he hit each key correctly. Once again the incorrect password message flashed on the screen. His heart sped up.

He tried again. "Access Denied."

Again. "Access Denied."

Heart pounding now, he grabbed his laptop from inside the desk drawer and logged on. He was once again greeted with "Incorrect Password. Access Denied."

Panic now.

He reached in his desk drawer for the key to his filing cabinet where he stored his back up memory drives.

The drawer was empty.

He anxiously pushed back from his desk and ran into the Zed Replicator lab where HELEN was housed in the locked window cabinet. A glance confirmed his fears. The cabinet doors stood open.

The dish was gone.

Shocked disbelief; then raging anger. There was only one person who could have done this.

"Devlin Matthews. You bastard."

His hand reflexively went to his shirt pocket. He breathed a sigh of relief. Thankfully the familiar bulge of his examining light, COLTEN was still there. Sweating profusely he took the steps two at a time and dashed out to the parking lot where his jeep was parked. He opened the trunk. Simon's black and grey backpack was still stuffed in the corner where he had thrown it. He unzipped the side pocket, relieved that the little ET tracker was still there. He removed it and put it in his pocket along with COLTEN.

He returned the backpack to the library's Great Knowledge room where he first found it.

Chapter 35

Something was not right. Peter could sense it. The energy at the falls was out of synch. The animals were acting strange. The grass and the trees seemed to be losing their color, not just around his house, everywhere. He could actually feel a difference in the air. It was not as fresh. It felt sluggish. He felt sluggish. His wife who was nine months pregnant was acting strange. She told him that she felt that the baby in her belly was acting wrong. The baby kicked and kicked all the time, like it wanted out. Today while hiking through the forest that surrounded the falls, he came across a dead fawn. A sense of dread was seeping through his consciousness.

With rifle in hand, he made his way once more around the top of the falls and began winding his way down the steep path to its base. The grass felt dry under his feet. The glint of the sun reflecting off a shiny surface caught his eye. What was that? He could just barely make out an object that obviously did not belong there. Probably just an empty beer can, abandoned by the latest batch of teenagers who came to jump from the cliff into the pond below.

It was not a beer can. The object that was reflecting the sun was something he had never seen before. It was round, like an umbrella but held hundreds of small projections all over its surface. The projections resembled a combination of mirror like waffles. The sun reflecting off the mist from the falls and the mirrored projections formed a rainbow around the dish. The dish itself was fastened to a concrete block and the inward curve was facing the direction of the pond. He circled the object inspecting it closer. There were flickering images, movements in the mirrors that did not seem to be reflected from the water. There was a large sign attached to the base with the word "Danger" and a picture of a hand in a circle and an X drawn through it indicating to not touch or handle. Under the picture were the words: "Property of the Government of New Brunswick."

In spite of the warning he reached out to touch the object. Before he could connect with the satellite, a zap of electricity shot through his outreached hand and knocked him to the ground. What the heck? Recovering from the shock, he picked up a twig and threw it at the dish. Before it could touch the dish, the stick was incinerated and fell to the ground in a mound of ash. He scratched his unshaven face in thought. How did this thing get here, and what was it?

Peter pulled his cell phone out of his jean jacket pocket. He would phone his father and notify the Elders. Whatever this thing was, he knew it was not good. He looked at his phone in amazement. It was dead. He shook it. Nothing. No power. He just charged it this morning. He looked at his watch to see what time it was and noticed that the second hand was not moving. He shook his wrist...nothing. Whatever this thing was, it was pulling energy.

***

The sun was high in the sky when Michael, Simon, and Marcus arrived at Mullen Stream Falls.

"What do you think it is?" Marcus asked.

"I don't know. But look." Simon pointed to a digital display at the top of the satellite. The flashing green number read 1750. As they watched it changed to 1751 then 1752, 1753."

"It is counting whatever it is collecting or transmitting."

"It is draining energy from the falls." Michael's voice was matter of fact.

"You mean like a dam does, to covert energy created from falling water into electricity?" Marcus asked.

"No. It is collecting energy intended for new life." Michael replied.

"Are you saying that you think each number on that digital display represents a unit of energy intended for a baby?" Simon asked incredulously.

"Yes, that is what I am saying," Michael replied. "This satellite dish is diverting souls, souls with a purpose to achieve on this earth."

"If what you are saying is true, then that means that the souls of seventeen hundred and fifty three people are captured in this thing. The entire population of Miramichi is only 30,000." Marcus stated. "That can't be right."

Peter put his arm on his father's shoulder. "It is as the Ancients foretold."

"The energy could be coming from anywhere, not just the Miramichi. This gate might service all of Eastern Canada and the United States for all we know." Simon contributed. "I can use ET to see if indeed it is life energy that is coming out of the pond. Maybe it is not what we think it is."

Reaching into his backpack to grab the familiar computer notebook, his face froze. His heart accelerated wildly. The electronic notebook with the ET application was not there. He anxiously ruffled through the contents of his bag in disbelief. Where was it? He was certain he put it in his back pack. He tried to re-play in his mind the last time he used it. He was so caught up in everything that was going on that he hadn't thought about the electronic device in days. The last time he used it, he was in the library with Francis They use it to download the image of Mr. Sandstrom's' energy heading to the falls. He distinctly recalled putting the device in his backpack where it lived since he arrived on the Miramichi. The backpack was right where he left it, under the desk in the Great Knowledge room. But ET was definitely missing. His face flushed with panic. Why hadn't he looked for it before? Someone took it from his pack. Who? Dr. Thomas? The kidnapper? Peter? His father? Anyone could be suspect. Gullible; that's what he was. Always trusting everyone. Gullible and stupid.

He thought that his ET device was of no interest to anyone but himself and Henrietta. In fact, anyone with an ulterior motive would be interested. Dr. Thomas; because it was his field of interest. Peter; because he would not want anyone to know about the energy coming into the falls. Marcus; because he just wanted Simon to fail. Hell it could be anyone of the 800 people at the fair that his father kept reminding him of. He felt paranoia setting in.

"My computer with the ET application is missing." Simon's voice was flat but resonated the horror he felt.

All eyes turned to him and the meaning of his words sunk in.

"This is all part of a scheme, a well thought out and planned scheme. Everything is related - the falls, ET, Francis's kidnapping. It is all related to collecting energy from the falls. Someone is wanting to use this energy and there is only one person that I know of who would know what to do with the energy." Simon stated with a disheartening sense of betrayal. Galen Thomas was the culprit after all.

Michael was the first to react. He grabbed a large boulder the size of a watermelon. Lifting it high over his head, he hurled it with all of his strength at the shimmering satellite dish. The rock ricocheted off the air 3 inches in front of the satellite. Michael jumped out of the way to avoid being hit by the flying missile. The satellite did not move. Whatever was surrounding the satellite was not going to be moved by brute force.

"This is my fault," Simon mourned. "I am so stupid."

"Stand back!" Peter removed his rifle from its scabbard, planted his feet in the isosceles stance, and firmly lodged the rifle butt into his right shoulder. With the barrel lined up perfectly with the center of the dish, he squeezed the trigger. The sound of the shotgun echoed against the walls of the canyon. The bullet reflected off the force field surrounding the satellite. It lodged in a tree 180 degrees away from where it was aimed and missed Peter by the breadth of a hair.

With one knee on the ground and one hand holding him upright, a cry of anguish erupted from Michael. He had to stop this. He had to find a way to stop further destruction of mankind. Again by the white man. This was his family's legacy. His job to protect. How had he let this happen?

Years of being a millwright, fixing problems to keep the paper mill functioning sometimes on a shoestring budget, taught Marcus that you always stay calm. Start with the simplest solution to fix the immediate problem first. Their immediate problem was the draining of energy from the falls. If they could not move the satellite then the simplest solution would be to deflect the energy coming to it.

"What if we put something between it and the pool to block the energy from coming into it?" Marcus pondered out loud.

Michael lifted his head from his chest with a look of hope. "That might work," he agreed.

His resignation lifted. "If we make a hoop from these willow branches, like our people used to do to stretch and dry animal hides, we could stretch a jacket or a blanket over it. We could use it as a barrier to deflect the energy flow."

"It is worth a try," Marcus agreed.

The pond was surrounded by willows. Peter selected the longest branches to work with while Michael stripped long threads of the dark bark to be used as rope to tie the ends together. Within 20 minutes a large hoop six feet in diameter was constructed and 3 denim jackets were stretched across its circumference. They then secured the makeshift barrier in front of the satellite dish, separating it from the front of the pond of souls.

The digital readout on the dish said 1772. With baited breath they watched. One minute, two minutes, three minutes. The number stayed the same. In unison the four men breathed a collective sigh of relief. Temporarily at least, the collection of life energy was stopped.

"This won't solve the problem forever. Who ever put this thing here, will be coming to check on it, to collect the energy. We need a plan for when they do," Simon said. He felt responsible for this nightmare and knew he needed to find a way to correct his wrong.

***

Michael and his son finished tying the last snare and setting the last trap, when they heard the low distant rumble of a motor. As nimble as a cat, Peter climbed a large elm tree. Perched in the highest crook in the ancient elm, binoculars in hand and rifle strapped to his back, he scanned the forest for movement.

The war paint on Michael's face camouflaged him with nature. He stood invisible in the forest, silent, still, waiting.

The men coming were not hunters. Nor were they one with nature. They crashed through the forest making enough noise to scare the remaining smattering of sparrows from their leafy perches into flight. From his vantage point Peter saw that one man was carrying a shoulder bag. He was middle aged, out of shape. The second man seemed to be just along for the trip. He was young, maybe in his mid twenties, tall and lean. He had a rifle strung across his shoulder. He was walking with a bounce in his step. Every once in a while he would reach up and grab a leaf from a tree, then pick up a pebble and toss it in the air and catch it. He gait was not like the older man's' in fact from Peters outlook, he appeared to be skipping. The men were not following the path in any orderly fashion and Peter shook his head in disappointment and disbelief as the duo managed to miraculously miss every trap that he and his father set.

***

Devlin was huffing and puffing and grabbing on to tree branches to aid his descent from the top of the falls to the pool below. He was most definitely out of shape. He vowed to himself that he would start working out at the gym, just as soon as he had this thing under control. He was not sure what was wrong with Allen. He was acting really peculiar. He did not want to bring him here, but the billionaire insisted that he see where the fountain of life was, and there was really no way to detract him from coming.

"It is just a little further," he told his companion. "You can hear the water."

Allen stopped whistling for a minute and looked curiously up at the trees, the clouds and the sky. "Feels like home."

"I put it up next to the pond at the base of the falls in the same position that Galen so nicely described in his book."

Allen left Devlin's comments unacknowledged. He was pressing his foot into the soft moss on the side of the trail in apparent wonder.

"If this thing really works the way that Galen indicated, we should be in business for a long time. The protective holograph your engineers designed is perfect. There is no way anyone can disturb the satellite. But I think it is smart for us to remove it today and then bring it back periodically."

Allen focused in on the conversation for a minute. "Why? No one knows what it is. People will think it is a counter of environmental gamma or of power being created by the gravity of the falls. By putting the property of the Government of New Brunswick on the sign, I think we have deterred any meddling. The people who are here will never question the government. They never have. That is how I came to be so rich; taking advantage of the trusting nature of the people of this beautiful province." He laughed. "People believe anything you tell them. Like taking candy from a baby. Their hope for a better life, for opportunities clouds all reason."

Devlin was not so sure that he shared Allen's view on people's gullibility. Where he grew up, no one trusted anyone or anything.

"Maybe. But Galen knows and it won't take long before that young physicist will figure something out about it. He was the one who discovered what the energy actually is."

`"Well then, like you said, they will need to be removed from the picture."

To emphasize his intent, Allen swung his rifle around, aimed it into the bush, slammed the magazine into place and pressed the trigger. The shot resounded through the canyon, echoing off the canyon walls and notifying every living creature within miles that they were here.

Devlin stared at Allen in disbelief. He changed from the innocent wonder of a child astonished by the carpet sponginess of moss to the volatile action of lunatic in less than a minute. He scanned the horizon to see if the shot would bring anyone running. The only sound was that of the churning of the water as it cascaded over the canyon walls. Perhaps the gunshot had been muffled by the water. He hoped so.

Now Allen was laughing like a fool. Rifle slung over his shoulder he jaunted down the path without a care or a worry in the world. Devlin followed behind cautiously scanning the brush for evidence of being followed. He did not know what to make of Allen's behavior, but it had him worried. Was the man losing his mind?

Rounding the final steep bend in the path leading to the base of the falls, they were blinded by the brilliant rays of the sun reflected off the many mirrored projections of the satellite dish sitting on the dirt bank in front of the pond. The mist of water tumbling from the 30 foot cliffs into the pond enveloped them in a surreal mist. It took Devlin a minute to notice that there was some kind of a barrier erected between the satellite dish and the edge of the water. The barrier was a large hoop that looked like it was made out of willow branches. Strung across the middle of the hoop, creating the barrier were what looked like jackets.

Before the word "Indians" materialized in his brain, an arrow whizzed by Devlin's right ear and lodged into the tree two feet away from him.

He instinctively fell to the ground.

The tall man beside him oblivious to what just happened, broke out into a loud laugh as he scanned the top of the canyon walls.

Devlin followed his gaze. Silhouetted against the burning blue sky stood a solid row of Indians complete with headdress, war paint and bows and arrows. From this distance he couldn't tell if they also held rifles. The familiar surge of adrenaline tingled in his arms and hands preparing him for flight. His heart beat wildly in his chest.

Not Allen. He emitted a loud banshee cry, shook his rifle in defiance and fell into a version of a war dance around the satellite, mocking and challenging the native population who glared down on them. He kicked the willow hoop into the pond and laughed in delight as the digital reader on the satellite dish immediately jumped by three numbers.

It was like being transcended into an old western movie and that the battle between cowboys and Indians was just about to begin. He did not feel like a cowboy though. Fear prickled his scalp and his chest felt like a locomotive pounding down the rails. While Allen danced wildly around the satellite dish singing and chanting, he scanned his surroundings for an escape route. Other than the steep path by which they had descended to get to the pool, there was no other path out. Water cascaded down three sides of the canyon wall into the emerald green pool in front of them. Water exited the pool by a rapid river flowing eastward. The water there was churning white, crashing around boulders and over rocks. He could swim, but swimming would not be much help. He would have to dodge the boulders to avoid being crushed and drowned in a watery death.

Kaboom! He was pulled from his thoughts by the crack of gunshot 5 feet away. My God, Allen was firing at the Indians.

He looked up just in time to see an old Indian dressed in rawhide and face paint jump out of the bush toward Allen.

At the same instant Allen turned, saw the man coming at him and fired. The Indian flew backwards landing on the ground in a heap.

The shot brought an instant reaction from the Indians at the top of the falls. Arrows came at them from every side. Allen was a madman, shooting wildly up at the crowd, who were no longer visible. Allen let out a yelp of pain and cursed as an arrow penetrated his shoulder.

Devlin had enough.

He could hear the natives descending the trail. They would be upon them in minutes.

He jumped over Allen, pressing the force field disarm button on his belt as he dove for the satellite.

Indians were pouring down the path.

He frantically worked to free the satellite dish from its holding stand, collapsed it in one easy movement and stuffed it into the empty shoulder bag. Without another thought, he dove into the deep pond.

The water was cold, moving fast. He surfaced just in time to see two Indians grab Innis and haul him to his feet. He let the current of the water carry him to the river exit. He couldn't hear above the raging of the falls all around him. He was aware of arrows piercing the water next to him. He dove below the surface again and followed the current toward the river exit where he was caught up in the force of the water. It grabbed him, tumbling and propelling him down the river. He held tight to the shoulder bag protecting it

from the oncoming path of rocks and boulders as the river,
oblivious of its passenger, made its frenzied journey to join the sea.

Chapter 36

Michael's breathing was ragged. The bullet shot at such close range tore through his chest. His face was splattered with blood. The ground around him was saturated with blood. Peter sat quietly, helplessly; his father's head in his lap. He put his ear to his father's lips to capture his last whispered words.

"I failed. You have to do it. You are the last protector. It is up to you. My son."

Michael drew one last torturous breath, squeezed his son's hand one last time, and was gone.

Tears rolled down Peter's cheeks streaking the war paint; revealing the human vulnerably it was intended to conceal.

A small group gathered. They surrounded the pair. Bows held down at their sides they circled at a respectful distance. The bond between father and son honored. The last moments shared in silent support. They came here today because Michael asked them to. He was their chief. Time and modernization may have changed their living habits, but not their culture, not their beliefs, not their bond. White man was the cause of this. Here on this scared ground, on their ground. The resolve for retribution was carved in each solemn face.

"We must stop this." Peter stood and faced his fellow tribesmen. "My father was too trusting. Too ready to work with the white man, as was I. They have no respect. No *Msit No'kmaq*. To take energy from this place, is to take life away from earth. Our women will have no children. There will be no new life. They don't know what they are doing. They are filled with greed. This man," he pointed to Allen who was being held up by two braves and who now looked and acted as harmless as a child. He was gazing around himself in wonder as if he had just been transplanted here and had no idea where he was. "This man shot my father. My father who did no harm to anyone. His purpose in life was to protect this place; to follow the directions of the Ancients. This man's God is money. He uses money for power. He does not know of the Creator's power. To the Creator he is nothing. In a thousand life times he will still be nothing. Take him. He needs to learn *Msit No'kmaq,* he needs to give back what he has taken."

The two men holding Innis dragged him away.

***

Simon and Marcus arrived at the now familiar fork in the road where the large fallen tree blocked further vehicle travel. Simon noticed that the leaves were already gone from the tree. The road looked much different than it had on the first day that he arrived here. He sighed at the memory of how vibrant and alive the place had been. Now the grass on either side of the wagon trail was yellow and dry. The leaves were falling from the trees. It was not yet August. There were no sounds of birds or bees or any living thing. The air felt still, thick. He thought about the story of the gateway, about the circle of life and his heart beat heavy in his chest as the realization that the sacred circle of life had been disrupted and he had not been able to help. In fact he was part of the reason it was so.

Marcus turned off the ignition and was about to open his door when the vehicle was surrounded by a group of men. A group of men in war paint, and head dress and carrying bows. Simon and Marcus shot a look of amazement at each other.

They were pulled roughly from the cab and escorted in silence, three miles through the thick woods to Peter's cabin. Something terrible must have happened during the few hours they were away, but their escorts would tell them nothing.

Finally they arrived at the top of the falls. Peter sat at the edge of the river, in the same cross legged position he had been when Simon had first sought him. His face was covered in war paint and he stared morosely toward the falls.

"What is going on?" Simon asked incredulously.

"My father is dead." Peters face was emotionless, his voice flat. "It was as you said. Two white men came for the satellite. They missed every snare we set. My father tried to stop them and he was shot."

Simon placed a hand on his shoulder in a gesture of sympathy. Michael recoiled under his touch. He quickly withdrew his hand.

"It is because of you and your people. You cannot stay away. You had to come here with your little machine. You had to share information that was not yours to share. You had to bring the future here. Now we will all pay the price." His voice was cold, solemn, and angry.

Simon hung his head. He was right. Again, he was responsible for death; first his own mother and now Peter's father. If it had not been for his big ideas and plans this would not have happened. It was he who had suggested that Michael and Peter remain at the falls and set up traps to detain anyone who came near the dish. It was he who suggested that Michael call the other members of the Mi'kmaq tribe for help to monitor the activity around the satellite. None of his ideas worked. He even failed at his side of the deal which was to find Galen and bring him here. The traps that Peter and Michael set had not deterred the intruders. And Michael Lifesong was dead. In his wildest imagination he had not anticipated that there would be shooting or killings. It seemed like everything he did was jinxed.

Marcus who stood silent during the exchange now asked. "Is the dish still there?"

"No, the one that got away disarmed it somehow and took it with him."

"Took it with him, where?" Marcus asked.

"He jumped into the pool and was swept down the river."

"You said there were two men. What happened to the other man?" Simon asked, rising from his self pity.

"He is under the south falls."

Not understanding, Marcus echoed his words "Under the south falls? Did he drown?"

"No the man who killed my father is still alive and I pray that each tortuous moment remaining in his life is one of pain, fear and anguish. His life is in the Creator's hands."

Both Simon and Marcus stared at him in confusion until he continued on.

"If we were in the desert we would bury him in the sand with just his head exposed to be burned by the sun and devoured by nature's scavengers. But we are here." He waved his arm toward the converging streams rushing to the canyon edge. "Surrounded by water. He is restrained under the waterfalls. Water will drip on him continually. Not enough to drown him, but eventually he will die. He will have time to think of his wrongs. His body will be overcome by the cold. It will not be a quick death."

Peter led them down the river that exited from the waterfall pool. The river divided into two streams and they walked toward the smaller of the streams which eventually led to second smaller set of waterfalls. There, under an outcropping of rock with water spilling over the edge, with bonds holding his feet and arms was the man who shot and killed Michael Lifesong.

Marcus waded through the water to the ledge. He grabbed the man by the collar and pulled him out from under the torrent.

"Who are you?" he demanded.

The man looked at him through bleary eyes making an attempt to focus.

"I am many people." He laughed, spitting water from his mouth and spraying Marcus in the process.

Ignoring the spray, Marcus reached into the man's jacket pocket and pulled out a wallet now sodden with water. Inside the billfold was a drivers' license with the name Allen Innis.

"Allen Innis. Isn't that the name of the kid who inherited all the money from old man Alfred?" Marcus turned to Simon.

"Yes, that's the name the sheriff gave us. I tried to research him but was not able to find any information about him at all. It is like he came out of thin air. No history. No background at all except that he is supposedly the son of Alfred Innis's sister, who died a number of years ago."

"Allen, if that is your name, where did you come from?"

The willowy man shook under Marcus' firm grasp. He eyed Marcus with contempt and then humour. "I came from here. I came from there." He shook his head back and forth and began laughing uncontrollably. The man was hysterical, delusional. "You can't kill me, I will live forever!" he yelled merrily.

"We will see about that," Peter muttered under his breath, as he grabbed Allen from Marcus and pushed him back to his perch under the tumbling water.

Chapter 37

His right leg screamed in agony as he dragged himself out of the water and onto a sandy beach. He must have banged it on one of the huge boulders protruding through the rapids. He could move it so he didn't think it was broken. At least the throbbing in his chest had stopped. There was no time to lament. He was too close to lose everything now. He patted the duffle bag still wrapped around his chest, feeling the dish inside. He still had the satellite. The last digital reading he noticed was over 1800. That would get his new company going. Hell it would take a long time to use up that much energy. He would charge a million dollars for every transfusion. That would be 1800 million dollars. That should last him for a while.

He sat on the shore getting his bearings. He had no idea where he was. After the current carried him down the river he was at its mercy. It was a miracle that he washed up here. But where exactly was here? He was sitting on a sand beach. It was littered with debris and junk that the river had washed ashore. It was a small inlet off the river where the water pooled before joining the heavy white rapids that would take it out to the Bay. The beach was surrounded by dense forest. There was no evidence of a road into the area. That was both good and bad. At least no one would easily find him here but it would make it difficult to find his way out.

He was alive. That was more than he could say for Innis who in all likelihood was burning at a stake this very minute. He was probably better off without Innis. Although his connections were good, he didn't need him. The man was a wild card anyway. Once he found a way to communicate his coordinates, help would be on the way. He was glad he took precautions, a little extra insurance for help before he started out on this trek with Innis. It would pay off now. He would need to revise his plan a little but that was doable.

The sun felt good. He was tired now, exhausted in fact. He needed to dry off and warm up. Spying a large log that he thought might provide good cover; he made his way to it and lay down behind it.

If anyone followed his joy ride down the river they would not see him there. He clutched the shoulder bag close to his chest and in minutes was asleep.

Chapter 38

It was nightfall. The sky was illuminated with millions of stars all the brighter in the absence of the lights of the town. The fire blazed and crackled sending glowing sparks to the heavens. They could barely see the deeper shadow of the man outlined among the rocks in the darkness of the night but they could hear him. He chanted, sang, and cursed. He sounded at once old and then young, a miserly, conniving, shrewd heartless, power monger and then an innocent child, whimsical, blameless. Marcus convinced Peter that he and Simon intended to make things right and restore the trust they had defiled. Their role was to guard this man. To be sure that he did not escape. To ensure he died at the foot of his Maker.

Both Marcus and Peter were emotionless toward the man. His ranting did not stir an ounce of attention. Simon on the other hand could not help but try to analyze Innis and why he was acting in such a bizarre fashion. It was like he had multiple personalities, all at a different stage of development. How could this man who was surely no older than he was be involved in something of this magnitude? Did he just fall into it? Was it something his uncle had been working on all along? Michael and Peter had noticed the energy around the falls changing for the past six months, yet Allen just appeared in the last week, was he a behind the scenes person who had been involved in this since the start? What about the connections he found with Living Energy Corporation? Was the other man someone from that company? He remembered the photo he copied from the computer showing Devlin Matthews. He wondered if Peter had gotten a good enough look at the man who had escaped in the river to identify him. He could hear Innis's teeth chattering now. Hypothermia was setting in. He knew the natives were doing what they felt was right but he felt sick in the pit of his stomach, bile rising into his throat. What they were doing was murder. Could he really sit here and watch this man die? Even though he deserved to die, was it his right to decide that?

He listened as Peter told Marcus of the native traditions around Mullen Stream Falls; how his people always donned the traditional dress when doing work of the Wheel. That is why the men were dressed the way they were. When Michael called his closest relatives and friends and told them about the strangers and the gadget they found at the base of the falls, they were quick to respond. Had it not been for them, they would not have been able to capture Innis.

"What do you think will happen now?" Marcus asked.

Peter, hung his head," It is not good. If there were 1800 souls in that satellite, souls that were intended for new life, that means that 1800 babies will not be born. The circle of life has been broken. Women who are pregnant now will give birth to dead babies. There is no spirit, no soul to bring life to a new baby." His voice hardened in anger. "My wife who is pregnant and due any day; my child who is about to be born will never see this world."

Simon's ears perked up. He did not even know that Peter had a wife, never mind a wife who was pregnant.

"What do you think is his story?" Marcus turned to Simon "He is ranting one minute and crying like a child the next."

Simon thought for a moment before answering.

"Maybe he is not Allen Innis."

The look of astonishment from his comrades encouraged him to continue to share the hypothesis formulating in his mind.

"What if he is actually old man Alfred Innis made young again?"

Silence.

"I have been thinking about that ever since we discovered the satellite dish," Simon said. "I believe a method to transfer the life energy coming from these falls to a living person has been discovered. The transfer of energy could keep a person destined to die, alive. It could extend life. The whole thing seems improbable, but nothing is impossible. Nothing else makes sense. I mean the

211

energy collected was destined for life, for human life. It is not capable of running machines or powering electricity. At least I don't think it is. Dr. Thomas is intrigued with life's energy and has been playing with this very theory. He is the common denominator in all of this. He would have the intelligence to create both a collecting device and a transfer device. What if that man is not actually Allen Innis...what if he is in fact the old man- Alfred infused with new life?"

Both Marcus and Peter looked at Simon in stunned amazement.

"Well we think that old man Innis died, right? Well what if he didn't actually die? I am thinking that Dr. Thomas found a way to inject him with new life energy. Life energy that was intended for new life, for babies being born to the world. If you thought of each baby requiring one unit of this energy perhaps Innis was injected with many units and so actually has many competing units or souls or lives or however you want to think of it within him. Peter, you told me about the circle of life. That every person has a purpose or destiny to fulfill and that if they do not achieve that purpose their energy returns to earth for another chance. If Innis was given many different streams of energy he would have many souls at cross purposes raging in his inner consciousness. I think his insanity is the result of multiple sources of energy inside of him."

"You mean you think that Allen Innis- that man over there", Marcus pointed "could actually be Alfred Innis?"

"Yeah, I think so. Alfred plus a multitude of other people."

"Okay. Let's assume that is true. So how does Francis's kidnapping and murder attempt fit in with this? Why would Dr. Thomas involve Francis in all of this?"

"I don't know. I can't figure that part out yet."

"Unless we go back to the idea that Francis was a pawn being used to influence Dr. Thomas to do something he did not want to do," Marcus offered.

"Like infuse the old man Innis with life energy destined for others?"

"Maybe. It makes sense. Innis was rich, dying and desperate. The doctor had a great discovery. Maybe he found out how to capture and transfuse life energy from one person to another. Maybe he wasn't working fast enough, or maybe did not want to play into their particular game. They put some pressure on him by attacking Francis. He heard us talking about this place, and somehow stumbled upon the fact that energy didn't just enter the falls as people died, it also exited the pond on its journey to its new body- new life, babies. He found a way to capture the pure energy of the young."

"If what Peter said is true, every soul that exits the stream has a new destiny to fulfill and so there are many competing needs of each energy source. If Galen actually transfused not just one energy stream but many into Innis, that might explain his conflicting behavior. There are many souls inside of him, not just one."

"It sounds fantastic, yet this whole thing is fantastic, beyond the realm of reality as we know it." Marcus stated.

"What do you make of your energy tracker being missing?"

"I don't know. Maybe Galen took it from my desk and used it to track the energy coming out of the falls."

"But the part that doesn't make sense is why he is involved in this." Marcus again pointed to the man under the falls who was now slumped over against the rocks." If he blackmailed Galen into infusing him with energy, he has what he wanted. Why is he here?"

"Maybe they stole the collector from Galen and decided to go into their own business?"

"But how would they know all they need to know to do this?"

"If we don't pull that man out of the water and get some answers from him, we may never find out what really happened and we will never know who really is at the bottom of this. We need him." Simon said, feeling a slight sense of relief for an excuse to pull Innis out from his watery grave.

Peter blew air out of his cheeks in disgust. "If it is as you say; that man is already dead. He died in a hospital bed two weeks ago. The human body is just a capsule containing life that is intended for others. That life must be returned."

The sun was coming up casting a golden glow upon the trees and the shore line.

"Maybe so, but maybe that body can give us some answers." Marcus waded into the water, grabbed Innis off his perch and hauled him to the shore.

Innis was no longer shivering but he was babbling like an idiot.

"Alfred." Simon began, using the old man's name.

The man's eyes fluttered briefly, but there was no other response.

Marcus grabbed the man by the shoulders and shook him roughly.

Innis collapsed like gelatin falling through his fingers into a heap on the ground.

The stars, bright a minute ago like millions of candles in the sky, were extinguished as thick cloud cover rolled in. A silence settled over the three men. The churning water in the pond before them seemed to stop. Time stopped. Simon did not need ET to know that the many energy streams housed in Allen alias Alfred's body had returned to the Wheel. The sense of silent fury in the air was undeniable.

Chapter 39

The three men sat at the kitchen table. A storm was rolling in. Wind howled around the cabin walls. All the windows were closed tight but the chill of the air found its way between the well mudded logs. Night had passed into day but darkness prevailed. Peter`s wife, Mary who was nine months pregnant, waddled across the well worn kitchen floor to retrieve the tea pot from the wood stove. The men were silent, listening to nature's rage rattling the windows and escalating the sense of panic in the room. It was more than the wind that chilled each man. They could not stop now. They had to get the satellite dish. Somehow they had to find a way to return the captured energy it held back to the Wheel. Then they had to destroy it.

Simon pulled the folded photocopied picture from his pocket and handed it to Peter.

"Does this look like the man that was with Innis?"

Peter stared at the picture for a moment.

"Yes. The man in the picture had shorter hair but was the same body shape and size and had the same posture. Yes this is the same man who took the dish, jumped into the pond and was carried down river."

"His name is Devlin Matthews. He is the CEO of a company called Living Energy Corporation. From what I was able to find out about him, he had a business relationship with Alfred Innis. There are numerous pictures of him at Innis' fishing lodge. Somehow they found out about the Medicine Wheel here at Mullen Stream Falls. They found a way, probably with Galen Thomas's help, to abstract and collect the energy leaving the Wheel. If that digital display on the satellite was correct and there really are 1800 separate energy streams or souls housed in its holding cells, they must have a plan for marketing and selling the energy. From the biography I read on Innis, he did nothing if it did not involve making money and gaining power. Devlin Matthews and he are alike in that regard.

They both use people to get ahead. They have no conscious, no obligation to anyone or anything. Life for both of them has been about money and power and they destroy anyone who gets in their way. I am hoping it is like Dad says and that Galen is a pawn in all of this. That he is the one being used at the moment, but I can't be sure about that."

Peter looked up from the conversation. Mary was leaning against the fireplace, one hand on the mantle for support, the other on her belly. She was quietly focusing her breathing. Blowing out long slow breaths through pursed lips. This was a familiar sight to Peter. Mary was stoic. She had been with the birth of their other children as well. There was no denying that she was in labor. He left the men at the table and went to her side.

"Our baby. Our baby will not live." she whispered. She clutched at Peter's arm; tears flowed freely down her cheeks.

Marcus overhearing the conversation rose to his feet. "Peter, where would the river take Devlin?"

"If he survives the rapids bashing him against rock and trees he should wash up about 5 miles down the river. There is a natural bend in the river there where the rapids slow and the water pools. If he made it past the rocks and let the river float him, he would most likely wash up on that shore line with other debris that has flushed there through the years."

"Simon and I will go after him. You need to stay here with Mary. We caused this, we will fix it. Simon and I will find a way to get the dish and return the energy to the Wheel before Mary delivers."

"Thank you." Mary's eyes brimmed with gratitude. She held her abdomen as another contraction began. As the pain subsided she pointed to the coat rack by the door. "It is going to rain."

"How do we get there- to the place where the river slows and washes debris ashore?" Simon asked grabbing a rain slicker from the coat rack in the hallway.

"Follow the river for about three miles. You will see an old rope bridge. You will need to cross it. The river pools on the other side about two miles further down. If he washed up, that is where he will be."

***

It was morning. The wind was howling. Devlin was chilled to the bone. His sodden clothes were still damp from his river trek. His right leg still throbbed when he moved it. He fashioned a walking stick from a large fallen tree branch and heaved himself to a stand. He couldn't stay here. People would be coming to look for him. He opened his back pack to check on the satellite and to make sure the gun he had packed in its water tight container was still there along with his cell phone. A quick look at the phone showed he had no reception. He was too far into the forest and surrounded by water and cliffs. He had to make his way up hill so he could call in help and put his backup plan into action. He slung his backpack over his shoulder and with his walking stick firmly lodged under his arm pit and the wind tearing at his damp clothes; he made his way up hill and away from the river.

***

When he made the connection that Peter's wife was in labor and that her baby would not be born alive unless the energy in the satellite was returned to the Wheel before she delivered, Marcus was out of his seat and out the door before Simon could tie his shoe laces. His father was fearless. Always had been. He tackled life and its obstacles head on with no apparent plan, figuring it out as he went. Simon wished he was more like him in that regard, instead of analyzing everything to the nth degree before making any moves. While he knew it was imperative to retrieve the satellite, this reckless approach was not his style. Marcus was already way ahead of him. He hoped he had a plan. He hurried to catch up.

The wind howled through the trees and threatened to blow them over the river bank. Simon grabbed on to trees and branches along the way to keep his balance and remain upright. They would never be able to find Devlin Matthews in this storm. Five miles downriver. That was what Peter had said. Follow the river for 3 miles, then cross over on a rope bridge that had been erected 50 years earlier by the Mi'qmak, then follow the river for another 2 miles and he would come to a natural shoreline where the water tended to pool. The shore line would be dotted with debris washed up on the beach from its journey down the falls and river. If Devlin had survived, or even if he hadn't, his body would most likely wash up there, like the garbage he was. They needed to find him and retrieve the satellite. Somehow. Once they had the dish they would seek out Galen and find out how to release the energy back into the Medicine Wheel to restore the balance of life. That was the extent of the plan. It sounded simple enough. If Galen wasn't just a pawn and he was actually in on this, he would need another plan.

His father forged ahead of him, setting the pace, breaking the trail. He was driven by a force beyond what Simon could understand. Maybe it was related to his inability to save his wife so many years ago, maybe it was to help an unborn child, or maybe it was just to help his own child. Maybe it was the need for a chance to make things right. He looked over his shoulder once in a while and Simon waved so he knew he was still there.

It was during one of those shoulder looks, that out of the corner of his eye, Simon saw the massive branched tree swaying toward his father. It was about to fall.

"Dad, look out!" The sound of his voice was whipped from his lips by the raging wind.

He watched in horror as the tree smashed his father to the ground. An insect crushed under the weight of a massive force. His father lost. Hidden, buried under a mountain of limbs and leaves.

"Oh my God, Dad! Dad!"

Panic immersed him. He pulled and pushed branches, fighting the wind to find his father. He was alive, not conscious, but breathing. Simon put his shoulder up against the enormous trunk. Pushed with all this strength. It would not budge. He began breaking branches to better visualize his father. The tree pinned him down. The largest part of the trunk which was at least three feet in circumference was sitting on his thighs. Simon grabbed him under the arms and tried to pull him free. It was no use. He was wedged solid.

Marcus winced with pain. His eyelids fluttered and opened. He took a minute to focus, trying to recall what happened.

The vulnerability on his father's face crushed him just as surely as the tree had crushed his father's legs. He had to do something. He had to save his father. This was his opportunity. Here. Now. He couldn't miss this opportunity as he had with his Mother. He couldn't fail again.

"Dad, I can't move the tree. It's too big," Simon slumped down beside his father.

"Lever," his father whispered "You need a lever."

Simon scanned the shore line for something to use. The wind was howling. The anger of the Gods was unleashed in the storm around them. Unrelenting as the wind was the fear and doubt that had established itself in Simon's heart. He was not capable of this. He was not this person. This person that his father always wanted him to be. He ran aimlessly through the trees; looking, looking for anything that could work, afraid his father was taking his last breath as he wasted his time aimlessly looking. Panic seized him.

"Don't die, Dad, Please don't die."

At last his eyes landed on something that seemed out of place in this sodden woodland. It was an old abandoned truck covered in an overgrowth of trees and moss. He pulled the branches away from the truck. He did not have time to reason how or why this old truck was here. Every vehicle had a jack didn't it? Usually tucked under or behind the front seat or sometimes under the hood? They were built in so that when you had a flat tire you could change it. The door squeaked open on rusted hinges. He pulled with all his strength to open it wide enough to get inside. The cab was still relatively intact. The window had many fractures but was whole. The wind and rain blessedly held at bay inside the cab. The seat was mouse eaten and decayed. It held his weight as he knelt on it to pull the back forward. Yes. The wheel jack and rod were still there. Feverishly he worked to unscrew the rusted nuts that held the jack in place. After what seemed like an eternity and with jack in hand, he made his way back to the fallen tree.

"Dad," His father was just barely conscious. "Dad, I found a wheel jack. I am going to try to lift this tree up off you and pull you out."

His father's eyelids barely fluttered in response.

Simon wedged the wheel jack under the heaviest part of the tree and screwed the lifting rod into place. He lifted and lowered the lever. First nothing, then slowly with each painstaking pump the jack inched the heavy tree upward. He continued pumping until the tree was an inch above his father's legs. He reached down and grabbed his father under his shoulders and pulled. He fell backwards. Got up and tried again, slowly he edged him out from under the massive tree.

Marcus grimaced but muffled any cry of pain. By the look of his legs, Simon knew the pain must be excruciating. Clear of the tree, Simon collapsed, exhausted.

The rain was unrelenting. It poured down on top of them. He had to get his father to shelter. The cab of the old truck would work, but how would he get him there? There was no way his father could walk, and no way he would be able to carry him.

In a moment of coherence his father seemed to understand the dilemma. "Use the branches that broke off the tree". His father gestured toward the fallen tree.

Simon looked at him uncomprehending.

"You can make a stretcher. Thread branches through the sleeves of your slicker."

Even in this much pain his father was reasoning; practical.

Simon ran back to the tree and selected two sturdy branches about 4 inches in diameter. He hurriedly stripped the branches of their leaves, shrugged off his slicker and worked a branch through each sleeve, leaving the body of the slicker as a makeshift stretcher.

He helped his father to roll on to the stretcher, then grabbed the two ends of the extending branches and bit by bit dragged him over the uneven ground to the abandoned truck. The cab door was still open as he had left it. He climbed into the truck first, secured his father under the shoulders and pulled him into the cab.

The inside of the cab provided blessed shelter from the wind and rain, shutting out the storm that raged around them. Marcus cried out in anguish as his legs hit the running boards before sliding into the cab. He was quiet now. Shivering uncontrollably. Shock was setting in.

Simon pulled his cell phone out of his pocket, said a silent prayer "Please God let this connection ring through". He dialed 911.

"What is your emergency?" The voice on the other end of the phone asked.

He closed his eyes and nodded a thank you.

"I need emergency medical assistance. A tree fell on my father. His legs are crushed. I think he is going into shock."

"What is your location?"

"I am not sure. We are in the cab of an abandoned truck about 2 miles south of Mullen Stream Falls. I am not sure how close you can get by road."

"No problem. I am tracking your location through the GPS device in your phone." the voice reassured him. "I will send out a unit immediately".

Simon collapsed back on the ragged seat in exhaustion and relief.

"Help is coming, Dad."

"Hurry then. You must go, Simon." His father's voice was barely audible. " Get the dish. Peter's wife could be having her baby. You have to go. Hurry. Follow the river. Find Devlin and the satellite dish. You have to find a way to put that energy back into the Medicine Wheel."

"Dad, I can't leave you here."

"I am fine." His father's voice gained strength."It is warm and dry. Nothing can get at me. The paramedics are on the way. There is nothing you can do here. Lives depend on you, Simon. Now you have to go. You can do this."

Simon shrugged back into the wet slicker before starting out. At least it would keep out the wind. Determination fueled his courage. He made his way back to the river and continued the trek along its bank.

Chapter 40

He was not sure how far he travelled. It felt like miles. The worry of Mary in labor and his father marooned in a truck in the middle of the forest with crushed legs and going into impending shock plagued him as he trudged forward through the wind and driving rain.

After what seemed an eternity, he saw it.

The bridge.

If you could call it a bridge. It consisted of two ropes, one above the other. One rope was intended for walking on and the other to hold on to for balance. He read about this type of contraption somewhere and recalled that it was called a Commando bridge. Too bad he was a clumsy physics geek instead of a commando with specialized training and no fear.

The bridge spanned the two sides of the river bank. He knew the river was only 100 feet across at most, but the bridge seemed to stretch out for a mile. It hovered about ten feet above the surface of the water. The river below was a white churning mass of rapids.

In spite of the cold and the wind, perspiration broke out on his forehead. His chest felt tight with fear. Self doubt flooded his every emotion. There was no way he could do this. He looked up to the heavens and then down to the rope and the churning river below.

He had to do it. There was no other way. Ten feet was not that high really. Devlin Matthews was a dangerous man. He had to be stopped. He did not know the power he had to end the world and his greed would never allow him to see it. If he didn't get the satellite dish and return the energy to the Wheel, it was the beginning of the end. There was no one else. It was up to him. He had to do it.

Simon jostled his back pack on his shoulders, took a deep breath, reached out and grabbed the top rope. It felt coarse and dry in his hands. The rope was old. He tugged it hard, testing its strength. It held.

He placed one foot tentatively on the bottom rope and felt the swing. His stomach swung with it.

He placed his second foot in front of his first. The rope swung. His stomach dropped.

He held tight to the balancing rope. He remembered reading that although the tendency when crossing a balancing beam was to creep slowly, it was actually better to step confidently, surely and briskly. Whoever said that had not been planning to walk across a rope spanning a river with raging rapids below. He was sure of that. He gingerly stepped forward.

The wind mercifully calmed and the rain ceased.

One step. Two. Three.

He was a third of the distance across. He tried to force himself to look straight ahead, yet his eyes were drawn downwards. He stole a quick glance at the rapids below.

In the instant he looked, his body wavered. He struggled to regain balance. His feet slipped off the rope. He hung onto the balance rope with both hands. The weight of his body hanging on the dry coarse rope drove the rope into his hands; hands that were unhardened by labor, familiar only with punching computer keys. He struggled to wrap his leg around the stepping rope, to help him stay above the rapids below. He managed to pull himself up and loop his leg over the rope. He pulled the rope with his leg as hard as he could, hoping to get a wrap. As he did, he felt some give in the rope and the momentary sense of hope was quickly replaced with dread as the rope gave way from years of weather and rot.

His body plummeted into the raging rapids below.

The cold of the water did not penetrate his fear. Miraculously he did not connect with the boulders below managing to somehow avoid them. The current whisked him down the river. He did his best to avoid being bashed but was at the mercy of the river.

Time had no meaning.

Was he in the river 5 minutes? An hour? It felt like an eternity. He reached for rocks and logs, but the slimy wetness denied a hold. Any thought of saving the world was flushed from his mind. His only thought was of survival until through no action of his own, he was catapulted onto solid ground.

Coughing and sputtering water from his lungs, he lay in a heap on solid ground. His slicker was suctioned to his body, water pouring from every crease as he pushed himself up on hands and knees and rolled to a sitting position. He was on a small beach that had seemed to resurrect from nowhere. It had to be the beach that Peter had spoken of. There was debris everywhere. Debris was a nice way to put it. The shore line looked like a junkman's back yard. Trees, branches, old car bodies, cans, bottles and shoes were scattered over the beach. The river religiously emptied its foreign contents on the beach, cleansing itself of any contaminants before finishing its journey to the sea. He was aghast at the sight. The beach stretched out for about five hundred feet. Beyond the shore line was dense forest.

He rose to his feet, wet jeans clinging to his legs and weighing him down. He scanned the shoreline in search of movement or anything that resembled a body. He looked for any evidence of footprints.

He was on his own. It was up to him to find Devlin Matthews, retrieve the satellite dish and somehow return the souls that were destined for new life to the Wheel. He needed to do this before Peter's wife delivered her baby. There was no time to waste, but he could not afford to be reckless.

Think probability and look for clues to support it.

If he were Devlin what would he be drawn to? Among the debris, his eye was drawn to a particular log that was at least 20 feet long and 4 feet in diameter. It was large enough to provide protection from the wind and was positioned in such a way as to block the water as well. It would provide some shelter and a hiding place for a man. He slogged his way across the beach to the tree remnants. His feet sunk into the wet sand, water squishing out from his sodden sneakers with every step. There was a slight indentation in the sand. The indentation could quite possibly have been from a man lying there for a period of time. There were other tell tale signs as well, a piece of torn shirt with fresh blood stains on it. Devlin must have holed up here for a while. He must have been injured and tore his shirt up for a bandage.

Thankful for the confirmation that the man he sought had indeed been here and was alive, Simon let his eyes follow the natural direction he would take if he were Devlin. The forest surrounding the beach was dense, but he could detect the semblance of a narrow path. He followed his instinct. At the mouth of the path he was encouraged to find what looked like a footprint in the soft moss covered spongy ground entering into the shaded wood. With a sense of anticipation, he slowed his breathing and listened for any tell tale signs that his adversary was near. There was no sound other than the birds chirping. His analytical brain kicked in. He looked for other signs to confirm he was going the right way.

Patience. Look. Listen.

Yes, there were bent branches where someone had passed through, trampled grass, ferns broken. He followed the subtle trail into the forest. The rain had stopped and the clouds were clearing but the sky was overcast and it was difficult to ascertain the position of the sun. The route climbed steeply up hill and knowing that moss grew on the north side of trees he realized that he must be heading north east. The trail seemed to be heading back to the head of the falls only on the opposite side of the river.

He had no idea how much time had passed since he and his father left Peter's cabin. It felt like he had been hiking for hours. His cell phone which had doubled as a time keeper for him he realized was water logged, the electronic mechanisms drowned. Not only could he not tell what time it was, he also had no way to connect with anyone to find out what was happening. Was Peter's wife in labor? Was his father okay? Had the paramedics arrived?

The mosquitoes were terrible. As soon as the sun broke through the clouds they came out in swarms. They surrounded him, getting in his nostrils, his ears and his mouth. He pulled his t-shirt collar up to cover his mouth and nose, fighting off the sense of desperation that had descended upon him. He was no closer to finding Devlin Matthews. In fact he was not even sure now if he was following the same trail. It could be a trail made by wildlife for all he knew. Once again, nagging self doubt singed the corners of his thinking.

The sound of a branch snapping broke into his reverie. He lifted his head and turned toward the sound.

From out of nowhere, a driving force knocked him to the ground. Pinned him there.

Winded, heart racing wildly; he looked up into the face of his attacker.

It was Dr. Galen Thomas.

"Shhhh." Galen put his finger to his lips and slowly removed his other hand from Simon's mouth.

"Up ahead," he pointed "you were about to trip over him."

"What are you doing here?" Simon whispered back, bewildered.

Galen motioned for Simon to follow him. They silently withdrew back the way Simon came. When it was fairly certain that they were at a distance where they would not be heard, Galen explained.

"I came to retrieve my satellite dish."

"You. You made that dish and have been collecting energy from "the pond!" Simon's voice was filled with anger. "How could you? Don't you know that the energy you collected is intended for new life? Do you know what you have done?"

"Slow down. Yes, I did invent the dish, but it was stolen from my office along with a book I wrote outlining that energy could be collected from the pool at the base of Mullen Falls. I put two and two together and figured out that the man I was partnering with, Devlin Matthews must have been at the bottom of it."

"So it's true. You are partners with Devlin Matthews. You are responsible for all of this, Francis's kidnapping, the stillbirths..."

"Devlin was providing me money to support my research. Francis was never supposed to be involved. We had a deal and I thought our deal was finished. I should have known; it is never finished with a man like Devlin. I didn't make the connection that the energy leaving the falls was destined for new life until I had supper with you the other night. I thought I hit the jackpot. All I could think about was how many lives I could save. It was "free" energy waiting to be harvested. Not just free, but pure too. Pride comes before the fall. I couldn't see beyond my own pride in what I thought I achieved. I did not expect this. "

Simon continued to look at him with a dumbfounded expression on his face. "I don't understand. How did you know that Devlin was here?"

"When I discovered that the dish was missing and neither Devlin nor Innis returned my calls or emails, I decided to come out here and see if my suspicions were correct. I expected to find my satellite dish set up at the base of the falls. It wasn't there. The satellite dish has a small GPS unit in it, so I just followed the directions it transmitted to my cell phone."

Galen held up his smart phone so Simon could see the flashing dot on the virtual map. It was no more than 200 yards away from where they were.

"When I saw you, I knew I had to stop you before you jumped in and got into serious trouble. You don't know Devlin Matthews. He is selfish to the core and would shoot you as quick as look at you if he thought you presented a risk to him. He will not give that dish up willingly. The dot has not moved in a while so I think he stopped for a rest. Maybe he is sleeping. We need to sneak in and see what we can see."

"Wait. Can you get a signal out on that phone?"

Galen checked the signal range display.

"Looks like it."

He handed the phone to Simon.

Simon dialed the only number he could think of.

The answer at the other end of the line was a relief.

"Hello this is Henrietta Stone."

"Henrietta. Thank God. This is Simon."

"Simon? Where are you?"

"I am out at Mullen Stream Falls. Henrietta, so much has happened, I can't talk right now, but I need your help.

"What do you need?"

"Two things. Check at the hospital to see if the paramedics brought my Dad in. A tree fell on him and crushed his legs. If they haven't brought him in yet, he is in an abandoned truck about 3 miles downriver from Peter Lifesong's cabin. And Henrietta, can you try to call Francis? I don't know why, but I have a bad feeling about her too."

"I am on it. Simon, are you okay?"

"Yes. I am okay. I will fill you in on the rest when I see you."

Simon breathed a sigh of relief. Henrietta would look after things. He had neglected to tell her of his own mess or to call the police, but the people he was worried the most about would be looked after. He handed the phone back to Galen.

Cautiously they crept forward to the place where the flashing dot suggested the dish and Devlin were waiting. In a small clearing, half hidden under the sweeping branches of a large fir tree they made out the form of a man lying on his side, his back to them. A duffle bag was exposed next to him.

Galen made a silent gesture to Simon pointing to the bag.

Simon edged forward. The bag was in reach. He stretched out to grab it. As his fingers wrapped around the handle he heard the distinctive sound of a gun being cocked.

"Stop right there."

Simon froze. He slowly turned his head to the voice.

Devlin Matthews was holding a gun. It was pointed directly at his head. Galen was standing next to him.

"I am sorry Simon. You were too close." The voice was not Devlin's it was Galen's. "I had to distract you and give Devlin a chance to get into position. We couldn't risk your getting the dish."

Simon stared at him in disbelief. "What? You are with him?"

Galen shrugged. "Yes. This is the greatest discovery since the beginning of mankind. I will be able to help thousands of people to overcome disease and trauma. I will be able to stop death."

"By stopping death, you stop birth."

"Stop talking and stand up." Devlin waved the gun at Simon.

Simon held the duffle bag handle firmly in his grasp. He slowly stood up bringing the bag to his side. He could hear the falls. They must be no more than 50 feet away. The duffle bag felt heavy in his hand. The souls of 1800 unborn who were captured, contained, and unable to reach their destined birth were in his hand. Eighteen hundred babies were born lifeless because the energy intended for their bodies was held in this bag. A deep sadness settled over his consciousness. Man at his worst. No hope for humanity. The muscles in his right arm tightened. This was his only chance. As fast as he could, before there was any chance for Devlin or Galen to read his mind, he heaved the bag high above his shoulders, extended his arm backwards and threw, as hard and as fast as he could throw in the direction of the river.

"That was stupid, Simon, very stupid." Devlin cocked the pistol.

The shot was muffled by the sound of the rapids below. Simon fell in a heap to the ground.

Galen and Devlin stepped over him like he was nothing and thrashed through the long grass along the steep river bank in a sudden panic to find the bag.

Chapter 41

Simon kept as still as he could. He slowed his breathing, willed his pulse to drop. His only chance of survival was if Galen and Devlin thought he was dead. The impact of the bullet had knocked him to the ground instantly. He was not sure why he wasn't dead. His chest felt like it was on fire and hurt like he had been hit with a sledge hammer. His skin felt sticky and wet. He hoped he wasn't bleeding to death. It didn't matter. He had to lie still. Pretend he was dead. They thought he was dead and his life depended upon them continuing to think that.

He waited. Listened, till he could no longer hear the two men. They must have descended down the steep incline toward the river's edge. He slowly rose up from the ground and edged his way out of the clearing. The wind which died down earlier was back. He was glad for the sound cover it provided. Dark clouds reconvened in the sky. The world was as dark as the moment they were in. He reached his hand under his jacket in search of the bullet wound that he must surely have sustained. His skin felt intact. He brought his hand to his face looking for blood. There was none. He smelled his fingers. There was a distinctive aroma of whiskey. He patted the chest of the thick canvas rain slicker he was wearing. There was something hard in the inner side chest pocket. He reached in and withdrew a metal whiskey flask. It was the flask he gave his father years ago as a birthday present. A bullet was lodged in the thick metal casing. It caused the metal to crack around it and the whiskey inside drained out. When he grabbed the jacket at Peter's house he must have grabbed his father's by mistake. After he used it to pull his father to the truck, he had put it back on. He shook his head in amazement.

"For once your drinking came in handy Dad," he whispered and prayed that his father was okay.

Knowing that he was not going to bleed to death, he appraised his bearings. The path they followed had actually taken them up the river. He could just make out Peter's cabin in the distance, on the opposite side of the river.

He could not stop now. He had to get to the bag before Devlin and Galen did. He considered the aim and direction at which he was standing when he threw the bag. The other men had not expected him to do that, so they may not have seen the direction in which it went. He replayed the scenario in his mind. He considered the trajectory of his throw, the angle of the bank and the direction of the wind. His mastery of physics plotted the most probable location. It was not where Devlin and Galen were.

He made his way toward the river bank, praying that he was more nimble at descending the steep bank than he was at any other activity that required balance and agility. He couldn't doubt his ability. There was no one else who could help him. He had to get the satellite.

The bank leading down to the raging river was steep. There were numerous shrubs and tall grasses growing out of the side of the bank, providing good cover but not much for a hand hold. The rain made the grass slick and as he descended the bank, his flat soled sneakers had little grip. He turned with his face toward the slope, feet splayed sideways and holding on the grasses for balance, he slowly edged down the bank. One false move and he knew he would begin a slide to the bottom that would not stop till he landed in the water. He was not up for another river ride.

Inch by inch he worked his way toward the area where he was sure the bag landed. His eyes moved slowly this way and that looking for a sign of the blue duffle bag. The bank was scattered with a dense mass of blueberry bushes. The shrubs were thick with the plump berries. He raised himself up slightly on his elbows. A glint of white caught his eye. The duffle bag was buried among the shrubs its white handle barely exposed.

He heard Devlin and Galen. They were close. Hidden for the moment by a screen of tall grass and shrubs. The bush that hid the bag was about 20 feet away. He dropped to the ground on his belly, digging his toes into the dirt to keep from sliding downward. Wiggling forward on elbows and knees he manoeuvred between the bushes. He was once again thankful to this father that the jacket

233

he was wearing was a dull brown color. It would help to provide him with at least some camouflage. Finally he reached the bag. He grabbed the handle and pulled it toward his chest. He gently unzipped the bag and removed its contents stuffing the folded satellite under his jacket. He left the bag on the ground hoping that Devlin and Galen would see it there. He continued on his belly with a goal of reaching the top of the bank and a cover of larger trees that would provide a screen for his escape.

As he crawled forward, the foremost thought in his mind was that Galen tricked him. Once again his gullibility led him to misjudge character. The second thought was that he had to find a way to release the captive energy held within the dish. There had to be a release mechanism. If Galen was the mastermind behind this device, there must be another device that allowed him to transfer the energy from the satellite holding cells to the targeted individual. The vision of Galen playing with the silver examining pen popped into his mind's eye. What if it were not an examining pen light at all? Galen was pre-occupied with the pen. That had to be it.

His thoughts were interrupted by the sound of voices below him. Devlin and Galen found the bag. From Devlin's loud curse he knew they opened the bag and found its contents missing. He was two yards away from the protection of the trees. Sweat ran down his face. His heart pumped wildly.

"Please let me make it," he prayed. The weight of 1800 souls was upon him.

He rose to his feet in a mad bolt for the trees.

"Stop right there." Devlin's voice followed by the distinctive click of a gun stopped him in his tracks. They were right behind him.

He turned to face the two men. He would not be lucky enough to escape death twice.

"Don't you die? I thought I already killed you once." Devlin was panting, out of breath. He was at least twice Simon's age and out of shape. Surely he could beat him.

"Where is it?"

"What? You want this?" Simon pulled the folded satellite dish from under his jacket. Its fabric sleeves flapped in the wind and threatened to unfold like the umbrella it was designed after.

"If I let it go now you will never get it. The wind will take it and you will never find it. You will have lost all of the energy that it holds. Are you prepared to do that?"

Devlin was edging toward him. Gun pointed at his chest.

Closer. Closer. He had to make a decision. His loosened his hold on the frame. The wings flapped wildly.

"I will let it go if you come any closer." He shifted his gaze to Galen. "Galen, how can you do this? You are a doctor. Your whole life has been about saving people. You are about to let 1800 babies die."

"They are already dead."

"It is just the beginning and you know that. You know that it won't end with these lives. It will lead to the end of the world. That is what you are starting- the end of the world."

As if in agreement with his words, a clap of thunder resounded and lightening flashed across the sky.

Simon sensed, more than saw Devlin move. It was now or never.

He pulled his arm back, away from Devlin's grasp and ducked low to the ground. The sudden move caused the floppy satellite to umbrella open. The wind snatched it from Simon's hand just as Devlin tackled him.

Their two bodies collided, crashing to the ground.

Devlin was on top of him. Heavy. Fist raised.

Simon squirmed out from under him. Managed to avoid the blow. Tried to stand. Devlin's legs entwined in his.

His body slammed into the ground.

Simon fought for his life. He grabbed Devlin around the shoulders in a bear hug.

Together they tumbled down the embankment toward the 30 foot drop off the edge of the cliff below. The combined weight and momentum of the men hurtled them down the bank.

Unimpeded by the bushes and shrubs they rolled in a tangle of arms and legs until they collided with the base of an enormous boulder 10 feet from the edge of the cliff.

He needed to be quicker than Devlin. His life depended on it. Muscles straining, Simon pushed away from Devlin.

Hands on the ground, arms extended, Simon raised both legs to his chest. He pushed his feet into Devlin's body with every ounce of remaining strength he had.

Devlin was not prepared. His body was driven away from the restraining boulder.

He slipped. Reached out for any handhold.

Rocks, grass, pebbles, sand sliding through his fingers.

Over the cliff's edge.

Air.

A scream. A splash.

Silence.

Devlin Matthews, CEO of Living Energy Corporation was gone.

Chapter 42

Rocks peppered his body from above. Simon tore his gaze away from the cliff below. Making his way down the embankment toward him was Galen. He held the flapping satellite in one hand, a gun in the other. There was no way he would succeed in a fight against Galen. He collapsed on the ground exhausted, defeated.

"Get up. We have no time to lose." Galen extended his hand to Simon.

He smiled at Simon's look of surprise.

"Really, Simon? Did you think I was truly a part of this? Back at the hill, Devlin caught me off guard. I had to pretend to be on his side I had no way to give you any kind of meaningful signal that you would have interpreted. And besides, you never looked my way."

"You let Devlin shoot me."

"I knew you weren't dead. The pistol that Galen was using was one I had in my office. I just use it for target practice. The bullets were under powdered. I knew it would hurt and maybe cause some damage, but wouldn't kill you."

Simon was sceptical of this sudden turn of events but accepted the outstretched hand and stood up.

"I thought you wanted to use this energy to prolong life for your patients?"

"Well yes, that was my plan; my grandiose plan for fame and fortune," Galen admitted.

"So what is making you change your mind?"

Galen was silent for a moment before answering.

"I guess you could say people. Good people. And the sacrifices they made. A little girl who died of leukemia, a woman who shot her husband to save her baby, and a nurse named Tirisa who has given so much to others she deserves to have her baby. It is also because of people like you and Francis. People who are still amazed by the world, who see the good in others and are not prepared to give up on them."

Simon nodded his head in acceptance. "OK then."

"I did lie to you about why I am here though. I did know the satellite was missing, but I did not come out here in this typhoon of my own accord. Devlin phoned me and told me that if I did not help him he would have Francis killed. He either has her locked up somewhere again, or else he has someone who is watching her. He is the one who was responsible for both the hit and run and the kidnapping. She is his ace in the hole. As you just saw, murder is not out of the question for him."

"I don't understand. Why? Why Francis?"

Galen shrugged. "He knew I would not stand by and let Francis be hurt. He knew it was a trump card he could play that would push me to meet his deadlines, push me to get what he wanted."

"Blackmail." Simon remembered his father's interpretation of why Francis was being targeted. He also heard something else in Galen's words. Emotion. The realization that Galen cared deeply for Francis hit him like a rock, in the pit of his stomach. He swallowed hard.

"So you and Francis...." he couldn't end the sentence for fear of the answer.

"No" Galen responded with a slight smile. "Francis and I have a connection; a mutual admiration for one another. I can't say that I didn't hope for more of a relationship with her, but no, we are just friends."

Simon nodded in response; a nod he hoped conveyed his feeling of gratitude.

"Okay. We need to get these souls returned to the Wheel. Do you have a way to do that?"

"Yes. If we can get to the spot where the energy entered the "Wheel" as you call it. My theory is that we can't just release the energy anywhere. If we could, I would have been able to collect it from anywhere."

Simon pointed to a spot at the top of the hill where two streams joined together at the head of the falls.

"When I tracked the energy from Mr. Sandstrom, it seemed to follow those streams. I am guessing each steam somehow acts as a conduit to transfer the energy into the Wheel."

Galen was already half way up the hill with Simon scrambling after him.

Reaching the top of the falls, both men stopped. A radiant sun burst through the clouds. A magnificent rainbow created by the sun's reflection through the mist of the falls was before them. It encased the merging streams in enchantment and wonder.

"Heaven's Gate." Simon whispered in reverent awe.

Galen reached into his chest pocket and withdrew Simon's ET tracker.

"You did take my tracker."

"Yes, how else do you think I discovered that there was energy actually leaving the wheel? Up until this, I thought I could only capture energy as it was leaving a dying person or as it entered the falls. I hadn't even considered that it actually left the Wheel downstream in a re-configured and purified form, free of the human flaws that it entered with."

Galen handed the device to Simon. "You are probably better with this thing than I am. See if you can tell where energy is entering the stream."

Simon touched the familiar ET icon on the touch screen and the device immediately sprung to life. There were several energy dots heading to the falls.

"Looks like we need to get it to that area over there," he pointed to the broad stream of water that was making its way toward the falls. "Maybe if we can actually empty the dish into the stream we will be successful."

They stepped precariously across stones into the middle of the stream. Galen opened the satellite. Its fabric stretched between the aluminum arms forming the familiar umbrella shape. He activated the on switch. A thousand projections opened within the fabric, each shimmering, catching the light, the gleam of living energy filling the projections. Galen withdrew another object from his pocket. It was the penlight Simon had seen him playing with back in the library so many days ago. He handed Simon the satellite dish. Using a digital compass and measurement guide in his cell phone, he positioned himself according to the direct angle and distance he previously calculated for successful energy transfer from the dish to the receiving cylinder in COLTEN.

Simon watched in awe as he felt more than saw the energy waves leaving the dish and entering the small penlight that Galen held. In less than 5 minutes the satellite dish was empty. The tiny projections lay flat against the holding fabric.

Galen placed the penlight on the surface of the water and pressed the release button. He held it suppressed for several seconds. He then returned the penlight to his pocket.

"That's it. I guess now we have to hope that the Wheel accepts the energy back and re-directs it out again. "

"Peter's wife; Mary. She is in labor. Will it be too late for her baby?"

"I don't know. How long does it take for the Wheel to determine if a soul enters through the Gates of Heaven or is kicked back to earth? Is it a millisecond or a million earth years? Where is Peter's cabin?"

Simon pointed to the opposite side of the river where smoke could be seen raising from the small cabin nestled among the pines.

Chapter 43

The air was crisp, clean and fresh. The grass and leaves of the trees still wet from the onslaught of rain shimmered in the late afternoon sun creating a world of wonder.

Thanking God that there was not a rope bridge spanning a 100 foot canyon and the worst they had to face was falling on slippery stones and rocks, Simon confidently waded into the water. Galen followed. At its deepest point the water rose to waist level, but his feet were still firmly on the ground. After his recent ordeals, the trek across the river and through the trees to reach the cabin's door seemed minor to Simon.

All feeling of optimism drained from Simon's heart when he opened the cabin door. The sense of despair in the room was palatable. Peter was kneeling beside his wife. Together they coddled the lifeless body of a small baby. Faces stained with dried tears. In unison they looked up as Simon and Galen entered.

Galen approached the couple and extended his arms.

"May I?" He asked.

Mary looked at him beseechingly. She surrendered the lifeless form of her daughter to the physician.

Galen cradled the baby gently in his arms. Her body was floppy. Her tiny arms hung limply to her side.

He touched her neck at the place where he should be able to feel a heartbeat, placed a trained hand on her chest. He thought he sensed rather than felt the faintest flicker of a heart beat. Imagined perhaps, that there was the slightest flutter of tiny lungs under the fragile chest wall.

He reached into his shirt pocket and withdrew the familiar silver penlight. He placed a finger into the baby's mouth, inserted the light and depressed the small button on its side.

He waited. Head bowed, he withdrew the penlight. He returned the baby girl to her mother's arms.

Mary looked at him, eyes wide in awe, then back to her baby. Tears streamed down her cheeks. The little girl's eyes fluttered and opened. She gazed at her mother with big bright eyes full of wonder and wisdom.

"What will you name her?" Galen asked softly.

Mary thought for a moment, looked up at her husband. He nodded his assent. She gently and lovingly stroked her baby's face.

"Her name is Sara."

"Sara." Galen nodded in agreement. "I once knew a Sara."

Chapter 44

The humming vibration of Galen's cell phone disrupted the shared moment of reverence.

"Hello. This is Galen Thomas."

After listening for a moment, he handed the phone to Simon.

"It is Henrietta."

Simon snatched the phone. "Henrietta. What is happening? Is my Dad okay? Did you find Francis?"

Galen, Peter and Mary watched him anxiously trying to determine from his occasional nod and facial gestures the information that was being shared. His expressions suggested that it was not good news.

When he handed the phone back to Galen his face was solemn.

"The paramedics found Dad and he is in the hospital. He is in rough shape. He is scheduled to have surgery any minute now. His legs were completely crushed. Henrietta said they don't know if they can save his legs or not. They may need to amputate." He choked on the last words.

The room was silent. Simon visualized his father in the hospital bed with no legs, then in a wheelchair. He imagined his father's feelings and reactions in that state. Despair. Despondent. Drunk. In the past month he had come to see his father in a different light. A man who could face any challenge, solve any problem. A father who had been there for him. A man who was not a drunk. He had a feeling this was the man his mother had married, the one he had never gotten to know. The thought of losing him to a cruel turn of fate weighed heavy in the pit of his stomach.

As if reading his mind Galen spoke. "Simon I don't know your father well, but in the little I do know of him, I know he is a survivor. He will handle this. I know the orthopedic surgeon on call tonight. If anyone can save his legs he will. There is nothing you can do. If they need to amputate, then they need to amputate. He is alive. That is better than the alternative."

"Yeah. I am not sure my Dad will see it that way. "

"Did Henrietta say if she was able to locate Francis?"

"No. Henrietta called the Sherriff and he is looking for her."

Simon was overwhelmed by the enormity of what still lay ahead. Getting the satellite dish and returning the souls to the Wheel was only half the battle. If Devlin had the plan he said he did, then Francis was in danger. They needed to get back to town.

Peter looked at him, knowingly. "Can you ride a horse?"

Galen and Simon looked at each other and in unison answered "Yes."

"Riding will be faster than walking. Come with me."

Simon and Galen followed Peter to a small barn and corral located in the trees just behind the cabin. In the corral were two stout sorrel geldings. The horses came up to the fence as the men approached. Peter rubbed each expectant head softly. He expertly haltered each horse, looping the rope over their neck to make a closed loop rein.

"We use these two for hunting and when we need to get to the road quicker. They know the way. Just head them to that path. He pointed to an opening in the trees. They will take you out to where your vehicle is parked. Tie them to a tree when you get there and I will come down to bring them back later."

He folded his hands into a step and helped first Simon and then Galen up onto the bare back of each horse. He pulled two slender wrapped packages out of his pocket and gave one to each man.

"Beef Jerky."

Simon did not realize how very hungry he was until he held the dried beef strips in his hand. He ravenously tore off a piece with his teeth and relished the smoky flavor in his mouth.

"Thank you, Peter."

"No. Thank you, Simon. You have saved my daughter. You have corrected the wrong. You have restored my faith in you. This is your path. You are chosen to be one of us- a protector of the Wheel and its secrets."

Riding bareback would be a new skill, but Simon was thankful that Francis taught him what she had. He stroked the neck of the big horse and talked to him softly. He looked at Galen, he wondered if Francis taught him to ride as well.

They started off at a quick trot toward the path that Peter indicated was the fastest route back to their vehicle. Sitting astride the strong gelding, Simon was filled with a renewed sense of confidence. It might have been the food in his belly or the horse or a combination of both. He could feel the strength of the powerful animal between his legs. Feel the purpose in his movements and the confidence the horse placed in him as a rider. There was nothing between him and the horse. No leather, no blanket. He felt like one with the animal. His energy which had hit rock bottom when he heard the news about his father and the fact that Francis was still missing was returning. It was just like Francis said. Horses had a way of infusing you with their energy, renewing your sense of purpose and well being. He wondered if Galen was having the same experience.

He was barely aware of the dabbling light flashing through the trees as the horses worked their way through the winding path, but by the golden glow that surrounded everything Simon figured it must be early evening. They had another couple of hours of daylight at best. So much had happened in the past 24 hours. Michael was shot and killed. Innis or whoever inhabited his body died of hypothermia. His father's legs were crushed, the paramedics rescued him and now he was on his way to surgery for possible amputation. Devlin shot him. Somehow he survived. He fought Devlin and won. Devlin tumbled to his death at the bottom of the canyon. Mary's baby was born dead but thanks to Galen was miraculously brought to life. Now they were on their way to try and find Francis. It was surreal. What happened to his life as a geeky physicist who barely left the computer lab?

The gleam of chrome bumpers reflecting the evening sun brought him back to the moment. They made it. The area behind the fallen tree was like a parking lot. Alfred Innis's luxury Lincoln Navigator, his father's old ¾ ton truck, and Galen's jeep lined the side of the narrow trail.

They dismounted. A sense of deep appreciation for the animal who navigated him here overcame him. The horse, he didn't know his name, provided him with more than transportation. In the three mile ride, he gave him renewed strength and clarity. He felt like he could handle whatever still lay ahead. He wished he had something to give back. Instead he gently rubbed the big sorrel's forehead. The horse nudged him and nestled his nose into the crook of his arm for a moment. Maybe it was enough.

Galen's Jeep was the last in the line and easiest to get out. The first turn of the key fired the engine and Galen expertly wheeled the 4 wheel drive around and headed toward town.

Simon sat quietly in the passenger seat watching Galen as he manoeuvred the jeep through the winding wagon trail, hugging the bush to avoid massive pot holes one minute, swerving to avoid fallen trees the next. They bumped and careened along as fast as the jeep could go without flipping over. Galen was intent on his mission with his eyes focused straight ahead, concentrating on the road. Simon realized how very little he knew about him. Who was he really? What kind of a man was he? Could he really depend upon him? His actions so far had been not very consistent. In the end, it didn't really matter. There was no choice. He needed to trust him.

When at last they reached pavement and swung onto the highway, Simon spoke.

"We need a plan."

"Got any ideas?"

"We can't just run around town aimlessly. How well did you know Devlin? What can you tell me about him? Maybe if I know more about him, I can think about what his backup plan was and where he might have Francis."

"Well like I told you, he was my financial partner. The deal was that he would provide me with resources to perfect my research and in return I would use the energy I collected to keep *his* money source, Alfred Innis, alive."

"So how did Francis get in the middle of this?"

"Devlin kept pushing me. Alfred was dying of cancer and there was not much time. My plan was to legitimately collect energy as it presented in the emergency department with people dying from trauma or a massive coronary, I would simply collect their energy as they took their last breath. I was still in the trial phase. It was not fast enough for Devlin, so he decided to put some pressure on me to work faster. He staged the hit and run with Francis when he knew I would be there. It was my warning. If I did not produce, he would hurt Francis."

"So the kidnapping? It was for the same reason?"

"I don't think it was originally a part of his plan. After the hit and run incident, he went to the library to wait for me, to make sure that I knew that it was not an accident. While he was there he discovered the work that you and Francis were doing and the rating scales outlining levels and quality of energy possessed by individuals in the town. He saw that Francis had the quality of energy needed to prolong Innis' life. When she arrived at the library for work, he grabbed her and formulated his plan after she was unconscious. If I did not come through with the energy to save Innis, he would use Francis as the energy donor. In his warped mind he felt there was no time to waste waiting for the perfect donor to present when the perfect donor was in his grasp."

"You mean he would have killed her to take her energy to infuse into Alfred Innis?"

"Yes. He called me from the fishing lodge. Told me he had Francis, and that he made another prototype of my collecting device. I convinced him that he would not be able to do it by himself. I told him that there was a special process to do it correctly and that I would need to do it. I convinced him that I was more interested in the money then Francis and that I would be willing to collect her energy if he did the killing. My plan as stupid as it sounds was to get him to take me to the lodge and find a way to overpower him and free Francis. Thankfully, I didn't have to because you and your father managed to get her out."

"Why didn't you call the police?"

"Arrogance, I suppose. I thought I could still control the situation. Once Francis was free I saw that you were looking out for her and so I focused back on my research again. It was actually your work that made me think of another way to get Devlin what he needed and get what I needed without harming anyone."

"My research?"

"Yes, you videotaped the energy of a dying man as it left his body, floated to the falls and descended into the pond or the Wheel as you call it at Mullen Falls. I hypothesized that I could collect the energy before it went into the wheel. That did not work. But inadvertently with the use of your ET tracker I discovered that there was also energy leaving the wheel. As it left the wheel, it was easy to collect and not only that it has the highest energy levels of any I had ever collected. I created an earlier version of that satellite," he pointed to the back seat, "that was not quite perfected.

250

It collected all of the energy leaving the Wheel but was not able to delineate the energy into separate streams. So when I infused Alfred, he received energy intended for at least 10 people not just one."

"That supports my theory about him. He really was crazy and acting like many people at once because he *was* many people."

They drove along in silence for a few minutes as Simon digested the information given to him.

"Devlin and Alfred are dead now. Francis is missing. Who else could be in this?"

"I don't know. Devlin's life has been one of using people. He got to be CEO of his company by using others and taking advantage of them. Selling people out, lying, stealing, cheating, blackmail, intimidation; that was his mottus operendum. The man had no scruples, no morals. He was driven by the need for money and power. His company is in desperate need right now so I would guess that it must be someone who he would think he had control over and who does not pose a threat to him. It would have to be someone he trusts or someone who helped him in the past."

"That doesn't help much. What would you say were his weaknesses?"

"Stupidity. He used others because he himself was stupid. He also did not trust anyone, so I can't see him involving anyone who could take his power away, like Innis might do. So he would want an ace in the hole, an insurance policy in case either Innis or I turned against him. "

"Okay. So we know his insurance policy with you was Francis. If he had someone else working with him who was not a perceived threat to his power, what do you think he would do?"

Galen smiled. "Well he would need to pull on past experiences so I think he would go back to doing something he had done before. In his idiocy he would think that no one would think he would do the same thing twice. I bet he took Francis back to the fishing lodge."

Simon nodded. It made sense.

"There is something else I have not told you."

Simon looked at Galen in silence, waiting for the next bomb.

"I think Devlin has both Francis and Tirisa."

"Why do you say that?"

"Because when Devlin called me, he told me if I didn't help him everyone I cared about would be harmed. He knows I care about Francis. But I think he also knows that I care about Tirisa. In his mind this would pose a double threat. One that I would not let go lightly. He knew I wouldn't risk their lives. It is just a hunch though. I tried to phone both Tirisa and Francis before I came out here, but there was no response from either. They are friends. They could just be out together shopping or volunteering at the soup kitchen or the animal shelter. I need to find out if Tirisa showed up for work this evening.

He used his cell phone to contact the hospital

The call was answered on the third ring.

"Miramichi Hospital Emergency Department."

"Hello, this is Dr. Galen Thomas."

"Good evening Dr. Thomas. How can I help you?"

"Two things. I need to know if Tirisa Case was scheduled to work this evening and if she came in and I also need to know the status of a Mr. Marcus Gallagher who was brought in by the Paramedics earlier today. I believe he was scheduled for surgery."

"Tirisa was scheduled for evening shift. But she did not show up. It is not like her. She didn't phone to say she was ill. We have been phoning her apartment but there has not been any answer."

Galen's heart skipped a beat. "Did you notify the police?"

"No. Should I?"

"Yes. She might have fallen or something. Call Sherriff Donavan. Ask him to go to her apartment to check on her. Also what can you tell me about Marcus Gallagher?"

"He is in surgery now."

"Okay thank you." Galen hung up.

From the one side of the conversation that Simon overhead, he knew the answers to his questions. It was not over yet.

Chapter 45

Pulling into the long paved circular driveway to Alfred Innis's mansion, a thought kept niggling at Sherriff Donavan's mind. How did Allen Innis know that the hostage was a woman? He didn't think he mentioned that it was Francis who was kidnapped. It had not been on the news.

He was still puzzling over the thought when an older white haired man, the butler he assumed answered the door bell.

"I am afraid Mr. Innis is out." The butler blocked the entrance to the mansion.

Donavan handed him an envelope and pushed his way into the foyer uninvited.

"I am not here to see Mr. Innis. I am here to see his house. That is what that piece of paper is that I just handed you. My formal invitation to search this house and all of its hiding places."

"Very well, then." The butler made a wide armed gesture motioning the Sherriff to enter.

Donavan started in the main office. Everything was neat and tidy and ordinary. He was not sure what he was looking for exactly. Perhaps a wall safe, a computer, files full of names and connections. Someone as rich as Innis would have a secret hiding place for his valuables. He toured the house, all three levels quickly getting a precursory overview of each room and the overall layout of the mansion. There was only one office but it was magnificent; cathedral ceiling, stone fireplace framed by two plush tan colored leather rocking chairs each with their own reading lamp, floor to ceiling windows overlooking the Miramichi valley, and two walls lined with red maple bookcases. A lavish red maple desk hand polished to a gleaming shine held a place of power in front of the big window. The window itself was framed on either side by a variety of tall growing plants with large leaves that created the sense of actually being outside. He imagined the billionaire sitting at this desk looking out over the valley that he believed he owned. The thought brought him back to the moment and made him realize what was missing from the room. Innis was a billionaire. He didn't get that way because he hadn't embraced technology. Yet there was not a single sign of technology in this room. There was no computer. No laptop, no monitor, no TV, not even a radio. He took his time now and slowly paced the room. It was large for sure. It must be at least 50 feet long and 30 feet wide.

There had to be a room with communication technology.

There was no way to knock on the walls to listen for the hollow sound that would suggest a hidden chamber because each wall was filled. The one large wall housed the stone fireplace, another wall held the window to outside and the remaining two walls were floor to ceiling bookshelves. He walked out into the hallway. There were no other rooms beside it. The office occupied the entire west side of the house. He walked outside. He looked into the library from the outside window. He paced the width of the house. It did not add up. The library was at least 20 feet short of what should take up the entire west side of the building. He re-entered the house and sought out the butler.

"Is there a larder or storage area behind the office that you get at from somewhere else in the house?"

"I am sorry Sherriff; I have only been working for Mr. Innis for the past two weeks. I am not aware of any room behind the office space."

Donavan went back to the library. It did not make sense. From the outside of the house it was apparent that the wall behind the fireplace was not the outside wall of the house. There was no exterior chimney. The true tell tale sign was that the chimney exiting from the roof gable was indeed 20 feet from the outside wall. There had to be a room behind the fireplace. He felt under the edge of each book shelf, searching for a button or a switch that might activate a hidden door. He remembered childhood movies of old castles. The hero would remove a book from the shelf and miraculously it would cause the wall to swing inward. He looked closely at all the books for a likely suspect. None appeared to have the power he needed. He lifted items off the fireplace mantel, pushed on fireplace stones, looked for a floor switch on the hearth.

After an hour of searching he found nothing.

In exasperation he flopped down into the desk chair and stared out at the vast tree lined lawn with their leaves already turning color. He ran his hand over the polished wood of the desk. There were no drawers in the desk. There was no filing cabinet in the room. Where, oh where, oh where did Innis hide his valuables and store his secrets? He supposed his main valuable was actually the land over which he ruled. That was why his desk faced outwards instead of into the room. He kept that which he treasured in plain sight.

Plain sight.

Donavan let his eyes wonder around the corners of the window where the plants framed the view. There was nothing notable. The walls on either side of the window were bare except for a furnace thermostat. Could it be? He bopped out of his chair. It looked like any thermostat. It was a round knob with a pointing arrow and degrees marked around the circumference. It was set at 0 degrees. It was summer so maybe the furnace was shut off. Still most people left the setting somewhere around 17 degrees Celsius in the summer. He reached a tentative hand to the knob and turned it toward the 20 degree mark. He did not hear the furnace engage. Instead out of the corner of his eye he saw the large stone fireplace wall begin to move.

He turned the knob further to 50 degrees. Miraculously the massive stone fireplace silently hinged inward revealing the hidden room he suspected.

Donavan entered the secret room in awe. It was outfitted with every piece of technology imaginable and even some that he couldn't imagine. Computers, a full wall of video monitors, and machines that looked like photocopiers but were obviously a type of replicator. The room was alive with motion. Each monitor was capturing a video feed of a different room. He looked closer. It was a live video feed of the library. He could see the front reception desk. It was empty. He looked at the other monitors. All showed the library empty. He looked at his watch. It was one o'clock. Francis should be there. He touched the monitor screen and instantly a digital menu was displayed. He selected history from the drop down menu and then selected the previous day's date. The screen instantly displayed Simon and Marcus rushing through the front door of the library. They called out Francis' name. He watched as they descended the stairs to the lower level of the library, knocked on the door, called out to Dr. Thomas. They then ascended the stairs to the Great Knowledge room where Simon pushed aside tables and chairs frantically looking for something. He watched as both men left the library and the monitors returned to scenes of inactivity.

He took his eyes away from the monitors to examine the rest of the room. There were several desks and filing cabinets. A large document was open on what looked like the main desk. The title of the document was "COLTEN- Collecting and Transferring Energy". The author was Dr. Galen Thomas.

Was it just a coincidence that the billionaire possessed a document with the good doctor's name on it?

Sitting down in the big leather chair he began flipping pages. A diagram of what looked like a satellite dish that was titled "HELEN – Using Heliostats to collect Living Energy" made him stop and read the section more closely. The text described how large amounts of energy could be collected in a satellite dish to be later used to extend human life. What was this? Had he just descended into a science fiction dimension shift?

He looked up from his reading in an attempt to ground himself in reality. His eyes were drawn to the monitor video feed from the library. There was still no activity. He decided to phone the library and see what happened. He could hear his phone call ringing over the computer monitors. No one came running to answer the phone however. He received the "please leave a message" response from the automated phone service and disconnected his call.

He once again selected history from the on screen menu. He selected July 28, two days previous to review. This time he saw Francis sitting at the reception desk, working on the computer. The time at the bottom of the screen read 1330h. A woman who he did not recognize came in to the library and approached the desk.

"Good afternoon. Welcome to the Old Manse Library." Francis welcomed the woman.

"Good afternoon. Are you Francis Simpson?"

Francis nodded.

The woman extended her hand in introduction.

Donavan selected the up arrow on the screen sound bar to capture the conversation.

"My name is Samantha Flewelling. I work with Dr. Thomas at the hospital. He needs your help with a project he is working on at the hospital and he asked me to stop by and ask if you might have some time to help him."

"Sure. What does he need?" Francis replied.

"He is not able to leave the hospital just now. I realize this is an inconvenience, but if there is any way you can help him I know he will be most appreciative. He seemed to think that you were the only one who knew how to access and maneuver around the journal data base he is searching," Samantha replied.

Francis raised her eyebrows in surprise but agreed to go. She grabbed her purse and followed the woman out of the library.

The Sherriff forwarded through the tapes slowly to the present time. Francis did not re-enter the library at any time nor did anyone else.

The hackles on the back of his neck stood on end. This was all wrong. Something was very wrong.

He picked up the phone and called the hospital.

"Dr. Galen Thomas, please."

"I am sorry Dr. Thomas is not in this evening."

"This is Sherriff Donavan. Can you tell me when he last worked and when he is scheduled to work again?"

"He just phoned in a little while ago to check on a patient, but he is not scheduled to work again until tomorrow night. In fact I just left a message with your office because he wanted someone to check on Tirisa, one of our nurses who didn't show up for work tonight."

"This is an emergency. Is there a phone number where Dr. Thomas can be reached?"

"I can give you his cell phone number."

"Thank you." Donavan wrote down the number and disconnected the call. What was going on?

Chapter 46

"The road that takes us to Innis's fishing lodge is just up ahead." Simon pointed to the narrow road where he and his father had rescued Francis previously.

Galen drove past the turn off.

"You missed the turn. Where are you going?"

"I know a back way in."

"Dad and I followed the fence right into the water and could not find another entrance. "

"That is why we are going by boat."

Galen drove another three miles past the turn off and pulled into a road with a boat dock sign posted on the side of the highway. They drove down a narrow road enclosed by deep forest on either side. Simon had a momentary sense of panic as his trust in Galen wavered and he wondered if he was taking him somewhere else. He breathed a sigh of relief when at last he saw the moon's reflection in the water ahead. There was a large pier with two boats tied to the dock. They dipped and bobbed in the moonlight. Both boats were tarped to protect them from the elements. Galen pulled the tarp off of the bigger of the two boats and they both jumped in. In the darkening evening it was difficult to get a full appreciation for the luxury of the boat but Simon guessed it was the best money could buy. It did after all belong to Alfred Innis.

The engine turned over at the first turn of the ignition. Galen idled the boat backwards away from the dock and followed the shore line toward Innis's lodge.

The lodge was aglow. Every light in the house was on. It shone out like a beacon, reflecting a golden translucence in the water. They could just make out the shadow of a boat tied to the dock at the front of the house. Galen killed the motor and allowed the boat to drift to shore. The lights inside the house would prevent the occupants from seeing outside into the darkness. It was not very smart of the occupant, but helpful to Simon and Galen.

A tall slim woman was pacing in front of the window. She was well dressed but slightly out of place in this setting. She wore blue dress pants, a white blouse and low heeled pumps. A business woman. She held a cigarette in one hand and a cell phone in the other. On the table in front of the sofa was a glass filled with amber fluid and ice. Scotch? Next to the glass was a hand gun.

The woman's anxiety was evident. She punched numbers into her cell phone, brought the phone to her ear for a minute then put it down. She sat down. She took a puff of her cigarette, inhaled slowly then blew the smoke out in a long exaggerated exhalation. She took a drink from the glass, stood up, walked to the end of the living room, returned to the sofa and repeated the sequence.

After four attempts of reaching whoever it was she was trying to reach, she left the room for a few minutes. She returned with an old fashioned rolodex. She placed the card holder in front of her and began flipping through the cards. She removed one card from the deck and punched a number into her cell phone. She put the phone to her ear.

The vibration of the phone in his shirt pocket startled him.

Galen looked at Simon in alarm. He looked in the room at the woman holding the phone to her ear and realized she was calling him! He backed away from the house and crouched in the bushes to answer the call.

"Hello."

"Hello. Is this Galen Thomas?"

"Yes it is. Who is calling please?"

There was a pause as the woman on the other end of the line took a long drag off her cigarette and slowly exhaled.

"You don't need to know that. What you need to know is that someone who you care about is in grave danger."

"What do you want?"

"Don't play coy with me. You know what I want. Bring the satellite dish and the pen to the fishing lodge by sunrise or else you will never see her again."

"How do I know you really have her?" From his cover in the bushes but through the illuminated windows, Galen watched the woman leave the room. A few seconds later there was a cry of anguish emitted from his cell phone that he knew was created by the distinctive sound of tape ripping off skin.

"Hello?" the voice was tentative.

It was Francis.

"Francis. This is Galen. Are you okay?"

"Galen. Yes. What is going on?" She burst into sobs.

Then the woman's voice was back on the phone.

"Believe me now?"

"Yes."

"Don't call the police. There are security cameras around the perimeter of the house. If I see anyone but you or Devlin, I will shoot her. Do you understand? Bring me the dish and the pen."

Galen slipped the phone back into his pocket. He slumped down onto the damp evening ground in resolution. What had he done? How could he have gotten Francis into this mess? This was the third time he put her life in danger. Conflicting emotions made his head feel like it was made of ceramic and would explode at any moment. He wanted it all. He wanted to keep the satellite dish and he wanted to save Francis. How could he do both?

"Galen, I don't know much about these people" Simon broke into his thoughts, "but what I do know is that it is not going to be easy. We can't let her get her hands on the satellite dish. There is too much at stake here. In the wrong hands that dish could lead to the end of mankind. Not only that, but I don't think she is that stable. I mean look at her. She is on her last nerve. Anything could throw her into a panic and she would shoot Francis."

For the first time in his life, Galen was shaken. They came here fully expecting to find both Francis and Tirisa being held captive, but they had no plan. He still did not know if Tirisa was there or if it was just Francis.

"What should we do?" he asked Simon.

"I think you need to go back to the Jeep and get the dish. I will block out the cameras that oversee the beach area. We will use the dish as a bargaining chip. She doesn't know about me and won't suspect that I am here. Somehow you will need to convince her to come outside and when you do I will be waiting."

Galen picked up on Simon's idea. "We don't know who she works for. It might be Devlin or it might be Innis but either way she won't know that they are both dead. I can convince her that I barely escaped the same fate as Innis and Devlin and that I need another partner. I will tell her that she needs me too because the dish will be useless to her if she does not know how to use it. From there I should be able to convince her to come outside the house so I can show her how it works. When she does, you be ready."

Galen looked solemnly at Simon. He was putting an enormous amount of faith in him and he didn't really even know him. Still he didn't have a choice. There was no way to do this alone. The medical charisma he had developed over the years and his ability to have people trust him would definitely be tested tonight. If he failed his life and the lives of both Francis and Simon were at stake. Their plan was risky.

"Can you use a gun?" Galen asked.

"I will figure it out." Simon said resolutely.

"Good. I will bring the handgun from the jeep then. How will you find the cameras?"

"My ET tracker should be able to pick up on any camera lens movement. I am assuming camera lenses must move to focus in and out. As long as they do, I should be able to determine their location by that movement. Where you would put surveillance cameras if you were setting them up?"

"I would put one at each corner of the house and probably one in the center. I might put one down by the dock looking up to the house as well."

Simon pulled off his shirt and tore strips of fabric. The night air was chilly but after the many ordeals he had just survived it was nothing.

"What will she think when the cameras go dark?"

"She might suspect something, but my guess is she is not expecting you till morning so will not be watching the monitors too closely tonight. Still I will just cover the ones that we need covered so that she still sees different angles of the yard, just not the angles we need."

Stealthily, Galen made his way to the boat being careful to stay hidden under the shadow of the trees.

They agreed to meet back at the river line in 20 minutes.

***

It had to be well over 20 minutes. Where was Galen? Did he use this opportunity to escape with the dish? Maybe he was not coming back. What if something happened to him? Maybe there was someone, a thug hired by Devlin waiting at the dock for him when he pulled in. It would make sense that the woman arranged for someone else to help with the deal. Man, they were stupid. They should have never split up. He needed to develop a backup plan in case Galen didn't return.

He looked back at the house. There was movement. Through the window he saw that the woman now held Francis at gunpoint. Francis looked terrified. Her hands were tied behind her back and the woman was gesturing toward the door. There was no sign of Tirisa. Panic clutched at his heart. His mind raced wildly.

They were leaving the house. He watched as they made their way to the shore line toward the dock and the boat that was tied there. His anxiety escaladed with the realization that the woman was taking Francis to the boat. Panic seized hold. What if Galen came around the bend in the river right now? There was no time to plan, no time to think. Belly crawling he made his way along the rock lined shore to the dock. He prayed that the woman was too occupied with the chore of moving her hostage forward to notice him.

They were on the opposite side of the boat from him now, on the dock. Hidden from their view, he slipped soundlessly into the water. The soft ripples created by his entrance quickly disappeared and he swam silently underwater to the boats hull. He said a silent thank you to his father who had insisted on swimming lessons. He held on to the boat's swim deck with his fingers, keeping his head just below it. The boat bobbed in the water as first Francis than the auburn haired woman stepped into it.

"Get up in the bow, where I can keep my eyes on you." It was the woman's voice. Her voice was cold and dispassionate.

"Where are you taking me? What do you want?" Francis asked.

Simon could tell from Francis's tone that she was trying to be calm and in control and the urge to protect her was overwhelming.

"Somewhere that the brilliant doctor won't suspect." The woman replied.

The boat's engine fired. He had one chance. This was it.

Simon hoisted himself up on to the swim deck and in one fluid movement rolled tight against the hull. He hoped the sound of the motor, the churning of its blades in the water along with the chore of driving the boat and watching her captive would distract the woman from his movement.

The boat slowly manoeuvred away from the dock.

Now or never. Adrenaline pumping, Simon leapt to his feet and hurdled over the seats to the helm. He lunged at the woman, tackling her around the waist in a football hold. Together they tumbled in a mass of arms and legs over the captain's seat.

Shocked by the unexpected attack and with the gun still in her hand she pulled the trigger.

Simons eyes widened in horror as the blast of the gun resounded in his ears, rendering him momentarily deaf.

He spun around just in time to see the look of panic and the silent scream on Francis's face before she fell forward onto the floor of the boat. The image forged into his memory like burning steel.

Precious moments lost. He was too slow. The woman was on her feet. Gun still in hand. It was pointed directly at his head.

"I don't know who you are," she said in a cold voice. "But I suggest you move up to the front of the boat with your girlfriend."

Deafened by the gunshot, Simon could not hear a word she spoke but by the way she waved the gun at him, understood he was to move to the bow of the boat. He lost no time scrambling through the narrow passage to Francis's side. A feeling of dread enveloped him as he gently lifted her into his arms.

"Francis. Oh my God." A pool of blood was collecting on the floor of the boat. He removed the rope that held her hands behind her back. His hands were sticky and wet with blood. Freed from the restraining ropes her arms fell limply at her sides. Her body was floppy in his arms. Her breathing was raspy and blood sprayed from her mouth. He brushed the hair from her face. Stroked her cheeks. Kissed her face. Whispered in her ear repeatedly. "Don't die." He removed the scarf she wore around her neck, balled it up and held it tightly to the bullet wound in her chest, hoping the pressure would limit the loss of the precious tincture of life seeping from her body.

He sensed the boat moving. Anger replaced sadness. He wanted to kill this woman. This stranger who had taken the life of the woman he had so completely fallen in love with. This stranger, who did not know them. This stranger whose greed had moved her to do this. He looked up at her. Her features were difficult to distinguish. She was focused on steering the boat out into the darkness of the night, out into the bay.

Out on the water, the night enveloped them.

The stranger drove without running lights. The only illumination was created by the millions of heavenly stars that unimpeded by city lights, dazzled in the sky and reflected in the water. All sound was drowned out by the roar of the motor and the churning of the water as it made way for the boat's passage leaving a large wake behind. By the position of the stars Simon realized where they were headed. There was a small uninhabited island located up the river that he remembered from his childhood. It was once an Acadian refugee camp and later the home of a wood ship building company. Beaubear Island. It had long ago been abandoned. The island still held the remnants of old buildings and an ancient cemetery. The only way to get on or off the island was by boat. She must intend to leave them there while she returned to the fishing lodge to await Galen.

The island loomed ahead. The motor slowed to an idle. There was no dock on the island. She would need to pull up on to the shore. She was focused on the task at hand and did not see what Simon saw.

Canoes. Three empty canoes were cloaked in the shadows of the shoreline.

"Hang in there, Francis." He whispered "It is not over yet." He gently leaned her against the bow rail.

A smidgen of hope. An opportunity. Be ready.

The motor stopped. The boat eased up on to the shore.

She was out of her seat now, coming toward him, gun in hand.

He stood up. Faked a stumble forward. Dove at her legs.

Shocked and caught off balance their captor fell backwards into the boat alleyway. Simon leveraged himself upwards and was on top of her. Legs straddling her middle, hands gripping her wrists, struggling to get the gun from her grasp. He repeatedly banged her wrist against the center tow pole until the gun dropped to the floor.

He held her there, pinned to the floor. Exhausted now. Not sure of his next move.

He became aware of eyes watching him. Men stepping into the boat. Hands grabbing him under his arms. Pulling him to his feet.

"Need some help?"

Simon looked up into the kind dark eyes of the man who was the protector of the Wheel, the keeper of the Gate.

Peter. A sense of relief flooded over him. He flashed Peter an ear to ear smile.

The men who were with Peter grabbed the woman and tousled her overboard to three man who were waiting on shore.

"Francis has been shot. She needs a ...."

The words were not out of his mouth when the sound of a motor boat travelling at high speed, the motor revved out, screamed its approach. The big boat that Simon and Galen first arrived at the fishing lodge in was beside them. Galen was already climbing from one boat to the next. Ignoring Simon and Peter, he was at Francis's side in an instant.

She was limp in his arms. Her respirations shallow. Even in the moonlight he could tell she was ghostly pale. She lost a great deal of blood. Too much blood. He removed the soaked scarf that was plugging the bullet wound. The bleeding seemed to have stopped but there was no way to know the amount of internal hemorrhaging that was occurring.

"Tirisa, bring me the medical bag out of the boat," he yelled.

For the first time Simon realized that Galen was not alone. He took his eyes off of Francis for a moment to see Tirisa scrambling over the side of the boat with a black medical bag and Sherriff Donavan putting hand cuffs on the woman.

It was all happening fast. Tirisa was beside Galen in the cramped bow. They worked soundlessly as a team. Tirisa seeming to read Galen's mind. She removed Francis' blouse and was now running a bag of fluid through a long tube. Galen was expertly threading a needle into Francis's arm. He nodded to Tirisa who connected the tubing to the hub of the needle and then held the bag high, pouring fluid from the bag into Francis veins.

"We need to get her to the hospital right away."

Simon nodded agreement, jumped into the driver's seat, put the boat in reverse, its large rotor churning up mud as it backed away from the shore, then turned the boat and pushed the forward lever into gear, pulling away from the island and racing toward the Miramichi Hospital as fast as the boat could go.

The hospital was located on the shore of the Miramichi River. It had its own dock and Simon pulled up alongside. Peter called ahead and told the Emergency department they were coming. The team was waiting on the dock with a stretcher ready. They transferred Francis to the stretcher and into the hospital at warp speed.

Both Galen and Tirisa ran alongside the stretcher with the Emergency team. A nurse wrapped a warm blanket around Simon's bare shoulders. He hadn't realized how cold he was. He secured the boat and then made his way into the Emergency department, terrified of what lie ahead.

The front entrance to the ER belied the activity that was going on behind the triage area walls. All seemed peaceful and serene. It was in complete juxtaposition to the anxiety that washed over him. A unit clerk directed him to a waiting room. A large room of subtle green and beige hues. There were only two other people, a young man in his late teens and a middle aged woman sitting a distance apart in the room, both were engrossed in their cellular devices, texting or gaming he supposed. Everyone had their own escape; activities to direct the mind elsewhere, away from the present moment in space and time.

Simon stared blankly at the wall. He sat alone. He supposed he should phone Henrietta, to tell her he was here and to find out about his father. Did they have to amputate? Did his father still have his legs? Was he even alive? He didn't know how he could deal with either answer right now. He should be praying for Francis, praying that she got here in time, that she had not exsanguated along the way. Instead his mind was numb. Empty. The power of life and death was not in his hands. He had to let fate play out. He had to believe in fate, that everything happens for a reason. Like Peter said, opportunity and events present themselves throughout our lives. Events are designed to guide one's destiny.

He was not sure how long he sat in silent reflection, dosing off and on before a gentle voice and a touch on his shoulder roused him. He looked up into Henrietta's smiling face. Galen was standing next to her. He was in OR greens. He still wore the green beanie on his head and a face mask hanging loosely at his neck. He looked exhausted. His face was devoid of any emotion.

"Come on, I will buy you both a coffee," Henrietta said.

They walked in painful silence to the cafeteria. Seated at a secluded table, Simon cradled the hot coffee cup in both hands. He willed the warmth to break through the chill in his heart, to fortify him for the news he dreaded to hear yet yearned to know.

"How is Francis?"

Galen brushed the beanie off his head and rubbed his scalp vigorously before beginning.

"The bullet went through her right lung. We had to remove the lower lobe. She lost a great deal of blood. We almost lost her. She is in ICU now, but in critical condition. She is on a ventilator. She has chest tubes in place and is receiving blood and massive antibiotics. We did all we could do, Simon. The next 24 to 48 hours will be critical. It is out of our hands now. All we can do is wait."

Simon accepted the information without flinching. There was hope. Francis would pull through. He knew it. He felt it. He looked at Galen with true appreciation. Galen had every opportunity to desert him back at the lodge, but he didn't. Instead he brought the cavalry. In spite of what must be exhaustion to the extreme, considering what they had both been through in the past 24 hours, he saved the life of the woman he loved. He owed him everything.

"Thank you Galen." He hoped the simple words were enough to convey his gratitude because there were no words that could adequately describe his emotion.

"Your father is alive too." Henrietta said. "He was in surgery for seven hours but is recovering on the Orthopedic Unit."

"His legs?" Simon looked beseechingly at Henrietta.

"He had to have one leg amputated."

Simon stared at her in silence for a moment allowing the competing emotions of relief and fear to settle in his mind before asking "Is he awake? Does he know?"

Henrietta sensing his conflict placed an ever gentle hand on his arm. "Yes, he is awake and he knows. He is going to need you, Simon"

"Need me? He has never needed me. Nor has he ever wanted me around."

"He was there for you. You need to be there for him."

Justice.

Simon met her eyes; eyes that could be full of compassion, but right now were full of determination and resolution. He knew she was right.

"Francis needs you too." Galen added with less resolution.

Chapter 47

Sherriff Donavan's office seemed a little less cold and a little less Spartan when the people sitting in the chairs were not suspicious of one another and when there was a shared feeling of accomplishment among those people. Donavan had invited Simon, Galen and Tirisa to his office to debrief the events of the past several days.

"I don't understand what happened after you left me at the lodge to go and get the satellite dish." Simon was talking to Galen.

"When I went back to get the dish, I was shocked to find the Sheriff and Tirisa there waiting for me. Sherriff, want to tell Simon the story you told me?"

"It was a bit of luck really. I went to Allen Innis's house with a search warrant. He wasn't at home so I had free range of the house. I found a hidden room where he was running surveillance videos from the library. The videos showed Francis leaving with a woman who I didn't know but who told Francis she was working with Dr. Thomas and that he needed her to go to the hospital. I ran a face recognition scan on her and found out that she was Devlin Matthew's secretary and that Devlin was the CEO of Living Energy Corporation. I phoned the hospital and found out Galen was off duty but had just phoned in to ask about Tirisa and Marcus who had come in by ambulance because of a crushing leg injury. I figured that Galen and this Devlin character must be in cahoots. The hospital gave me Galen's cell phone number but when I phoned, the line was busy. He must have been talking to Galen's secretary. Using our GPS tracking system at the police station, I was able to lock into the location of his phone. When I discovered it was in the vicinity of the fishing lodge where Francis was held captive before, I decided to go there."

"The Sherriff was just leaving the police station when I pulled up," Tirisa jumped in. "I was coming to see him because Francis was missing. When he told me he was going to find Galen and that

Galen had phoned the hospital looking for me, I insisted on going with him."

"When I pulled up to the dock, Sherriff was there, ready to arrest me," Galen said. "I had to do some fancy talking, put on my best doctor's voice to get him to believe me."

"It was a good thing that I was there," Tirisa clarified with a grin. "If it hadn't of been for me, the Sherriff would never have believed Galen, he had been pegged for a criminal."

"The gunshot was the convincing factor though," Galen said.

"We came around the inlet to the lodge just as the boat you were in was pulling away. Samantha's voice carried across the water and we figured out that you were still alive but Francis was hit. We cut the motor to idle along behind you. We were afraid that if Samantha knew we were there she would do something drastic. When your boat touched shore and we heard the ruckus, we motored to you as fast as we could," Galen said.

"What about Peter? How did he get there with the men from his tribe? I can tell you it was the sight of those canoes on the shore that gave me the courage to tackle her."

"I don't know how or why the natives were at Beaubear Island ahead of us. When I asked Peter he mumbled something about a visit from a spirit or a dream. I think he had a sixth sense or something. " Sherriff Donavan said.

"I still don't understand why Devlin's secretary was involved," Simon said.

"Samantha and Devlin had a relationship. They were partners in a number of crimes involving coercion and money diversion from investors. She has a history of misdemeanors but no previous murder charges." Donavan said.

"Devlin promised her richness beyond her wildest dreams. He told her he had the discovery of the century. All she was supposed to do was convince Francis to come with her and then bring her to the lodge and wait for Devlin to return with some satellite dish that would make them a fortune. When she didn't hear from Devlin at the time she was supposed to, she decided that she would try to work the deal herself." Galen interjected.

"She grew up in Boiestown and so knew the area well. She knew about Beaubear Island and bringing Francis there was her own idea. She thought if Francis was not at the house when Galen returned with the satellite dish there was less risk of anything going wrong. You messed things up." Donavan said with a smile.

"So what happens next, Sherriff? Michael is dead, Innis is dead and Devlin is dead. Are we in trouble here?" Simon asked.

"Well the way I see it is, Michael and Innis had a fight and killed one another. Samantha Flewelling is in jail for kidnapping and attempted murder. As for Devlin we don't have any proof that he is dead. You know that pool is bottomless. My men dove down as far as they could go, but there was no sign of a body. The rapids may have moved him down river, and his body might wash up somewhere, sometime, and when it does, well we will need to do an investigation. As for now, there is no proof that he is dead, he is just missing. In my mind, I think justice has been served. You three good with that?"

"Yes," they replied in unison.

Chapter 48

It was dusk; the time of evening when day faded into night and the world lost all definition, when the human eye was unable to distinguish earth from sky as the two merged into one. A time of day when anything seemed possible and reality was just a moment in time. Simon and Galen sat on the hospital dock. It had been a week since their adventure had come to an end. Francis was expected to make a full recovery. Marcus was being fitted for a prosthesis. He and Henrietta had become very close in the past week. In spite of his loss, he was full of hope and optimism. Henrietta had a way of doing that to people. The adventure they had been through seemed surreal.

"We have been through a lot together, Galen. I need to tell you some things that I am not sure you are going to believe, but you need to know." Simon's voice was low, confidential.

Galen looked at him with interest.

"What if I told you that the survival of another world depends upon the transfer of pure life energy from earth and that earth is actually one big factory created by another race of people; a factory that grows pure life energy to sustain life on another planet?"

Galen gave Simon a quizzical look. "I would say that you are delusional."

"You know that the reason I developed ET was to find out where life energy goes after it leaves the body at death. Using ET, I was able to track life energy entering into Mullen Falls through one of three streams. You discovered that energy intended for new life exits out of the pool at the bottom of the falls. So we know that the pool serves as a gateway or portal for energy flow."

"I would say that what we know is that energy enters the falls and leaves through the pool, that it gets re-directed or re-energized in some way. I don't think it means there is a gateway to another planet there."

Simon continued. "The natives have been protecting this secret for centuries. The name of this other world that needs energy from earth is called Heaven. The inhabitants of Heaven do not have a human form. Their physical make up is one of pure energy and they are unable to reproduce offspring. Any new life in their world must come from another source. Earth is that source. Earth is an energy factory that was created by that race. The pool at the bottom of Mullen Falls acts as a gateway to transfer energy from Earth to Heaven. The pool at the bottom of Mullen Stream Falls is Heaven's Gate."

"You are out there, but considering what we have been through, I am listening."

"Only the finest of products, the purest levels of energy can be used by the other race. Energy that is not of the highest caliber still enters the gate but is rejected and returned for re-processing. Re-processing happens as the returned energy is instilled into a baby when it is born here. Of course it might also be instilled into a tree, a plant or an animal depending upon the level of purity."

"The reincarnation theory?"

"Yes. The recipients of the re-processed energy on earth must achieve certain goals; overcome weaknesses in their life span to move up the ladder of purity that is acceptable to the other world. The attainment of pure energy occurs only when the individual achieves virtue. Well four virtues actually, the ones described in the Bible and picked up on by Ranger at the library; temperance, wisdom, justice and fortitude. When an individual dies, their energy travels to the "Wheel" as Peter calls it. Once in the wheel, it is evaluated and directed accordingly. Only when virtue is achieved in all four categories does the individual's energy pass through Heaven's Gate to that other world."

The look on Galen's face told Simon that he thought he had lost touch with reality.

"Think about it. Everything I have described fits with religious teachings about the need to live a good life to pass through the gates of heaven. You noticed it too. You found that some people had higher energy levels then others and those who lived corrupt lives emitted low energy levels."

Galen nodded in agreement. 'I can't argue with that part of your explanation."

"What is mind bending for me is that our religious beliefs are true, just not in the context that we imagined. But think about it. We do have a Creator. We strive to follow his laws so that we may be admitted into his realm; Heaven. Heaven; where we will know everlasting life, peace and happiness. My goal was to find out where energy went after death. Now I know. It travels through a gateway. It is evaluated and based on that evaluation is either returned to earth for another opportunity to improve or passed through to Heaven. It is just that man did not consider for a moment that God was actually the leader or the manager of another planet. Nor did we envision Heaven as the name of another planet. But the underlying truth is that God is real. Heaven is real. It is just not how I saw it in my mind."

There was nothing more to say. The two men sat in silence, processing and synthesizing information and experiences until night overcame dusk and the sky was filled with the illuminescense of a million stars.

Galen spoke first.

"That is all well and good but it really does not change anything does it? Heaven is not what we thought; only really it is. In fact the piece that is so unnerving is that *it is*. It is not an illusion, not something that priests and ministers preached about. Heaven is not some figment of our imagination. It is real. But that knowledge does not change anything. We still need to live our lives here on earth today. We need to tackle life every day. Nothing has changed except the perception and knowledge of God and Heaven. The rules are still the same. Right and wrong is still right and wrong. We still all have a job to do and a life to live."

"Mullen Falls is not the only Gate."

"What?"

"Henrietta has discovered that there are at least six other Gates. We believe three of them have shut down."

"Why do you say that?"

"Well one area is the pyramids of Egypt, one is Stonehenge, and one is the Mayan temple. When I list those areas, do you get the idea of lush growth and abundant life?"

"No. They are all located in desert or inhabitable parts of the world. Mind you, some of those areas are rejuvenating."

"Exactly. The land was not like that when they were first built though. In fact it is known now that at one time the Sahara desert was a labyrinth of water ways and rivers surrounded by lush growth and vibrant life that supported the pharaohs and their cities for over two centuries before becoming a waste land."

"So how is that related to these Gates to Heaven that you describe, being closed?"

"Do you think the Bible is to be interpreted verbatim or do you think it is actually a collection of stories and parables hinting at a deeper meaning?"

"I believe it is written in parables, stories told to help man understand and to make connections about things that are beyond his realm of knowledge."

"Me too. I know I am just presenting a theory here, but everything we have discovered so far is evidence that the theory is true. Think about stories like Noah's flood and the great plagues. Man became

279

too evil, his energy was not worthy of harvesting and so the population was left to die without rebirth. Gates were shut down in the areas of the earth that were the worst inflicted with man's degradation. In Christian literature the story of Jesus coming to earth as the son of God, the King of Heaven, tells how he assured man that no more gates would be shut down. The gate to heaven would remain open. He told how man would continue to have a chance to correct himself to eventually pass through a gate to his Father's world-Heaven. By our intervening, removing energy before it enters the gate and has an opportunity to be rerouted, **we** are actually closing the gate, not God. Just like the Sahara, Miramichi will become a desert devoid of life."

"What are you suggesting?"

"No one can find out what we discovered. I have to destroy ET and you have to destroy HELEN and COLTEN. We have to eliminate any evidence that we ever discovered this. In the wrong hands, even in hands like ours, people who intended only good, look what we have caused."

"You are asking me to destroy my research? To deny the greatest discovery since the dawn of time? To not answer the question that everyone wants answered. That does not make sense, Simon. You must not want to do this either. I mean this is your life's work...to answer the question about where life's energy goes upon death. My God, man, you answered it. And I discovered how to re direct it. How can we keep this quiet? We owe it to mankind to share the knowledge. That is what we do, we are researchers. We bring knowledge to the world. We answer the questions that need answering."

"We need to keep it quiet because it is the right thing to do. I think the categories that my energy ratings fell under were in order. You have to achieve the first two and then the last two. Peter says that we each have opportunities in our life time to develop these virtues. Temperance is not just about living life in moderation; it is about realizing we don't need to use everything up just because we can. We just need enough. It is about managing pride, greed and self-indulgence. It is about sharing and caring about others. Once you have achieved that you move on to justice. Justice is not just knowing right from wrong, it is about treating others as they deserve to be treated based on how well they do with the first virtue. Devlin and Innis never got past their greed and self indulgence; they never got to the point of knowing right from wrong. Wisdom is not just about gaining knowledge and bringing knowledge to the world. It is about knowing what to do with the knowledge we gain. I think that is our challenge now. We have to have the wisdom to know what to do with this knowledge we have gained."

"You are saying we can never share our research? No articles to publish, No Nobel Prize, No opportunity to save lives of good people- people whose lives deserve to be saved. People like Peter's baby and Francis?" Galen asked pointedly.

"I am saying we need to do what is right. Not what is easy."

Galen was silent for a long while, digesting the information Simon shared before replying.

"Forgetting about our inventions for a minute, maybe there was a reason we were led to this discovery. Maybe people have a right to know the truth about the purpose of life."

"You mean that we exist to keep another world alive?" Simon asked.

"No. Just the first part; that the real purpose of life on earth is to simply live a good life."

Simon smiled. "Do you think anyone will believe that?"

Epilogue

The sun rising above the tree tops cast a golden glow on the small group of people standing at the top of the raging falls. The churning water below created an ethereal mist over all. A feeling of reverence surrounded them. Simon felt present in the moment, yet at the same time he was an observer. He looked around at the small group: his wife Francis, Henrietta and his father, Peter Lifesong and his family. He felt a soul connection with each person. Galen was not among them. Simon wished he were. After the wedding, Galen decided to go on a medical mission to areas that were less fortunate. At this moment he was somewhere in India. Simon did not ask him if he still had COLTEN or if it still held energy. He suspected it did.

As they watched, a brilliant bright light rose from the pool below. It hovered in front of them, radiant.

"The great spirit, Nisgam," Peter whispered. "Kisu'lk's messenger." He fell to his knees.

Simon held out the collapsed satellite dish in offering. Nisgam engulfed it in its essence.

The group watched as all evidence of the satellite disappeared.

The spirit spoke with no sound; yet the message was heard and understood by each one standing there.

"My children, you have done well. You are the chosen ones. It is for you to protect this sacred area. This place holds man's future, as it does ours. I trust in you and in your protégé to keep it sacred and safe for all eternity."

The message delivered, the form evaporated into the mist of the falls and was gone.

About the Author

Deborah Leitch has been a practicing Registered Nurse for over 30 years. Caring for patients in their last moments of life, she often reflected upon life energy and where it goes when it is no longer needed by the body. That reflection and the question: "Where does your energy go when you die?" formed the impetus for this novel.

Deborah was born and grew up in Miramichi, New Brunswick. She currently resides with her husband and son in a small town in central Alberta.

19054363R00153

Made in the USA
Charleston, SC
04 May 2013